PAST GLORY

First published in paperback in 2024 by Sixth Element Publishing
on behalf of Franco Renrow

Sixth Element Publishing
Arthur Robinson House
13-14 The Green
Billingham
Stockton on Tees
TS23 1EU
www.6epublishing.net

© 2024 Franco Renrow

ISBN 978-1-914170-62-1

British Library Cataloguing in Publication Data.
A catalogue record for this book is available from the British Library.

All rights reserved. No part of this publication may be reproduced, stored
in a retrieval system or transmitted, in any form or by any means, electronic,
mechanical, photocopying, recording and/or otherwise without the prior
written permission of the publishers. This book may not be lent, resold,
hired out or disposed of by way of trade in any form, binding or cover
other than that in which it is published without the prior written consent
of the publishers.

Franco Renrow asserts the moral right to be identified
as the author of this work.

Printed in Great Britain.

This is a work of fiction. Names, characters, businesses, places, events
and incidents are either the products of the author's imagination or used
in a fictitious manner. Any resemblance to actual persons, living or dead,
or actual events and places is purely coincidental.

PAST GLORY

Franco Renrow

ONE

The Friday lunch routine had been established for a couple of years now where James O'Connell and Caitlin Tate escaped the office for an hour to sort the world out, and enjoy each other's company. Even the post-Covid working model, where working from home mixed with time in the office had yet to find a balance, had not disrupted their ritual. Friday had been established as the most popular working from home day, bringing some calm to the working day and with it no pressure to cut the lunch hour by hastily called or overrunning meetings.

They made an unlikely pair. James was studiously on trend, with a trimmed beard, a fade cut, just the right oversized check shirt, an old Ramones t-shirt, a pair of cargo trousers and Doctor Martens. Caitlin had a slightly hippy look of a floral skirt and a t-shirt with a cardigan, complete with brightly coloured boots. There was an age difference of ten years between them but that wasn't an issue for either of them as they'd found the sort of genuine uncomplicated friendship that's often found between colleagues.

The venue for lunch varied a little from a handful of places they'd discovered within walking distance of the office. The current favourite was a small café. All Scandinavian lights, a chipboard finish on the walls, an eclectic mix of roughly made furniture with a sheen from the varnish with upcycled pieces, a couple of tribal rugs hung on the wall to damp the sound, a tasteful scattering of design classics blended with vintage curios that adorned the surfaces, all finished off by a good selection of dangling succulent plants and cacti. The sound of the coffee machine and the clatter of crockery gave the place a nice atmosphere which was not overrun by the house Spotify list playing on the discreetly set speakers around the café. The smell of the café: ground coffee, toasted paninis, the waft from the cauldron of soup that bubbled on the edge of the counter gave them both an appetite.

The hipster uniform, formed by thousands of pictures from Instagram, and a global cultural identity that had become totally homogenous and distinct, was a great comfort to James. The hipster movement had extended beyond clothing and had permeated into eateries and boutique shops serving the global community of hipsters. The full hipster package was something that James fully embraced.

James suggested a table. They settled down to lunch. The two of them sat next to each other when James first started working at the office. They would have snatches of conversation, generally in the morning or at lunchtime, and occasionally a coffee break. It was one day when there had been some big announcement in the office that they'd suggested it might be good to discuss it over lunch. They had long forgotten the big announcement along with whatever implications it had. Importantly, it had set in train a regular weekly outing for lunch.

When they first began their Friday lunchtime outings it had generally been to the Bay House around the corner. There was nothing special about it: a standard tied pub, with a standard lunchtime pub menu that rarely changed and had long given up on the chalkboard of daily specials. The seats were comfy and the service was efficient meaning they could comfortably get back to the office within the hour. The appearance of new, trendier cafés in the last few years with more interesting menus, such as the Eastern Mediterranean influenced one they began going to which had a lovely spread of mezzes and spicy stews, to the one they were in northern Italian themed, offered more excitement than the Bay Horse. The pubs had evolved from the sticky carpeted, dark mahogany and horse brasses theme to stripped wood, chalk boards and sharing plates, but what had changed is that it became less acceptable at work to have a drink at lunchtime, so they tended to stick to pubs after work.

There had been a drama at the office this week. No doubt bound to be top of the agenda for today's lunch. The office being a small publisher of magazines and websites for niche businesses called Davidson and Sons. Although nobody in living memory knew who either Davidson or his sons were. There had not been a Davidson in charge for a very long time. Davidson and Sons published *Earth Mover Weekly*, *The Weekly Undertaker* and *Cold Storage Monthly*, amongst a string of other titles. Davidson's was run by an eccentric Mr Pickles, who never revealed his first name, in his mid-sixties with a full head of white curly hair and a wispy beard. Mr Pickles cultivated the eccentricity in his fashion sense, favouring corduroy jackets irrespective of what the fashion trends were, a collection of white shirts and the same brand of jeans. Mr Pickles, it was believed, was married but nobody knew much beyond that. He kept a work focus while steadfastly not talking about life outside of work. Despite the eccentricities, he'd somehow managed to adapt the business at the right time to produce both printed and online versions of their publications. The publishing world had gone through a big shake up as advertisers moved to the online world and not all publishing houses moved quickly enough. This helped Davidson's grow, as they picked up the publications from other businesses who were running into trouble or closing down, often due to retirement. The team at Davidson's understood the online market, punching above their weight in the industry by being more agile than the big publishing houses, more savvy than some of their equally sized competitors.

The sales team, where Caitlin worked, was at the noisy end of the office, with their monthly targets for new subscriptions, in parallel to making sure the existing customers were renewing. A large whiteboard was mounted on the wall behind the team with the targets for the month set out, how much they'd achieved scribbled onto the board. The board looked tired, developing a green hue from the continuous writing and wiping. The information was all on their sales system which they all had access to, but setting everything out for all to see was how it always was. A nod to tradition. The sales team had a klaxon that they sounded every time they made a sale which, if they were having a good set of sales, could be more than a little annoying for the rest of the team as they were all in a big open office.

Davidson and Sons had been in the same offices for decades. The offices had begun as a rabbit warren of small offices, a big panelled meeting room referred to as the board room, and a small staff kitchen. Sometime in the early 1990s there was a modernisation when they tore down the walls to create an open plan office. The thinking at the time, along with many other companies, was that it would magically engender people to speak with each other and communication would flow. This new transparency improved communication would make the company better, or so the modern thinking at the time suggested.

Thirty years on and the open plan office was looking a bit ragged around the edges. Those who needed to focus brought in their noise-cancelling headphones. This triggered more communication by staff using the company messaging app, both in the office and with those working from home. If anything people spoke less with each other than when they had their own offices. They were used to getting up and walking to see people in their offices, often clutching papers or a notepad. Otherwise they used their phones to dial the extension numbers, remembering the old days when all outside calls went through a switchboard that made sure the calls had a business purpose by listening in.

James was part of the content team, and from time to time he helped the editorial team. He'd moved from the sales team when it was discovered that he had a talent for writing. He had written a couple of thoroughly researched sales reports with forecasts for the trends which was very well received, importantly getting a mention from Mr Pickles himself as good work in the weekly meeting. The trigger for his move was when the dependable Sally, who seemed like the furniture, announced out of the blue that she was going to Australia for a year. Sally was a bit evasive about whether it was for just a year, saying that she would see what happened next. James was swiftly moved into her position rather than go through the lengthy recruitment and onboarding process. The handover from Sally was thorough as Sally was very conscientious, making sure everything was documented so that James got a good start to his new role.

The office drama kicked off with dynamic duo George and Hitesh, from the sales team, getting angry with Editorial about feedback they were getting on the *Fruit Nursery* magazine. The issue began when they had a couple of grumpy customers saying the content had gone down the pan. Amanda from Editorial, James's boss, had been carefully navigating the transition from very traditional to more progressive content with advances and innovation in horticultural and arboreal technology based on a big market survey she'd commissioned. This had greatly increased the online subscriptions and even lifted the sales of the printed magazine; nonetheless, it had caused tension with a corner of their old customer base.

'Well, that was brutal when George and Hitesh were kicking off to Amanda about the articles on GPS mapping of orchards, and the soil robots,' said Caitlin. 'I can see where Amanda is going with this as the online metrics are showing a big increase in subscriptions, but it seems to be making a vocal minority of the traditional magazine buyers upset.'

'There's been something simmering for a while between Hitesh and Amanda. Hitesh seems to have pulled George in to stir things up to the next level,' replied James. 'I can see it ending badly for either Hitesh or Amanda… or both of them. The gaffer knows that we need to move with the times, offering both physical and digital. Mr Pickles will go with the numbers. He's not sentimental, and if he can increase sales at the cost of losing a couple of loyal customers then he will follow the money.'

'On a different note, did you notice that Sam took last

Tuesday afternoon off? Do you think she went for an interview? I know she has met someone in Leeds on that dating app. Since then she's there most weekends,' said James while shuffling around to get a better look at the specials menu which was on a chalkboard just over to one side of the counter by the coffee machine.

'I wondered that too. Shall we order? What have you spotted? I was thinking of the minestrone and a cheese panini. I'm starving,' replied Caitlin. 'The kids were late getting ready for school. Richard was off at silly o'clock to go to a meeting in Nottingham, so I skipped breakfast.'

'It has to be the pasta special with Pisto sausage and sage sauce for me. I hope they douse it in parmesan cheese,' said James with gusto.

There's a paradox between the ethos of local, sustainable eateries and the adoption of highly regional dishes of other countries. Would it have made a scrap of difference to the diners if the café served artisan sausages sourced from a local farm over an obscure sausage from a region in Italy? It could only be about outdoing the other local cafés in a race to conform more to the hipster ideal, and produce Instagrammable menus. Hipsters playing hard and fast with the term authenticity was the likely driver.

James caught the waitress's eye, and she made her way over to their table to take their orders. With lunch ordered the two lunchtime conspirators continued their conversation.

Caitlin said, 'Isn't it two years since you moved to Editorial? Is it more fun than the sales team? No regrets? I couldn't stand doing your job. I love the thrill of closing a deal.'

James looked like he was carrying a heavy weight. He

took a short pause before speaking. 'It pays the bills. I enjoy it more than having to meet more and more unachievable targets. I guess, when it comes down to it, I do enjoy the writing and even the editing. Fundamentally it's little to do with why I started my history degree. Then again, there are precious few jobs other than teaching that are linked to history. It would be nice to get into something in that area.'

There was an itch that needed scratching. James had been happily going along in life with whatever came up, but he was starting to think more about what direction he should be taking. There was a lingering question that seemed to have be unanswered for a couple of years. Was he just drifting along? He had a good set of friends and work was okay, even if it wasn't that exciting. Was that okay or should he strive for more?

James had been thinking that he needed to be more ambitious. There were unexplored territories, although it was all a bit daunting. James had begun a history degree at Birmingham University several years ago but dropped out after the first year, and it still felt a bit unfulfilling that he'd not completed his degree. He'd since taken up history as a cause, and in particular he was drawn to the medieval guilds of England.

It was this new interest that first brought him to York as he wanted to see for himself what the guildhall actually looked like. James wanted to walk amongst the medieval streets such as the Shambles, imagining how they once looked and smelled. He could picture a noisy market, animals being herded, people shouting and selling their goods, the rumble of cart wheels on cobbled streets. How would it have smelled? There was some drainage so it would've smelled less of fetid water, assuming the drains had been kept up to wash the dirt away? Would it really have stunk of animal faeces, urine and wood smoke all mixed together? It was one thing reading about how they'd lived but could you ever imagine how it had smelled and sounded? One of the highlights in medieval York were the stained glass windows in the Minster that look as beautiful today as when they were first installed.

James recalled reading how many people were involved in the making of the windows, the phenomenal time it took to painstakingly assemble each panel. A recent restoration had brought back the vivid colours as they would've been when they were first assembled.

It was not entirely planned, but the history connection could've been the pull that meant he ended up applying for a job looking for trainees in York as he began to think about life after studying. He was ready to move from Birmingham. Not because he didn't like it, but because he'd had a messy breakup of a relationship with a fellow student, Pauline, who was studying archaeology in her fourth year. The big source of tension was about their plans and where they would move to after she'd graduated. Pauline had spent a year out in the east of Turkey at a prestigious dig in her sandwich year, and she was keen to go back as a full-time archaeologist. James didn't really have an idea on what he would do there. Languages weren't his thing, so the idea of learning Turkish didn't appeal. To make it worse, he didn't really relish the thought of living in the camp with all the other archaeologists, who seemed to only ever talk about the dig, artefacts they were finding, and what other interesting digs were going on. It would feel very claustrophobic being amongst them. He could've stayed in Birmingham as he had a good network of non-student friends. He knew his way around. Birmingham was comfortably familiar but James needed to draw the line, move away and have a fresh start.

•

'I saw something in LinkedIn recently where someone was posting about a job at the county archives in York. That could be up your street and would fit with what you're interested in?' replied Caitlin.

'I'm not sure about that. I bet the pay is rubbish. I don't think being in a dusty basement cataloguing stuff would be much better than editing the *Refrigeration Times*?' said James a bit defensively. 'Maybe I should have a look at having another go at university? It could help me rediscover my passion for history, although I have no idea how I could fund it. I don't have much in savings. I suspect that at the end of it I'd be in the same position as I am now... only broke.'

'I guess you're right, unless it's a path to something more interesting. Oh, look here comes lunch! I need a quick picture before I start.'

They tucked into lunch, exchanging plans for the weekend. The normal routine was that they finished lunch with a coffee, which was a treat as the café had a supply of beans from an artisan roaster on some industrial estate just outside of York. The roaster had a remarkable source of single estate coffee beans, and an expert blender. Caitlin suggested they skip the coffee and pop into the second-hand bookshop on the way back to the office as they had a spare twenty minutes. This was a regular occurrence especially if time allowed, otherwise a coffee nicely filled the gap.

One of the routes back to the office was slightly longer but went past several antiques, vintage and second-hand book shops clustered in a couple of connecting streets away from the tourist bustle. They had over the past few months been into all of them and bought bits and pieces. An old Arabic coffee pot with a few dents, barely decipherable lettering and an obvious repair done a long time ago to the handle. An elaborate French mirror with a couple of missing finials, spotted flecks where the mirror had come off and a handwritten label at the back with an address in Orleans. A stuffed hen harrier, slightly cross-eyed, with its claws on a moth-eaten mouse in a domed glass.

The favourite place at the moment was the bookshop in a passageway that led off the street next to their office. It was an intriguing place as it was a confusing mix of buildings of various ages. The most noticeable thing was that there was not much of a shop front, or even a shop sign, as there was barely room.

The main door opened into a narrow hallway paved with stone flags that stretched into the rooms beyond. A small glass storage unit stood resplendent in the middle of the room where the prize books were displayed, and a lingering perfume of musty books mixed with a whiff of damp and the aroma that old books give off. There was a small, weathered, painted sign above the door Nesbitt's Second-hand Books with the slightly scruffy strapline 'All books in any condition wanted' written below in an old-fashioned font.

Once in the shop there were a series of rooms, roughly grouped into subject matter. Aside from the big collection of novels that were further categorised into true crime books, romance, and, for some inexplicable reason, an extensive section of guidebooks and old maps. An intriguing section held the older but not especially rare or collectible books or those that were dumped there as they didn't neatly fit the other sections.

The rare and collectible section was compact and had a very visible CCTV set-up. The room was sparse and had a couple of sturdy old cabinets with glass covers which were locked. If a prospective buyer wanted to examine the books they had to go through a process of finding one of the members of staff who would then disappear to get the keys, then unlock the various locks, open up the cabinet and hover while the prospective customer examined the books. It was a good way to ensure only the serious buyers ever looked at the books, and there was usually a reverential silence between the prospective buyer and the member of staff.

James and Caitlin liked to rummage through the old but not rare section. The subject matters of the books varied from household management tomes, volumes of encyclopaedias, hefty memoirs and autobiographies of long forgotten people, shepherding, fishing and obscure gardening books specialising in plants for heated glass houses. It was always a lottery. It depended on what books had come in, whether some of the book dealers had already raided the shelves, and sometimes new books had appeared where they'd been moved from other sections. There were even rumours of people surreptitiously photographing the books, listing them on the online auction sites, and hiding them so they only needed to buy them if the book had reached the reserve price.

James made his way along the racks, selecting a couple of books. One was a history book of York with some engravings of the main landmarks of the city. The book had suffered from minor water damage on some of the pages. The discounted price reflected this. The other was an old cookbook which had some interesting pickling recipes, and recipes for unusual cordials which he'd spotted thumbing through the book.

Caitlin had found a gem of a gardening book which she was thrilled about as she was planning to spend some time at the weekend designing her garden. She'd been on the hunt for some inspiration for a cottage garden, especially more about the old-fashioned plants and vegetables that grew in them.

They talked excitedly as they walked back to the office, weaving through the groups of tourists, clutching their books that had been carefully placed in paper bags with the simple text of Nesbitt's Books stamped on.

They were pleased that they'd found some books as the last few visits they'd come out empty-handed. There had been some tempting books, such as the one on the medieval castles of the Dordogne which James had dithered about. In the end he decided that the tiny print and long passages of italicised medieval French, made the book a bit hard to read. Caitlin explained that she'd spent ages trawling websites of the seed merchants creating all sorts of lists. She had to get moving with the orders for fruit trees from the nurseries as she wanted to buy bare-root trees rather than paying much more for the convenience of container grown trees. The gardening book offered promise of planting ideas and help with the structure. James was looking forward to getting his nose into his new books.

TWO

Caitlin made time to maintain a social life outside of the whirlwind of family life. As well as the Friday lunchtime routine with James, which she found light-hearted, especially with James's knack for scurrilous gossip, she also met with Verity.

Verity and Caitlin worked briefly together at a hectic digital agency and they quickly became friends. A monthly wine-o-clock was their usual get together at one of the many wine bars in the city centre. Caitlin had moved to Davidson and Sons, while Verity stayed at the agency, continuing as a graphic designer.

The two friends hugged, settling down to order a glass of wine and a bowl of olives.

'I had lunch with James from work today at the slightly pretentious Italian café which he loves. We had a good gossip and went for a rummage around Nesbitt's afterwards. I got myself a nice gardening book to help with my project. James snapped up an old cook book and a dusty one on the history of York,' said Caitlin.

'Which pretentious Italian is that? There seem to be a few that have popped up recently!'

'Oh, I think it's a northern Italian one, can't remember the name of it. Hang on, it's on my phone. James sent me the link in WhatsApp.' Caitlin scrolled though and showed Verity the website.

'I know where it is, although I haven't been yet. Is James still on his history mission? I thought that had gone quiet for a while?'

'Yes, he seems to be back on it. He'd gone to a talk at

the museum given by a professor from the University of Birmingham on medieval trade routes, and that had fired him up again. I think he was sat on the front row again,' said Caitlin, and chuckled. Then she asked, 'How are your renovations going?'

Verity's flat was part of a small industrial building which she'd taken on as a shell, making it exactly how she wanted it to be using her joinery skills to the full. The landlord had plans to demolish the building one day, and in the meantime let it out on the understanding the tenant would be expected to leave once he'd navigated the planning processes to get his scheme approved. It entertained Caitlin that Verity, a twenty-something socialite, would have taken on such a project and done all the work herself.

'Pretty good. I've stripped back some of the walls, got the lighting sorted and have put up a nice insulated internal wall to make a cosy bedroom.'

'I don't know where you find the time to do that!'

'The walls were easy. I cheated and left the chipboard with a coat of varnish.'

'Amazing. I should get you round to ours. We have a long list of to-dos.' Caitlin laughed.

'I might, but I'm not quite finished at the flat yet. I am making a massive chandelier out of bottles and a big chain to hang in the main room.'

'I need to see that when you have finished!'

'Too right. I'm long overdue a house warming party.'

They stayed for another glass, and a small mezze selection, trading gossip.

•

James woke with a start. There was a crashing noise outside the window, and he glanced at the bedside alarm radio. It showed an uncivilised 07:45. He padded to the window to see what the noise was. The wind had blown over a propped-up sheet of timber in the garden next door. To make matters worse it had fallen on a collection of various sized terracotta pots, sending them flying. What James saw was the sheet fluttering on the ground with fragments of pots swirling around on the paved section of next door's garden. He had a busy day ahead but it felt too early to start it quite yet. He returned to bed for another half hour's sleep.

The night before had begun as a normal Friday night. The band in the Angel would not have been James's first choice but an old work colleague Rick, who played saxophone, had messaged him to suggest he go and see them. James had seen them play before at another venue and was a bit taken aback as they'd veered to jazz. It had been a pleasant surprise as he was not normally a fan of the genre. He'd bumped into a couple of people he knew and caught up on the gossip while the music played.

It was nice to be out listening to live music. It brought back memories of the band he was in, Blinding Bongo Beats, and the fun they had doing the pub and club circuit, along with a couple of minor festivals. James had enjoyed the camaraderie of the band, always getting on well with the drummers who seemed to be constantly rotating. He still kept his bass guitars, some pedal effects, an old amplifier, a mixer and studio speakers. He hadn't felt the urge to play in ages.

The first couple of years of the band were great. They rehearsed plenty and were prolific writers. James co-wrote some of the songs with the singer contributing to the lyrics. They had a spin on indie rock infused with some ska... it sounded much better than described. They'd even made an LP, which he had a couple of copies of in a box somewhere. It was on the streaming platforms but not generating the plays to get excited about, let alone bring any significant income.

The wheels started coming off the band when the singer, Leslie, and the keyboard player, Matt, were pushing to do more, sending demos to record labels, applying to festivals across Europe.

For James it became less fun as he didn't dream of being a star in a successful band. He harboured no ambition for the big time. He stuck with it for a while but didn't want to commit to take summers off to tour the festivals. His temporary job wasn't an obstacle, more that he was worried that being in the band would become a job rather than a hobby. It was one thing doing a two-day festival, playing one set, and a whole other commitment doing three months of back-to-back festivals. The travel in between gigs and festivals in a cramped minibus staying in those sketchy two-star hotels seen on the outskirts of towns or in the town centres near the main shopping street. It all came to a head when Matt gave James an ultimatum right after one of their regular gigs at the Social Club... unless James was committed to the new direction, willing to go all in with the touring, Matt would bring his mate Chloe from the punk band he occasionally played in. It was a tense moment. James was not very comfortable with confrontation, and followed his instinct to tell Matt that he would leave to make way for Chloe. It felt quite a relief when he made his decision, even though he would miss playing, being with the band and being part of something. James never saw the band members again, which was a shame as he genuinely liked them. They went on to tour the festivals for a couple of years, attracting a steady following but they never made it big, eventually going their separate ways.

Rick had joined him after the set. The band was followed by a DJ playing Northern Soul to an appreciative crowd. They had a good spot which was handy for the bar, avoiding the worst of the crush as the bar filled up as the DJ set progressed.

'That's a big pivot. I wouldn't have had you down as a jazz musician,' said James.

'Yeah, it was one of those things when we were messing around in the studio. For some inexplicable reason someone started with some chords and it developed before transforming into a jazz piece. When we stopped, we were all grinning, so we started again, played some more and it evolved from that.'

'The best way to find out is by playing.'

'How about playing bass again? A friend of mine, who's a drummer, wants to do something new and we are missing bass.'

'I was thinking about it the other day. I haven't picked my guitar up in ages and kind of miss it. I'm also very honoured to be asked.'

'You know it makes sense to get back into it. Besides which, this will be something different to what you did before.'

'I want to have a bit of a think about it before I commit.'

'Don't take too long. We have a bunch of ideas we want to get moving with. We even have a couple of gigs lined up based on some dodgy demos, especially as I'd programmed the bass.'

•

That morning, as James had his weekend breakfast of smashed avocado with poached eggs on sourdough toast washed down with freshly ground coffee, he dithered whether he should share it on his Instagram feed. He procrastinated for a while wondering whether he should go to the cricket match or finally get round to finishing decorating the bathroom. He made another coffee, pondering, eventually making his decision. He sent a message to the WhatsApp group saying he wouldn't be able to make it before he changed his mind again. The trip to the hardware shop was successful. He came back with paint, brushes, decorators caulk and sandpaper, along with a much better bathroom light fitting. He then set to with the mission to finish the job.

James's terraced house was once the home of the railway workers and there had been a cobbled street of grey setts at the front and back, but that only survived at the back of the houses. The street was named after a famous railway engineer of the time. He was a bit reluctant to be tied to owning a house, but he'd saved up enough money for a deposit and rather than keep building his savings he figured it would make more sense to buy a place.

He had, after all, been in York for nearly seven years so he was as settled as he could be. He figured that if he wanted to move on he could sell it or rent it out. The house was well maintained when he had bought it so didn't need any major work. It mainly needed decorative attention, making it more the way he liked it. The only work needed was replacing a couple of windows. His final project was finishing off the bathroom, which was a lean-to off the kitchen that he'd reconfigured. The main work had been done: new shower, sink, loo fitted, and it had been freshly tiled. The last piece was down to James. All he needed to do was the painting, and put up a shelf and a unit.

He was in the middle of washing his brushes having finally completed the bathroom project when the doorbell rang. It was Luke, popping by to see if he wanted to go to the cinema later as there was a sci-fi festival on. The cinema was showing the original Dune film from the 1980s. James offered Luke a cup of tea. While he was getting the cups out and boiling the kettle, Luke filled him in.

'You missed out on an epic match today. The visitors started off hitting sixes, fours in rapid succession. Strangely they then seemed to collapse with a string of LBWs. When it couldn't get any worse for them their star batter was run out. I wouldn't like to have been in their dressing room at the end of the match.'

'Yeah, I wish I'd been there. Sounds like a great match. I'm feeling a bit pleased with myself… I finally got the bathroom finished this afternoon.'

'I thought the plumber and tiling guy had been in months ago?'

'That's right. It has taken me forever to get my act together to visit the hardware shop to get the bits I needed. Never mind, it's done now. What time does the film start? Do we have time for an early meal at the Star?'

'The film starts at eight. No doubt the first twenty

minutes will be adverts followed by trailers. We should have plenty of time to eat before. I haven't been to the Star for ages. They do a wicked garlic chilli curry. Good call. Why don't I pick you up at half six?'

James poured the tea as Luke continued to give a blow-by-blow account of the match. After Luke left, James had plenty of time to clean up, and have a shower, slowly getting himself ready to go out.

•

James had a leisurely start to Sunday morning. He gathered his walking gear, filled his water bottles, rummaged in the cupboard for his usual snacks, made a flask of coffee and packed them all into his day bag before driving to the North York Moors. He'd read about a walk starting from the village of Boltby, nestled into the lush hills. The path led out of the village, meandering through the trees while climbing up to the ridge, connecting with the old Drovers Way in a loop before descending back down into the village.

He liked the solitude of the moors, the wide sweeping landscapes tinged with a purple haze from the heather. He couldn't help wondering what it would look like if the moor tops were mixed moorland and forest like he'd seen in Scandinavia, rather than the slightly bleak moorland which looked dreary even with the valiant attempts of the purple of the heather at the right time of year.

There was a light breeze, and clear skies were framed with a few clouds skipping across the sky. The Drovers Way threaded along the top of the hills, offering lovely views across the Vale of York. It was near perfect walking conditions, marred only by a couple of very boggy sections despite the recent dry weather. The bogs were an enigma as they were on top of a hill which in theory meant the water should flow away instead of collecting. The tracks of a quad bike through the bog mixed with some trampling by horses made it worse; however, James was able to jump some of the sections. He did find a squelchy passage where it was unavoidably long and he had to adopt the technique where he had to walk briskly through to avoid sinking too far, getting his boots muddy but not wet.

James walked along the old Drovers Way framed by drystone walls each side, undulating along the tops of the hill. The walls were in various states of repair; in some places ingeniously patched with timber or sheep netting, the mottled, healthy mix of lichen and moss gave a sense of permanence rooted in history. He approached a mixed wood made up of Scots pines, alder, and birch, with patches of bracken in the glades interspersed with clumps of gorse. He caught sight, in one of the openings, of an old agricultural implement, long-forgotten with a vibrant rusty colour, covered in dried goosegrass.

He reached an abandoned house lacking a roof with a barn that looked in use next to the wood. It was a good position for a dwelling with a nice view and yet sheltered from the breeze, making it feel warm when the sun shone. James decided it made a nice spot to stop for a coffee from his flask, and some cake he'd brought with him, as the long climb from Boltby had given him an appetite.

James had read in one of his many guides of the moors how the house had been a pub built to accommodate the passing drovers and their herds. He could imagine the scene where a few hundred sheep corralled in the enclosures would make a noisy backdrop of bleating, with the odd cough. The mules or horses snugly housed in the stables. The roaring fire of the pub being the centrepiece where the evening's conversation would flow with the drovers catching up on the gossip over a pot of beer, joined by the local farmers. The reality was probably very different but it was always nice to let the imagination wander.

As James settled down, he laid down his waterproof jacket to sit on, and opened up his Tupperware with the cake and a packet of biscuits. He munched on a piece of cake while pouring the steaming coffee into his enamel cup. From the corner of his eye he noticed a small group of walkers approaching.

Rick waved as he approached, and said, 'You can't go anywhere to get away from things. I didn't expect to see you today.'

'I like to get out into the countryside and get some fresh air. I didn't know you liked to walk too. Funny that we worked together and met at music events but neither of us has ever talked about walking.'

'I guess neither of us brought it up.'

'Have you had some further thoughts about joining the new band I mentioned at the bar after the gig?'

'I was going to message you when I got back. I think it would be fun to play in a band again. Could I join you the next time you get together to see how we all get on? You know how it is between bass and drums. It has to click or it becomes an endless battle.'

'Good. I'll message you with details.' Rick nodded

towards the group he was walking with as they disappeared slowly down the path, and said, 'I'd better get going or I might get lost.'

Rick set off at a rapid pace. He was pleased he'd persuaded James to join the band, they really needed someone on bass, even if James was a big ditherer he made up for it by being fun to be around and he was a good musician.

James continued his walk, mulling over the idea of playing in a new band. The prospect was exciting, especially as he got on well with Rick, who was unlikely to surround himself with idiots. It would be good to try some different sounds and styles. He was glad that Rick had asked him again as he felt that it was meant genuinely, not done out of politeness. That said, James had some reservations about committing to a band as he didn't really relish the thought of giving up all of his Friday and Saturday nights to playing gigs, and still felt the scars from his previous experience. He needed to think through both the positives and negatives, but didn't need to do that now. He soon put it to the back of his mind as he followed the path and let his mind wander, embracing the countryside, spotting birds and looking at ruins along the way. He followed his circular route through a combination of his map and a handy app on his phone with GPS to show him where he was. After a couple of hours he arrived back in the village of Boltby where he'd parked, feeling nicely tired and refreshed from being out in the countryside.

•

The normal routine for James when he came home from a walk involved washing his boots if they were muddy and putting his walking trousers in the wash. He was feeling hungry after a day in the fresh air. He took out a chilli con carne from the freezer and cooked it with some rice and a tin of refried beans.

After he had finished eating and cleared away the dishes, he sat down to have a look at the new books he had bought on Friday from the second-hand bookshop.

He picked up the cookbook and began flicking through the pages and stopped at the pickling recipes… a project he'd been half planning for a while. James liked the idea of doing pickled beans in a mustard preserve. He bookmarked a page, being curious about the pickled apples with sultanas. There was a comforting thought about having jars with pickles lined up on his rustic kitchen shelves. He liked the idea of knowing what was in the jars, especially that they were not brimming with sugar, colouring agents and flavourings.

James had also toyed with the idea of making a mini larder with shelves all round lined with greaseproof gingham wallpaper, complete with a vent to the outside to keep it cool.

He continued flicking through the book until he came to the bread section, which was not as interesting as he'd expected. He was expecting more rustic loaves or sourdough recipes but there seemed to be only tea loaves and recipes for white bread.

The other section of interest was the cordials – lemon and barley, elderflower with gooseberry, and blackcurrant – which seemed very straightforward to make.

The book ended with recipes for fruit wine, which he was curious about but had little inclination to do as it seemed quite involved, and he didn't have the kit, nor could he imagine drinking a slightly sweet, low alcohol concoction tasting vaguely of blackberries or raspberries.

He put the cookbook in the kitchen, while he was there making himself a cup of tea, before settling down to look at the history book.

There was something James was talented at, and that was procrastinating. He was very prone to distraction. The cookbook could very well have led to a burst of pickling, jam making or a fit of baking. For some reason, the history theme was the topic he was absorbing himself with. Although it was not total absorption. He still had time for his music, and keeping up with Instagram.

•

The book on the history of York was bound in some kind of leather, but there was hardly a trace of the original colour of the binding. Whatever it was had faded to a dullish yellowy brown colour, the lettering on the spine had totally disappeared, and the end of the spine had a few stray threads. The first couple of pages were damaged by water. Given the state of the page it was impossible to figure out when it was printed, or where or who the author was. Apart from the first few pages and a couple of pages towards the back of the book, the book was in a good condition and the text readable.

Although James had started a degree of history, he'd dropped out before acquiring much of the knowledge or an academic approach to the subject. His interest in history was driven by a passion for learning and stimulating his imagination.

The book that James had found began with the pre-Roman settlement of York, and followed with chapters on Eboracum and the Roman era. The more relevant chapters for James were those on medieval York, how the walls had been built on the remains of the Roman walls, the layout of the streets that were first adopted by the Romans and incorporated into the medieval development. The book contained illustrations of the gates, known as Bars, connected by the wall around the city. The illustrations were very detailed, drawn with a good sense of perspective and grouped two per page with the last two being one per page. The illustrations were a complete set of the Bars of York, and had two additional ones named Frenchgate Bar and Finkle Bar, both with elaborate barbicans or towers and structural arches to support sustained damage should they be attacked.

James had selectively read the book, skipping chapters that were of less interest or subjects he thought he already knew, and made his way to the medieval section. The first flick though the chapter revealed the illustrations.

•

'Hi, Luke, how are things?' said James. Without waiting for an answer, he continued, 'You know how I've been going to history lectures at various times and buying the odd book at the second-hand shops? I bought one last Friday which was an old, battered, history of York. I was flicking through it just now when I came across a series of illustrations of the walls and the bars. There were all the ones we know such as Bootham and Micklegate Bars, but intriguingly a couple I didn't know. The mystery ones are called Frenchgate Bar and Finkle Bar. Anyway, I did a bit of online sleuthing and drew a blank. Frenchgate came up with pictures of a shopping centre in Doncaster, and some Georgian buildings in Richmond but nothing in York. Finkle came up with images from Norwich, a tea room in Richmond, and again nothing from York. I even tried searching for the Bars of York but had endless results aimed at hen and stag groups. I then got on a mission, trying Street View and walking around the walls, going onto sites that archived old maps. All of it drew a blank. So I'm either looking at an exciting discovery or a fake. The other possibility is that they are genuine but aren't from York and were accidently included in the book.'

'Woah fella! You're on one of your mad missions again. You didn't even take a breath.'

'Yeah, sorry. I needed to get it all out.'

'It seems you got lucky with the book. Surely it would be worth digging a bit more to see if you can find anything to connect these pictures or find clues about where they might have been?' said Luke.

'I was thinking that too. There's a good archive at the Yorkshire Museum library that I plan to try. I'm going to contact that lecturer that did a talk recently.'

'That sounds like a good plan. If you reach a blank after that, you can always say at least you tried and you won't be left wondering.'

'The only problem is that I might be off on some mad mission to prove that the pictures in an old book existed or didn't. If I find nothing, then what? I prove the book has a dodgy illustration in it. Then that could take me down another rabbit hole of why the illustration was included? Mischievously or designed to confuse? The simpler version is that they may have existed but for some reason haven't been documented elsewhere? After all they aren't even referenced in the text of the book.'

'Don't worry about that yet. You have a load of things you can do before you really hit a wall. Besides which, if you're going to go off to visit the old towns, then I quite fancy coming with you as I haven't been to many of those places before. It would be interesting to see them.'

'That's a deal then. It'll be fun being tourists at the weekends, not just doing the investigating and research. I have no doubt that we'll become experts on where the best cakes are in the tea rooms of Yorkshire.'

'Nice. Let me know how your research goes. It's really intriguing. Thinking about it, it's hard to imagine how you could lose two bloody great fortified towers, even in a city like York… or come to think of it any town or city? It would be a feat to demolish buildings put up as defences and designed to withstand cannon balls or great lumps of stuff fired out of trebuchets.'

With that they finished the call with a bit of chat about the next cricket match.

Luke was left a bit puzzled by the call. He was used to James's flights of fancy and his habit of jumping on a subject to the point of obsession. Luke found it endearing, rather than annoying, especially as he enjoyed James's company. Luke also wondered whether he should've been encouraging James to embark on the project, but the prospect of a couple of day trips to places he hadn't visited before overrode any reservations he may have had.

Luke was not a native of York, he'd moved from the Midlands to join a mid-size firm of estate agents specialising in commercial and industrial property. He missed his extended family, even though they were only a few hours' drive away, and spent weekends visiting or having his relatives visit him.

He had met James at a cricket match, a mutual friend having organised a big group to go and watch an evening twenty-twenty game. They'd got chatting, and instantly began trading stories, one more outlandish than the other as they drank more and more beer. As they got to know each other they didn't seem to run out of stories to tell, and they thoroughly enjoyed their gentle teasing of each other, about James's being a hipster or Luke being an estate agent.

THREE

James had been to several lectures that Professor Angela Jeffries, an expert in medieval history, had given and had become a bit of a fan. Angela was in her mid-fifties with a distinguished academic career in the UK and on the continent. She'd made her reputation with her research and publications on medieval trade systems, which were far more complex than had previously been thought. She'd appeared on a TV series, explaining how medieval trade was extensive and made it come alive by filming all over Europe, North Africa and into Asia Minor showing the traces of that era. Her life was the academic world and she enjoyed not only the research and some lecturing but also encouraging the next generation to continue the work into understanding the long span of history referred to as the medieval period.

Angela had come to know James, who always sat on the front row, and always asked lots of questions. Though she liked his enthusiasm for the subject, and while it was flattering that she had a fan, she had a tinge of regret that she'd given him her number.

The last lecture that Angela had given was on her research of the Hanseatic League, and as part of that she'd found some interesting connections between Groningen in the Netherlands and Newcastle upon Tyne based on the export of wool and the import of tools used in glassmaking. She'd found some documentation which was backed up by a recent excavation in Newcastle. The site was on the ground where an old warehouse was making way for a block of flats overlooking the river, which unearthed a rich collection of artefacts from the right era. She'd worked closely with the archaeology team in identifying the items, using the literary references while the archaeologists did the scientific cross-checking using carbon dating and dendrochronology on the timber.

- Hi Angela, have you ever come across these? I found them in a book on the history of York but something doesn't look right.

While he was waiting for Angela to reply he dug out his book on medieval military architecture and began looking through the section on defences. The construction of gates served as both defensive and controlling people entering and leaving the towns that were encircled by walls.

The topic James was interested in was the role of the barbicans which were built before the fifteenth century, until the siege engines and advancement of battlefield tactics made them redundant. Although, after the fifteenth century they were built as decorative buildings as some kind of pageant or pomp. The illustrations of the gates looked like they were utilitarian rather than the later decorative form. Looking closely at the illustrations, it was hard to see the detail, there were mainly without much flourish or coats of arms as a statement piece as you might expect from a later romanticised version.

The book was helpful in describing how and why the barbicans were built, but James knew he would need more information to find Frenchgate Bar and Finkle Bar. He was beginning to question whether they were in York at all. He picked up the book again, looking at the illustrations again to see if he'd missed something obvious. The illustrations had captions with the names of the gates. Nothing else. He went back over the text which described the four gates he knew about, again no mention of the two mystery gates. Could they have been a hoax or a stab at humour from the illustrator? It seemed very unlikely as the rest of the book was a serious one, the text was studious in meticulously describing the history of York. An editor would not let that pass.

The first step would be a process of elimination establishing whether they could've been in York. He would need to dig into the history, researching documents, and notes from excavations of the walls of York. If he drew a blank then he would need to make a list of medieval towns around York, such as Middleham, Knaresborough, Richmond, Helmsley, Pickering, Scarborough and Pontefract. Starting with those towns and cities, he would do his research into which of them were castles or whether they had significant walls with gates to narrow down the list of candidates. It would also give him an excuse to make some trips in the coming weekends, even if it might be a bit of a wild goose chase. He had a thing for medieval history, and this would be a nice project to get stuck into.

James's phone buzzed

- Hi James, no I haven't seen anything like these in York, but I'll show them to a colleague who specialises in medieval military architecture. What makes you interested in these?

- Thanks for the quick reply. I recently bought a book on the history of York in the second-hand place. Knowing the city walls of York I was curious to find out more about the ones I didn't recognise.

- Good luck. I'll let you know if I hear anything at my end.

James decided to have a break from his research as his head was getting full with the possibilities. He put the book to one side with his laptop, reached for the remote, and flicked though the TV channels to find something to watch. Eventually he settled on a series he'd been meaning to watch for a while.

As he watched TV, the doubts in James's mind came back. He wondered whether it was worth pursuing. After all, what would he do if he did find the gates in Middleham or Helmsley? What if they were just fragments in the ground? What would he achieve by proving that an illustration in an old history book was wrong? The worst scenario was that he could not conclusively prove that they existed at all in York or indeed anywhere else in the surrounding area. He would be left with two prints that were clearly labelled Frenchgate Bar and Finkle Bar and not much else to show. He knew Luke had a point about him embarking on a mad mission, but chose to ignore it as the thrill of the project started to take hold.

•

- Hi Grace! I bumped into James, the bassist I was telling you about, on a walk at the weekend. He's in and wants to come to the next session.

- Rick, that's great. I've also had some luck with Helen, the electronics whizz. She's also on for the next session.

- Brilliant. If it all works out, we have ourselves a band.

•

James was a little early for work on Monday, despite making a detour to pick up a coffee and a pastry along the way. James's vice was to stop at a small café that did the most wonderful cappuccino made by a man with an unfeasibly long beard. What made it special was the man's total concentration to ensure that each drink that left his workstation was the embodiment of perfection. The pastries came from an artisan bakery that worked through the night to make sure they were as fresh as could be for the morning rush. He took his prized possessions to work.

Caitlin smiled as James came into the office.

'Have you been to the usual café? What were the queues like?'

'Good morning. The queue was okay this morning. How was your weekend? Did you make any progress in the garden?'

'Yeah, that book I got was handy even if it was a bit old-fashioned. What about you?'

'I went for a nice walk and had a look through the books I got on Friday. The cookbook was interesting although it might lead me down a rabbit hole.

'The history book was intriguing, especially the illustrations. I'll tell you all about it later.'

'I look forward to it,' replied Caitlin with a smile. She wondered what he was getting himself into. Most people would've given the illustrations not much further thought, some may have taken them along to either the museum or the university to find out more, and then there was James, who looked like he was about to embark on a quest.

They both consciously started work as Mr Pickles took a dim view of people chatting at work, especially first thing.

The illustrations in the book posed a few questions. Were they in York as the book suggested and, if so, was it a reasonable assumption they'd long since been demolished? There was the other thesis that James was adopting: a mistake was made and they didn't belong in the book about York and were of another town or city. The places needed to have been significant in the medieval times when these Bars were built and the Bars, by definition, could only have been in towns or cities that had fortified walls. There was nothing in the literature that they existed at all, but James clung on to the book as evidence they did.

•

The county archives were a natural place for James to visit as they contained a vast number of documents and maps of York. There was a lot of relevant information about the walls and how they'd evolved over the years, much of it in documents on the financing of various initiatives. It takes rigour and training to navigate the archives, two attributes that James was short of but made up for with tenacity and enthusiasm.

While he came out of the archives none the wiser having spent a couple of hours working through the digital collection and assorted maps, the information he was looking for was there. It was not in one tidy document, rather it was scattered through the archives. The walls of York served different purposes in history and they were naturally adapted to meet the needs of the city, such as defending it from attacks and being able to control the coming and going of people in order to tax them. The documentation in the archive had details going back centuries on when there were additions, repairs, demolitions and additions, from this information it would be possible to chart the history of walls. Importantly for James he would have had a much better understanding of Bars and would have the answer whether Frenchgate and Finkle Bars were indeed in York…

•

The afternoon passed quickly as James threw himself into work, and he found time to message Caitlin.

 - Do you have time for a swift sharpener after work today? J.
 - Yeah, Rob is looking after the kids. I'll only have an hour as he's going out later and I need to be back.

James and Caitlin left work promptly and went to the Bay Horse just around the corner from the office where they found a quiet corner. James got a pint of IPA, Caitlin a cider and a bag of mixed nuts to nibble on.

'So tell me what are you up to,' said Caitlin. 'Did you discover anything interesting?'

'It's both baffling and compelling at the same time.' James showed Caitlin the pictures of Frenchgate Bar and Finkle Bar on his phone. 'Baffling as they are big defensive structures that would be hard to demolish without leaving a trace, but there's no documentation about them, and they aren't on the old maps. Yet they were in a book about York. This has made me more determined to track them down.'

'It seems a bit strange that these illustrations are in a book about York, and yet they were not built in York. Do you think there's a chance that they were put in by accident, and for some reason nobody picked up on it when they printed them?'

'That's what struck me at first. I also wondered about the scenario where the illustrations were put in as a joke of sorts. The rest of the book is a serious one so I doubt it would even cross the author's or editor's minds to do something like that.'

'What next? You can't go digging up the walls of York looking for them. The walls are scheduled monuments.'

James filled Caitlin in on his progress and plans to visit a bunch of places with Luke, joking that they would become experts on the tea rooms of Yorkshire if nothing else.

'That sounds like you're going to be busy for a while at the weekends. I hope you manage to track something down. It will, as you say, be a bit of fun doing the search,' said Caitlin.

They spent a while chatting about Caitlin's garden design. Caitlin got more animated, making elaborate arrangements with the beer mats to explain the layout, using the condiments to show where the trees would go. They left just as the crowd started filling the pub, the noise levels rose. Caitlin left in a hurry to get back to take over from Rob.

- Hi Verity! I just had an after work drink with James and he seems to be obsessed about the history book he bought recently. He's about to spend the next couple of weekends visiting a bunch of towns looking for some old Bars. I just went along with it. Do you think I should discourage him?

- Caitlin! Lucky you… having a drink after work. Nobody wanted to go out here, although I'm out later. He's an adult and no doubt going into it with his eyes wide open?

- I guess so but I don't want to be the one encouraging him.

- Fair enough. I wouldn't worry about it. Are we still on for wine-o-clock in a couple of weeks?

- Wouldn't miss it for anything! xx

•

When he got home, James messaged Angela to see if she was free for a call. Nobody seemed to make spontaneous calls; there was the unwritten etiquette that messages needed to be exchanged to make sure it was a convenient time to call. While he waited for a response he pottered around the house, watering his plants, making a cup of tea, rechecking his bookshelves to see if there were any books he'd forgotten.

- Hi James, I'm available for the next couple of hours, looking forward to speaking soon. Angela

James thought it polite to wait a little before ringing her.

'Hi Angela, James here. How are you? I enjoyed your last talk.'

'I'm fine thanks and you?'

'Good, thanks. I wanted to ask your advice. As you know I've been looking into these illustrations and found no references to them anywhere in York. My theory is that, rather than being in York, they are illustrations from structures in one of the North Yorkshire towns or cities.'

'Interesting. What makes you think they are in North Yorkshire and not anywhere else in the country?'

'I thought about that. When you look at illustrations, the stone work in the detailing matches the other pictures. From that connection, my thoughts are that the stones will have come from a similar geological area.'

'That's a good start, but do consider a wider area as it may not necessarily be as connected as you think.'

'I was also going on the names. Finkle seems to be of northern origin, and while the word French may well be derived from an older word, gate in Yorkshire is a road.'

'Well, you have done your research, and I can see you're enjoying yourself, so I don't want to grill you too much. But keep an open mind,' said Angela. 'I passed your images on to my colleague, the medieval defence expert, but he's away at a conference presenting some important work that he and his team had been working on recently. He did acknowledge receiving the images and promised to have a look on his return.'

'Thank you. I really appreciate your help.'

'My pleasure. I'm not by any means an expert in military architecture, but to my untrained eye the illustrations show a structure build before 1500. Nor am I an expert on York so I can't confirm either way that they are buildings from the walls.'

'Thanks for all your help and I look forward to hearing from you with news from your colleague in due course.'

James was buoyed by the call and next on his list was to message Luke to arrange the weekend.

- Luke! Are you free at the weekend? Fancy a trip out?

- James! You bet, I'm looking forward to a tour of the tea shops and having a nosy around.

- I was thinking beginning in Scarborough and coming back via Pickering and Helmsley. How about Sunday at 10:00?

- OK, are you picking me up?

- Yes! See you soon.

•

The journey to Scarborough was uneventful. James drove following the satnav instructions and they chatted for most of the journey after having had a discussion on whose phone was in charge of the music. They found their way to a pay and display car park near the castle. After faffing about with the ticket machine and consulting the information board with a handy map of the town, they went off to explore. There was a fresh breeze coming off the North Sea, the horizon was grey, and noisy gulls circled. James was not sure what he was looking for so they began by walking around the walls. While there was an impressive gate it didn't match the illustrations in the book, either stylistically or in design. They extended their search, looking carefully at the houses and the walls between them for traces of older stones. No luck. They didn't uncover anything that they were looking for.

James suggested as they were at the seaside they should have an early lunch of fish and chips. It didn't take them long to find a suitable café with Formica covered tables decorated with salt shakers and vinegar bottles. They enjoyed fish and chips, mushy peas, doused in malt vinegar, liberally sprinkled with salt, washed down with a big mug of disturbingly brown tea accompanied by bread and margarine. Far from a trendy café in James's eyes but authentic in its own way, he dutifully took photos and posted them to his foodie social media account.

They walked back up to the car discussing the medieval remains, the gates, the quality of the fish and chips, and argued about the way back to the car park. Scarborough could be crossed off the list, and with that they set off to Pickering on the main road.

The stops at Pickering and Helmsley followed the same pattern as they experienced in Scarborough: a walk around the castle and ruins, an extended walk in the nearby streets looking for evidence of earlier structures, and the mandatory café stop. There was something inevitable about the visits. There was nothing visible to the keen amateur and it stretched the imagination that they would stumble across clear evidence of the Bars that was not already widely written about in guide or local history books. It was not the sole purpose of the trip as there was an element of a day out and all that came with it.

'That was a grand day out. It's great being a tourist and not having to travel miles. I had no idea that these places were on our doorstep and how nice they were,' said Luke. 'The important debate is what was the best cake we had? Was it a carrot cake, coffee and walnut or a lemon drizzle?'

'A good carrot cake wallops the others,' replied James.

'Good choice but what makes a great carrot cake? I have had some dry, tasteless ones in my time!'

'You have half got it right. For starters it has to be a moist cake, with a few plump sultanas in, and the crucial part is that the butter icing is thinly spread or it quickly becomes sickly.'

'Fair point about the butter icing, but I don't need sultanas in the cake. Similar idea with a good chocolate cake: never with white chocolate, the darker the better, not too much filling, and doesn't need icing.'

'I can't argue with that either. I have a good feeling that we are going to continue our cake odyssey over the next couple of weekends. I was thinking we go up to Richmond next weekend, and come back via Knaresborough?'

'If it's as good as today then count me in!'

'It was a shame we didn't discover anything on the history front today, but we have a couple more weekends of exploring to do. Although there's a risk we don't find anything and it remains as a mystery known only to the engraver, editor and publisher.'

'I wouldn't get too bogged down in what may be until we have completed the tour?'

'Yeah, you're right.'

The rest of the journey's conversation covered the cricket, and their plans for the following week.

•

Luke enjoyed his day trip, exploring places nearby that he didn't know and, it went without saying, the tea rooms. It was easy to get carried along with James's enthusiasm and zeal for discovery. There was a niggle in Luke's mind about the purpose of the trips and the research James was doing. On the face of it, there were two illustrations in a book he'd bought that made little sense. Was James developing a whole narrative out of very shallow fundamentals? Luke reconciled minor conflict by deciding that the weekend trips were fun and the excuse of research was enough to go and enjoy visiting new places and sampling cakes.

FOUR

The local, late-night grocers sold everything you would ever need for a weekday evening meal, a decent selection of booze, a strange collection of household cleaning goods, and stationery. Importantly they also acted as a delivery hub. James was a frequent visitor due to his insatiable appetite for ordering things online, and, as was his habit, he combined it with a basket full of ingredients for his evening meal.

When faced with trying to find out more about a subject, the answer for James was to hit the online bookshops. There was a small issue with this particular line of enquiry in that the books on the history of York or medieval Yorkshire wrote of the major historical events, such as battles, or the narration of the way of life. There was a small amount of space dedicated to the architecture, often describing what the major buildings such as cathedrals, castles and monuments looked like, along with what has survived into the modern era. So there was unlikely to be a single source detailing the walls, and the various entrances, and how the structures evolved to meet the needs of the towns and cities. James, ever the optimist, kept ordering more books, reading them, and building a pile that he didn't know what to do with.

•

As promised, Rick had organised the room as everyone could make Thursday at 7 p.m. It was clear there was not one style they all subscribed to. James was in his usual checked shirt, T-shirt and jeans. Rick wore combat trousers and a utilitarian gilet with his hair worn in a man bun. Helen wore a hoodie, black jeans and had strands of pink hair coming out of a multi-coloured beanie. Grace was in jean shorts, tights and a striped cotton jumper with her hair tied back. Rick introduced everyone, setting them at ease before explaining what he and Grace had come up with. Helen did electronics, which she carried in a robust looking case, containing boxes with a lot of cables that James assumed were modular synthesisers. Grace, the drummer, came from a background in jazz bands before she'd started collaborating with Rick.

Rick played them some tracks he'd worked on with Grace as an introduction. It was clearly a work in progress. Rick was keen to know what Helen and James thought and how they could develop it a bit further. They experimented with some dub style bass with matching percussion, Helen coming in with some backgrounds as Rick joined with his saxophone that he'd routed through some pedal effects to add some delay and reverb. They continued playing around for a while as they got to know each other a bit better. It worked well as they seemed to bounce off each other, beginning to create some sounds they were all happy with.

Of the group, James was least comfortable with improvisation but with a bit of encouragement he quickly picked it up. Helen had not often played with others, as she was mainly a solo artist with some studio collaborations, and enjoyed the experience.

The two-hour slot they had seemed to pass in no time. They packed up feeling very happy with the session they'd had. To finish off the evening they went for a quick drink at the local around the corner so they could chat and get to know each other a bit better. They all wanted to continue and Rick said he would book the rehearsal room as a regular session, with the caveat that if someone was busy and couldn't make it the others would carry on.

•

Friday had come around quickly for James and Caitlin. Their regular lunch was at the Italian café as the week before but this time their favourite table had gone. Left with little choice, they sat at the table by the window. The specials on the board advertised gnocchi with wild mushrooms, and homemade ravioli filled with spinach and ricotta, which made the choice difficult. They decided to order one of each. There was a lot to catch up on.

James began by telling Caitlin all about his road trip with Luke at the weekend and how they'd had a lovely time but had drawn a blank.

'How frustrating,' said Caitlin, 'but on the other hand it has been good to eliminate a couple of candidates. You may have better luck in Richmond or Knaresborough next week.'

'Yes, another trip to look forward to,' said James. 'I have also been filling my evenings with lots of online searching, and reading a bunch of books I bought online. What I've found so far is some nice background on medieval Yorkshire, a lot about battles, castles and the like, but nothing that's directly relevant to my search. I am sure that if I keep going something will turn up.'

Changing the subject, he went on to the familiar topic of work gossip. 'That argument from last week seems to have settled down. I think Mr Pickles stepped in, knocking their heads together.'

'Well, you say that but I caught George and Hitesh conspiring at the coffee machine. I don't think they heard me approach. I heard a snippet complaining about the focus on digital, and that web adverts were all well and good but you couldn't beat the old-fashioned telephone and having appointments.'

'It sounds like that will simmer for a while. No doubt that Mr Pickles will keep a sharp eye on them.'

'How was your band practice?' asked Caitlin. 'What were the others like? What sort of music did you play?'

'It went really well. Rick was really good at getting everyone organised. Helen was on electronics, with some weird boxes and a couple of small modular synths. Grace on drums was amazing. We clicked very quickly. We messed about for a bit trying a few things out. Out of that we slowly started developing some nice sounds combining a rhythm with the layers of electronics topped off with Rick on saxophone routed through some effects. Helen was a bit shy until she started with the electronics when her whole body changed and she really got into it. Grace comes from a jazz background, and improvising is her big strength. It also helps that she has a wicked sense of humour. The music we played was very experimental but wasn't anything too strange or atonal. Luckily we didn't veer into free jazz.'

'That sounds very different from the stuff you used to play. I wouldn't have you down as liking experimental music. It will be interesting how the band dynamics evolve.'

'It took me by surprise how much I enjoyed playing

with them. Clearly it's a bit early to tell what everyone is like. Obviously I know Rick well. Helen seems a bit quiet and serious but she may come out of her shell. Grace is a lot of fun.'

There wasn't enough time to visit the bookshops so they opted for a coffee and a piece of tiramisu instead before walking straight back to the office following the direct route, weaving through the tourists that thronged the streets.

•

Luke arrived at James's house on Saturday at ten o'clock sharp. Rather than getting out of the car and ringing the bell, he messaged:

- *Yo! I'm here, double parked and ready to roll.*

James emerged immediately as if he were waiting behind the door, carrying his bag and jacket. Throwing his stuff on the back seats, they set off following the satnav out of York due north to Richmond, their first stop.

'Seeing as I was first in the car, my phone is connected. You'll have to put up with my playlists,' said Luke. 'Are you feeling it for Richmond and Knaresborough? Or do you think they'll be like last weekend?'

'I'm going in with an open mind,' said James a little pompously. 'I guess each place has been put on the candidate list and one of them may come good. If not then it's back to the drawing board.'

'Fair enough. What do you think will be on offer on the cake front?'

'As long as there's a minimum of carrot, chocolate, and lemon drizzle, I don't think we can go far wrong. Unless you go the savoury route of cheese scones or fruit cake and cheese.'

They continued the journey debating tea rooms, dissecting the recent cricket game and Luke's complicated love life.

Luke followed the signs for a long stay, public car park, and managed to pay through one of the apps he had on his phone. They followed the signs to the town centre, walking past the cricket grounds along the road they had come in on. Crossing the road to Rosemary Lane into a street leading to a cobbled market place which was called Finkle Street. The name of Finkle Street piqued James's interest.

'Hang on. Finkle Street might be something as one of the illustrations was labelled Finkle Bar,' said James, 'although there's no obvious building resembling the illustration.'

'Let's keep going and see what there is along here.'

Luke spotted a small plaque attached to one of the buildings on Finkle Street that described how it was the site of the bar or gateway. 'Have a look at that, James! It talks about the gateway you're looking for.' James stood silent while he read it before replying, 'Luke, I think we might be in the right place. From what I remember there's a street called Frenchgate in Richmond.'

There was nothing on the wall to suggest an ancient gate that had once stood. No trace of heavy masonry. It was clearly long gone.

James said, 'Seeing there's nothing left of Finkle Bar, let's go and have a look to see if there's anything that remains in the other place. According to the map it's at the bottom of the square. Although I'm not holding my hopes up too much'.

With that they crossed a large open space, mostly cobbled with a tarmac road crossing it with a mix of mainly Georgian buildings framing the square. A castle tower stood prominently above the town as a sentinel, adding to the drama of the setting along with a church in the centre and an obelisk. Although the square, called simply the market place, looked timeless with the cobbles and the old houses, the modern use as a car park and thoroughfare ensured it didn't look like a theme park or outdoor museum.

Much as with Finkle Street there was no evidence of any structure. Again the Bar or gate must have been demolished a long time ago. A street called Frenchgate led out of the market place. A narrow road, now restricted to a one-way system before it reached a larger road, connected the upper part of the town to the river, branching off the road upwards to a cobbled street lined with Georgian era town houses where Frenchgate continued.

'What now?' asked Luke. 'How about a visit to the castle to see if we can go up the tower to get a bird's eye view of the town? I've also spotted a couple of places selling cakes which will need some further investigation.' They retraced their steps to the market place, crossing diagonally, to a road leading to the castle. James got the tickets. Getting their bearings before climbing to the top of the tower, they traced the perimeter, taking in the spectacular views to the river. The tower had a series of steps that followed its inside before a final climb to the very top. Here they could see the layout of the market place. The buildings on the edge of the market place looking very much like a line where a wall could've been. James took many photos from all sides of the tower which he could examine later and study in conjunction with maps of the town, both ancient and modern.

It was still a bit early for lunch, so they went for a wander through the narrow streets near the castle. The collection of houses along the streets wore the badges of holiday cottages with the eponymous key safes fixed next to their doors. The quiet was punctuated by ambling tourists, some of whom tugged their trolleyed cases over a mix of stone flags and cobbles with a distinct rumble. The commerce was centred around the open square, and some side streets. It was amongst the shops where James, unable to resist, had to check out the bookshop with a nice selection of local history books.

Lunch was at one of the tea rooms that Luke had spotted. He expounded on the art of having something light like a soup, so he had room for cake as his preferred tea room strategy. The tea room had none of the airs and graces of a hipster café. No baristas intently plying their craft. Instead there was predominantly an older demographic mingled with a handful of families generating a cheerful hum of chatter.

Luke picked a salad, and James opted for a ham and cheese panini. The tea room was busy, meaning they had a bit of a wait until their food arrived.

'What we have found is two good candidates of where the gates may have been with no trace of them left,' said Luke. 'That in itself is a much better result than last week's sleuthing. The next challenge will be to find some evidence that the gates were on that street. Even better to find something that matches your pictures. I can imagine that's going to be difficult as I doubt that they would be in history books unless you get lucky finding another print. I don't suppose that we can call Time Team, and set them a challenge to dig up the streets to see if they can find the foundations?'

'I couldn't have summed it up better myself, you have a gift,' James replied, partly joking as Luke was a very successful commercial estate agent. 'Time Team haven't done anything for ages. What I'm thinking is that there may be some documentation around the demolition, perhaps in the context of an upgrade to the road, or maybe it was remodelled in the fifteenth century. Maybe find a ledger or contract somewhere with the costs, or contracts hiring people to do the work.'

'There's a total lack of any evidence so far. What you have is two pictures. You know there was a gate in Finkle Street but not what it looked like. While there is a street called Frenchgate, there's no sign of a gate. Let alone one that looks like your picture,' said Luke. 'Although, I do concede that it's very likely that the illustrations you have once stood in Richmond.'

Their lunch arrived and, after James dutifully uploaded a picture to his foodie account, they wolfed it down as they'd built up an appetite. Once they were done with their main course, cakes were ordered after some discussion.

'I'm convinced that we have come to the right place, but still want to swing by Knaresborough on the way back in case this is a red herring. Before we leave I'd like to walk around the castle to get a feel for things, and see if we can spot anything else? I saw a path at the bottom of the walls when we were in the castle,' said James.

'That would be good to walk off the cake before we get into the car. Does that mean that we cancel the Skipton and Pontefract trip?'

'I suppose it depends a bit on what I find in the meantime,' said James as they were paying their bill, and gathering up their things.

It didn't take long to find the path which started off the market place, which hugged the castle. As they left the square the view opened up, and they caught sight of a folly. A helpful information board told the story of Culloden Tower. They stopped, leaning on the wall, admiring the setting and the grand architecture of the tower. Luke pointed out a small arch over a footpath that was below the allotments laid out below the wall they were leaning on. He suggested they retrace their steps and have a look to see if it was anything to do with the gates.

They approached the arch down a narrow, cobbled street with cottages on each side strewn with window boxes of varying degrees of colour, though some cottages had an air of neglect. Grass grew between the cobbles of the path, suggesting it was a less well used lane. The arch was clearly an entrance into Richmond, with a fragment that was all that remained of the wall. The street widened as it went down the hill with houses on each side. A steel plaque inscribed with a brief history said that it was known as Bargate and explained that it was one of the old entrances into the medieval town. The arch had been preserved with a layer of cement resembling a thick slice of marzipan and could easily have had more structure. While it was clearly the remnants of an old gate, it was definitely not one of the gates from the illustration. James took some photos of the arch, the plaque and the walls which he would look into when he got back.

FIVE

'Oh, fuck! Darling, did you take the booking for those people arriving tomorrow? I thought we had a free weekend?' shouted Henry through the open study door. He had just received an email from some soon-to-be-guests, who were looking forward to their stay and asking if Henry and his wife could suggest somewhere nice to eat for lunch.

'That was ages ago. I updated the book. Not that you checked it.'

'Did you make the rooms up? Have we got stuff in for their breakfasts or do I have to go to the butchers before they shut?'

'I've done it all. You have remembered that you're collecting the boys at four o'clock, haven't you?'

Henry swore silently. He was in what he grandly called his study. It was more of a small room off the kitchen, possibly a pantry when it was first built, with a very small window looking out onto a wall of the neighbouring house. The house, a ramshackle Georgian in one of the historic streets of Richmond, was where Henry Heckroy, his wife Lucinda, and their two boys Hugo and Harold lived with a geriatric black Labrador. They used one of the floors for their bed and breakfast business, which gave them a nice income in the summer months with the steady flow of walkers doing the Wainwright's Coast to Coast Walk, making up for the erratic income that Henry made as an antique dealer.

Henry had a mop of thinning hair, and was dressed in a loud blue-and-white checked shirt with fraying collars and cuffs, a tweed waistcoat, and burgundy-coloured corduroys. He sat on a farmhouse chair that had seen better days, and his desk was piled up with papers that some may unkindly consider junk. There was just enough room for his laptop. The room had a distinctive smell of damp tweed, hay, musty books, and a whiff of something that strangely resembled tobacco, despite nobody in the house having smoked in years. The smell was probably deeply engrained in the old brown furniture.

He was trying to shift some things he'd bought in a job lot at a farm sale recently on eBay. There was half an hour to go before the auction finished. He often bought the job lots of boxes with the hope of finding a couple of interesting things. In a recent job lot purchase, the real prize had been a snuff box that he knew a collector would be interested in, once he'd given it a bit of a clean. The rest of the job lot was stuff to shift on eBay or sell to a couple of car booters he knew who would always give him a tenner or so.

Henry's business involved doing the circuit of auction houses, farm sales and the odd car boot sale to pick up a steady stream of antiques or curios that he was confident he could sell on with a bit of margin. Every so often he would get lucky finding a miscatalogued item that was undersold, but that was getting harder with online bidding at auctions, where the catalogues were open to view days before. He enjoyed the dealing as it gave him some welcome cash flow. More than that he loved the tactics and strategies he'd fine-tuned over the years. The house was an inheritance and had been his family home since he'd married Lucinda. The B&B was a godsend at times, even if the stream of guests could be a bit annoying.

He left his laptop on so he could see whether the lots sold above the reserves when he got back. A few things had bids and a number of watchers but the old biscuit tin that he fancied had nothing. Grabbing his keys and phone he dashed out of the house and walked down the road to his old Discovery. With a dark belch of smoke, he pulled away and went off to collect the boys.

The boys were at a friend of Henry's, who had boys the similar age. The gang enjoyed being feral in the fields with their air rifles, or messing about on their bikes. Henry stopped for a cup of tea and a chat while the boys were rounded up ready to go back with him. When they were finally ready, he bundled them into the Discovery.

'Our turn next week. Why don't you drop them off in the morning? They can stay for lunch,' shouted Henry as he started the engine. 'Give you a bit of peace and quiet. Thanks for having them.'

He turned off the drive into the narrow country lane that was just about wide enough for two cars. In places it even had a faint white line down the middle. The high hedges and scraggy trees gave a dappled light on the road.

'Boys, I need to stop off quickly in Leyburn to collect some boxes. How about I get you a nice cake too?' shouted Henry to the boys, who were sat in the back totally ignoring him as they had their earbuds in.

'Did you hear me or have you got those bloody ear things in? Hello! Can you hear me?' bellowed Henry while waving and simultaneously looking hard at them in the mirror.

At that moment a horn blared. Henry looked up to see an oncoming car flashing its lights. He'd drifted over the white lines, and tugged at the steering wheel to avoid the car, rejoining his side of the road.

'Idiots. They think they own the road!'

Henry made his stop in Leyburn, where he went into an antiques shop where he was expected. He made his way to the store room, ducking underneath a moth-eaten stag's head complete with strange bulgy eyes that had a distinct faraway stare. He was careful not to trip over the badly placed umbrella stand filled with carpet beaters, old lacrosse sticks and a couple of lacquered walking sticks with battered brass tops that had seen better days. He gave his friend the wad of cash they'd agreed on, which neither of them counted, and concluded their business with a quick chat cut short by customers. He then loaded the boxes in the back of the car while scowling at the boys. Resolutely not going to the bakery.

On arriving home, the boxes were taken to his study where he could have a rummage through without being disturbed. His friend in Leyburn, knowing he was interested in old papers and books relating to Richmond, had called him and offered the two boxes at a cheeky price. Henry promptly negotiated the price down, with a set of expletives, to something sensible for a collection of uncatalogued papers. There were a couple of boxes with letters in from the nineteenth century which Henry skipped through as they didn't look at all special: dull documents mainly about the sale of sheep and wool, a set of ledgers from one of the smaller lead mines in Arkengathdale from a similar era, a bundle of letters wrapped in old copies of the *Darlington & Stockton Times* dating from 1921 and tied with a blue ribbon, and a couple books on livestock management. Henry untied the bundle to find some correspondence dating from the early eighteenth century, which he was pleased about.

He went through the dozen or so letters, skim-reading them and pausing occasionally where he struggled with some of the handwriting. They were letters written by his ancestors, the likely reason why he got the call about them, although his family name was not unusual in the area. Henry knew about the subject matter as he'd found other letters over the years. Knowing their significance, he'd decided these documents needed looking after. The eighteenth-century papers belonged with his collection in the armoire in the attic. He carefully rewrapped the letters, retying the bow.

Making his way up the creaking stairs to the top of the house, he turned left towards a small door that led into the attic. He was feeling pleased with himself that the boys had not spotted him as they were always up for a rummage and a play in the attic, which was normally off limits. The boys were downstairs in a sulk with him.

The attic was full of family relics: old furniture they no longer wanted but Henry could not sell out of some loyal family duty, various boxes of unknown items that were on the 'one day I'll sort these out' list, and towards the back stood the armoire, near one of the vast chimney breasts. The armoire had been painted in some pastoral scene but the detail was no longer very clear. Not that it could be studied as it was draped in a dust sheet, covered in spiders' webs, dust, the long dead bodies of insects, and punctuated with bits of mortar and soot. The attic was warm. The air fusty and strangely quiet beyond the odd mysterious creak.

Henry pulled the dust sheet to one side and fished

out his key. Then he carefully opened the doors, which protested with a low creak, and he got a waft of musty paper and pungent mothballs. Inside there were a series of shelves that contained stacks of papers and books, all of which were ledgers, correspondence and papers relating to the family. He moved some papers around, carefully placing his bundle into the gap he'd created before checking the mothballs. With the papers secured, Henry closed the door, replaced the dust sheet, and retraced his way downstairs.

Henry's collection of papers in the attic were extensive, spanned a long period of time and contained a wealth of information about family matters. Henry's ancestors were part of a small group of individuals that had had a big impact on the townscape of Richmond and had caused large social change. The group had taken it upon themselves to modernise Richmond at the time of George I, demolishing the old medieval buildings that were a mix of poorly built constructions that needed something doing to them and some grander buildings that were not at all fashionable. To achieve that they'd schemed to take over the important buildings, and use their position of wealth and growing power to mandate the renovation programme. Henry's papers contained correspondence of the group discussing their plans, as well as the paperwork around the demolition and construction of the buildings.

SIX

There was a loud knock on the door. Lucinda was about to shout to Henry but remembered he'd gone out earlier, so she went to the door and saw two police officers at the door.

'Are you Mrs Heckroy?'

Lucinda nodded.

'Can we come in?'

Lucinda led them to the kitchen. The younger police officer asked Lucinda to sit down. They explained that Henry had been involved in a fatal accident on the road from Hawes. He'd come off the road, hitting a tree, and was pronounced dead at the scene. The officer added that it was likely that speed was a factor in the accident. Thankfully nobody else was involved.

The younger officer asked Lucinda if she would like a cup of tea, and without waiting for an answer, put the kettle on, rummaging in the cupboards for mugs, tea bags and sugar.

Before they left, the police officers checked if she had friends or relatives that could come and help and explained that they would be in touch as they needed her to identify her husband's body. With that they left.

The days passed in a blur for Lucinda as she grieved for Henry. She faced a mountain of things to do, like cancelling the B&B bookings for the next month, letting everyone know, dealing with Henry's many business contacts, while trying to stay strong for Hugo and Harold. The boys took it badly. Although their dad could be grumpy and aloof at times, he was still their dad. They really missed him.

Her sister, Geraldine, came to stay for a few days helping with the formalities and letting everyone know the sad news.

'Henry could be exasperating at times. Annoyingly impractical but I really miss him,' said Lucinda. 'It's going to be very strange not having him around. It's already weirdly quiet.'

'Hugo and Harry are going to miss having him around, even if they pretended to be indifferent,' replied Geraldine. 'Are you going to manage with your part-time job, the B&B and being there for the boys?'

'It's a bit early to tell. I could go full-time. They always ask me to up my hours. It's very tempting to stop the B&B. The B&B was Henry's sideline when his antiques business was slow. If I do go full-time, I can be more organised with the boys. They're fifteen and fourteen, so less dependent on me now.'

'You're right. It'll become clear with time. Necessity will help focus things. Shall I ring round the undertakers to get things moving?'

'Would you? I don't think I can face it. I really don't want to be deciding on coffins or headstone shapes. I'll organise drinks and nibbles for after the service as it'll occupy my mind.'

The day of the funeral was a bright morning. A steady flow of people called in before they all went to the church for the service. Henry's best friend, who'd been his friend from school, delivered a fabulous eulogy, mixing the themes of his old family lineage, his love of shooting and some funny snippets from school and university. There was a big contingent from his wider family, who were mostly based in and around Richmond, with a small number coming back from around the UK, as well as the cousin who lived in Luxembourg.

The boys broke up for half term just after the funeral. Lucinda took them off to stay with some friends who'd moved to Normandy after the 2016 referendum as she badly needed to get away to make some space to think.

The long journey to the docks at Portsmouth was uneventful with a stop at one of the more run-down service stations, giving them all time to remember Henry by retelling their favourite stories, anecdotes and recollections. Once they got on the ferry, passed the Isle of Wight and reached the open sea, Lucinda felt that she could breathe again.

Andrew and Samantha were pleased to see Lucinda, Hugo and Harry, making them feel at home right away. They went on long walks with some well-placed stops at cafés and restaurants. The boys had some time to go out and explore the immediate surroundings themselves.

There were lengthy discussions about whether Lucinda should carry on the antiques business in memory of Henry. They concluded that all the connections and contacts were Henry's that he kept very much to himself. In theory, Lucinda could've worked her way through Henry's address book, making contact with everyone explaining what had happened. The reality was that Lucinda was not comfortable doing that. The other, not insignificant hiccup, was that Lucinda knew little about the world of antiques or curios other than knowing what she liked.

Once they returned to Richmond, Lucinda decided it was time for a big decluttering. She called a friend who worked at the local auction house, asking him to value and catalogue all the things she wanted to clear out. Lucinda's approach was by the room not by the piece, starting with the attic, moving down the house. There were a few pictures and a small selection of furniture she wanted to keep. There were lots of things she didn't want. Neither could she see the boys wanting the old furniture or paintings even when they got their first places to live.

•

It was Thursday, and band practice night at the rehearsal room. There was a strange lingering smell, possibly patchouli, from the previous band that had used the room. A hoodie lay crumpled in the corner. The bin was full of takeaway wrappers. The room was rich in echoes of the many songs played there, layered into its very fabric.

Rick got there early. Not that he had to set up much, apart from his saxophone and the microphone with the effects pedal. He was keen to help Grace with the drums, and to see if Helen needed a hand with her electronics. Grace was glad of the help with the carrying of kit. Helen didn't need much help, having a system in place, a sequence of plugging in the boxes, and knowing exactly what went where.

'James sends his apologies and says he will be ten minutes late and that we should start without him,' said Rick. 'We should manage without bass for a bit. Unless you have a simple bass loop you can use, Helen?'

'Sure. How about something like this?' replied Helen. She fiddled with one of her bits of kit, and Grace began playing the drums along to it. Helen stopped the looped bass and Grace did a final flourish before stopping too.

'That'll do nicely until James turns up,' said Rick, beaming. 'He's normally reliable, so it shouldn't become a problem.'

Grace, Helen and Rick played a few pieces together until James arrived with a flurry, apologising profusely, and promptly getting his bass ready and plugged in.

Rick led the evening with calm purpose without being bossy or not asking for input. They experimented in approaches. Building up from Helen who crafted layers of sound, James and Grace following, and giving space for Rick and Helen to weave their sounds on top. The simpler approach was for the rhythm section to begin, with Rick and Helen joining in. There was no real preference. As accomplished musicians, they were happy to adapt. In no time they were starting to find their style and writing tracks.

Rick signalled that time was up. They needed to pack their things as the next band was due in twenty minutes. They worked as a team, gathering their kit and putting the drum kit into the store room. The others took their instruments home. It turned out that Grace had an electronic drum kit that she could play at home without annoying her neighbours.

As they were busy packing up, James suggested a quick drink. Helen had to collect a friend from the station and Rick needed an early night as he was due to go to London on the early train in the morning for a work trip. That left James and Grace, who went to the pub to finish the evening off.

•

James and Grace found a table... which was a bonus. Thursday nights could get busy as it was a popular place with locals, a big selection of guest ales being one draw, as was the eclectic collection of curios. The interior was either the result of years of random purchases or a very carefully curated collection from an interior designer. The level of noise was about right: enough to create an atmosphere but not too much to make conversation difficult. The effect was achieved by a clever combination of soft surfaces, playful flags, hessian sacks from exotic places advertising coffee beans, and the right number of sofas and armchairs that were decked in wildly patterned covers.

James set the drinks on the table, taking his seat.

'What bands have you played in? Have you always played bass? Sorry, too many questions at once,' said Grace.

James laughed before replying, 'I was in an indie band that played the pub and club scene in and around York. We also did the odd festival gig. I was with them for about three years. I left when they began talking about touring the festivals all summer. Luckily they knew a bass player who could step in. Before that I played in student bands. I've always played bass apart from doing piano at school. What about you?'

'I'm in a few jazz bands, including a mad free jazz trio that has a double bass player who uses a bow to make some very strange sounds. The other is a cellist who goes through strings like they are going out of fashion. I like the free jazz sessions, although they're physically very demanding, especially when the tempo goes up. I came across Rick at a couple of gigs. He talked me into playing as he said he was looking for a versatile drummer for a project he had in mind. I enjoyed what we are playing tonight. Where did you study?'

'I studied history in Birmingham, but dropped out in the first year. I first came to York as I was curious about the medieval period, wanting to see the place, the medieval remains, for myself. It's a nice city. When I dropped out of uni, I ended up here. I've made some good friends here. I was happy that Rick asked me to join the band. It's good to be able to continue playing music. What about you? Are you from York?' said James.

'I'm from Bristol originally. I came here to study ecology and never left. As you probably know, being a drummer you're always in demand.'

They continued talking, had some more drinks, started telling each other stories that got sillier, ending in more laughter and giggles. The bar staff were cleaning up around them when they noticed they were almost the last ones, and at that point they decided to call it an evening.

•

The venue for the customary Friday lunch was chosen by Caitlin, who had been recommended it by her friend Verity. It had some strange symbol in the place of a conventional name. The attraction was that it did a fusion of dim sum with something that escaped them. As the restaurant had recently opened it was full of people like them, curious to sample the food. It had yet to get traction on the review websites.

The restaurant had the mandatory trestle tables made from rough-hewn wood and matching benches with some comfy cushions. There was a reclaimed enamel number screwed into each table.

The waiter handed them a small electronic screen with the drinks and food menu listed, briefly explaining how things worked, how he was happy to be of assistance, and left them to browse the menu.

As neither of them were dim sum connoisseurs and didn't fully appreciate how it was fused, they sensibly went for a set lunch menu, along with a pot of jasmine tea… and the mandatory photo to James's Instagram page.

The interior was covered in a statement pattern of bamboo plants with a few contemporary pieces of art, breaking up an effect that could otherwise have been overbearing. There was a good collection of plants of various shapes and sizes dangling from various places to give the place a warm, tropical atmosphere.

They chatted about the office gossip, beginning with how Mr Pickles had put George and Hitesh on a formal warning as they were beginning to make their issue more personal than about a genuine business disagreement. A new intern had joined James's team. James gave Caitlin the background on what she was like, where she'd studied, and how long she would be on the team.

'I saw something in the papers about an auction in Richmond,' said Caitlin. 'The widow of a man who died recently is clearing out his stock of antique furniture and books from his business. It might be interesting to see the catalogue if nothing else. Especially after your breakthrough at the weekend. There might be medieval treasures hidden in the boxes.'

'I'll definitely check it out,' said James. 'I've also started looking at the period that followed the medieval times for references of the demolition of the walls and gates. It's very heavy going and quite repetitive at times as there is a fair bit of work that all references the same source. I'm still enjoying it though. It's been good to narrow down the possible locations in Richmond.'

'How sure are you that Richmond is the right place? Can you be sure that the illustrations are from there and not York?' asked Caitlin.

'I'm pretty confident that the gates were not in York. The street names, the references in the history books to there being gates in Richmond with those names, and the positioning of Richmond all point to it being the right place. What I don't have is any other documents or pictures that would tie in with the illustrations I have.'

The first of their sharing plates arrived, along with their pot of jasmine tea accompanied by two small porcelain tea bowls.

'These dumplings look interesting. Do you think those dipping sauces are hot?' asked James.

'Only one way to find out,' replied Caitlin as she scooped up a dumpling, plonked it into the dipping sauce and popped it into her mouth. She chewed the dumpling, carefully holding a blank face to keep James guessing.

'Really tasty. Although there's a bit of a bite to the sauce but nothing you can't handle,' she said teasingly. Then she said, 'I've drawn my plans up for the garden. It's all been written down on the calendar what I should be planting, whether in pots for replanting or direct into the ground. I've even had an offer from Rob to dig the beds for me, help me with the paths, and do general labouring. It could be fun to get the kids involved, if I can persuade them.

On the other hand, it's nice to get some time doing what I want to do.'

'Tough one that. I guess they'll see you busy in the garden and want to come and help?'

Given that lunch was served quickly and the benches were not too comfortable, they debated whether they should have another visit to Nesbitt's bookshop to see if they had anything new or whether they should go to somewhere different. They concluded that it was possibly too soon to go back to Nesbitt's. They would go to the shop that was a confusion of antiques, curios, vintage, and some very obvious modern reproductions all stacked from floor to ceiling in a haphazard way. The shop was made worse by the layout of a maze of corridors lined with glass cabinets which looked much more fragile than they actually were.

James made a beeline for the books section. He was quickly disappointed as there were no old or interesting-looking books. The only vaguely old ones seemed to be a collection of Wesleyan sermons, and household management books. Caitlin, on the other hand, soon found a pair of porcelain Staffordshire dogs with a very funny expression of googly eyes and undersized noses at the right price.

SEVEN

The online catalogue featuring the collection of the late Henry Heckroy was live on the auction house website.

The lots were divided into furniture (mostly brown, heavy items), paintings that were Victorian or Georgian portraits of either red-faced men or horses, plus books and miscellaneous.

There were a lot of books in the collection. Each one had a photograph in the catalogue of the front and back as well as a short summary. The miscellaneous section contained some decorative pieces that Lucinda hated, and boxes of documents, letters and diaries that Henry had collected. There were few photographs of the papers, and very succinct paragraphs of descriptions, such as nineteenth-century correspondence or diaries. The miscellaneous lots had low guide prices to ensure they would be sold, and to generate interest from people who may get excited about buying bargains.

James put in some bids for the lots he was interested in, leaving it to the auction house to manage them. He'd briefly considered going to the auction. He'd never been very successful in the past. The lots he'd been interested in going for way more than the estimate, past his upper limits, and normally in a frenzy of bidding that he could not follow. James found it all the more overwhelming with bids coming from the room, the phone and the screen.

James didn't have to wait long as the auction was to take place in two days. He'd subscribed to text alerts so he'd be notified if his bids were successful.

He shut his laptop, settling down with a cup of tea

to watch a programme on the Vikings on one of the streaming channels when his phone rang.

'Hi James, how are you getting on?' asked Angela.

'Angela, nice to hear from you. I've had a small breakthrough with a trip to Richmond, finding the possible locations of the two missing gates. On the downside there's nothing visible other than a plaque on Finkle Street at the site of the former gate, and nothing obvious on Frenchgate.'

'That sounds like a good start,' said Angela. 'I imagine that eliminates York now that you have a more likely location. I suppose that there's little left as they were formidable buildings but were narrow entrances, by design, into the towns and cities they defended. Once they were no longer needed they were often enthusiastically demolished to widen the streets. The added bonus was that they were a good source of solid stones that could be reused as building materials.'

'Good point. A part of me wished there were some traces left behind, like part of the walls incorporated into the more modern buildings. But as you say, this is less likely if they were widening the streets.'

'I have some good news and bad news,' said Angela. 'Starting with the bad news, I emailed the images you sent me to a couple of professors I know at different universities. Nobody was familiar with them, although the style of building fits with the medieval architecture seen in northern England. The good news is that I was doing some research for my Hanseatic League project in Newcastle when I came across an interesting reference to a glassworks in Richmond that fits in with the dates you're investigating. I wouldn't have connected the two but for a reference to the Dutch craftsmen who'd previously worked on the Martinikerk in Groningen replacing the stained-glass windows which had been damaged by a fire around that time. The document refers to a journey they'd made to Richmond, which they described as a heavily fortified town. The glassworks were sited on a river near the walls.'

'Now that's an interesting reference to the walls. It's starting to make sense, although frustrating that there are no other direct references or illustrations that've emerged.'

'I have much more to go through including some correspondence which I need to decipher. Now I know you're focusing on Richmond I'll keep it in mind. I'll definitely email you anything interesting.'

'Thanks. That's brilliant. How about you? Is your research progressing well?'

Angela gave James a short summary of the project along with the latest finds from the digs in Newcastle.

•

The day of the auction arrived. Luckily James had some deadlines for *Cold Storage Monthly*, along with an overdue piece for *Earth Moving Weekly*, which kept him nicely occupied. He was busy enough not to furtively check his phone every ten minutes. While phones were tolerated in the workplace, Mr Pickles had an eagle eye for spotting people fiddling with them and had the art of directing some sharp comments at the offenders who would promptly put their phones on silent, out of sight. Mr Pickles had at one point got some people in to look at fitting some phone lockers with charging slots so the phones could kept away from peoples' desks. It was dressed up as stopping people posting scoops or taking pictures of their screens but it was seen through right away as the publications they worked on were hardly scoop material. The rumblings it caused, along with the threat of a staff rebellion, pushed the project into the 'we will do it next year' territory.

Lunchtime arrived quickly. James went out for a lunchtime walk, partly to check his phone but mainly to get some fresh air. As he left the office, he reached for his phone. There were a bunch of notifications, including one telling him he had a text message. He'd won the bids at below the upper prices he had put in for the lots he really wanted, apart from one of the book lots that had almost reached his top limit.

He rang the auction house to ask about collecting the lots. They went through the options of collecting it from them, their delivery van would be out in the York area in ten days' time, or they had a list of van companies they worked with. James thanked them for their help, arranging to collect the items on Saturday morning as they were open until noon.

- Luke! How do you fancy a trip out on Saturday? I won some lots at the auction that I've arranged to collect.

- Yeah, I'd be on for that. What time will you pick me up? I'd offer to drive but I don't want a load of dusty old things in the boot.

- Would 8:30 be okay?

- OK. Talking of going out, I was thinking of going to Jaipur tonight. Are you up for a curry?

- You bet. Yours at 7:30 and we can walk from there?

- Perfecto.

Jaipur had recently had a makeover… gone was the garish, heavily embossed red and gold wallpaper. In its place were bright, white walls decorated with mirrors to make the place look less long and thin, plush upholstered leatherette seats with deep buttons, and the table cloths were a crisp white matching the walls. There was also a change in generation, at least for the front of house, the smartly dressed waiter, deftly distributed menus while taking drinks orders.

'What exciting things have you been buying at auction?' Luke asked.

'I got a collection of papers, documents and certificates that was part of a bunch of things being sold from what I gather was a big clear out from a house in Richmond. I also picked up a couple of interesting books. The papers are a bit of a punt as I couldn't really tell from the catalogue what they were, but they did seem interesting enough to put a bid on. Are we doing poppadoms and starters or just starters and main or poppadoms and mains?'

'I'm not starving so how about the classic poppadom/mains combo?'

'Excellent, I know exactly what I'm having,' said James. 'I spoke with Angela, you know, the professor who gave that lecture recently that I went to?'

Luke nodded.

James said, 'She told me that she'd come across a reference to a glass factory in Richmond by the river, describing Richmond as being heavily fortified. It isn't a direct reference to the gates but it suggests that there were some hefty walls which must have had fortified gates in place to guard the entrance.'

'Yeah, that'd make sense but be careful you're not putting two and two together and getting five. The glass making factory sounds interesting. There was no sign of that when we walked around Richmond. I guess it's long been dismantled? The stones reused?' said Luke. 'Where are you heading with this investigation? From what I can make out we have found the likely location of the gates you were looking for in Richmond. What we will never know is who made those illustrations, and why they were in a book about York?'

'I guess you're right. I'm getting a bit deep into this. At times I think it's a big bloody wild goose chase with no clear goal in mind other than some challenge to find out for sure where two pictures were actually located.

'It's beginning to gnaw at me. I want to find out how you go from a massively fortified town with barbican gates to very little evidence of any of the defences. Yet as we see in other towns and cities, they left them in place. It seems like a lot of trouble that people went to?'

'It has morphed into a new mission. One without really knowing what the destination is, other than you'll know you're there at some point,' said Luke philosophically. Lifting the mood he enthusiastically asked, 'Shall we get another pint in?'

•

Band practice night was something that they all looked forward to. The band had developed a deep understanding amongst themselves. It felt like they'd played together for years rather than very recently, feeling very comfortable with each other.

They had, in the very short space of time, built a set that they enjoyed playing, leaving a enough space to improvise. This was new to James but he was a quick learner, getting the hang of it very quickly. He could try things out confident that Grace would keep the beat moving. He could play with a bit of freedom and keep coming back to where he'd set off from.

The routine was that they would rehearse their set. Rick was keen to book them a gig at a mini festival of experimental music that was going on in and around York. Once done with the rehearsal of the set they always played some new material that one or more of them would begin with the others joining in.

Helen was chatty after they finished rehearsing while she unplugged and put all her kit into the padded cases she carried it in, and generally had a reason to go home or was meeting friends. She was keen to play gigs and spend time rehearsing but clearly had a busy life.

For Rick, Grace and James the drink after rehearsal was a nice way to finish off the evening, although Rick often skipped the drink, leaving James and Grace. This was one of those evenings when James and Grace went to the usual pub and, once they'd got their drinks, found a table.

They shared their news, although James hadn't at this point told Grace of his obsession with finding Finkle Bar and Frenchgate Bar. Grace suggested they went to a club where a funk band she knew were playing. They were, by all accounts, worth seeing as they were a big collective including guitars, keyboard, brass, a string section topped off with multiple percussionists. The club was a short walk from the pub, not one that James had been to before.

The club was down a side street. A short queue of people lined up outside while the bouncers did their job of assessing who was who, whether they matched the mysterious policy that only the bouncers and the manager knew, along with a routine check for weapons and drugs. Once they got into the club and paid their entry, they left their coats in the cloak room, following the crowd into the bar area which was three deep at the bar. James made his way through the queue and got a couple of beers, after which they went through the doors to where the music was coming from. The walls were a mix of concrete, exposed brickwork, and some steel structures on the ceiling left from an industrial past, creating a nice structure to hang lights from. The stage was painted matt black. The only colour was a video projected to the back of the stage. The band were squeezed onto the stage, and were, as Grace promised, a big collection of musicians who had just begun their set.

The dance floor was packed as the band gave it their all, slickly playing a good set of covers, with their own pieces interspersed. James and Grace pushed their way into the middle, finding a bit of space to dance, where they stayed until the end of the set and the two encores. The band was followed by a DJ, and at that point they decided to call it a night.

They collected their coats and headed out to the quiet streets to the taxi rank. On the way to the taxi rank Grace asked James if he would like to go back to her house. James said yes without any hesitation.

The board members of Rufus Investments met in their London offices, which were in one of the less fashionable streets of St James, equidistant between the Piccadilly and Green Park underground stations. The board room, wood-panelled with artwork designed neither to offend nor make an impact, had an old mahogany sideboard serving as a combined stationery cupboard and drinks cabinet. In the middle was a huge table, which had notepads and pencils at each place, plus a glass and bottles of still and sparkling water at regular intervals.

The board members were a composition of the major stakeholders, the managing director, and the heads of finance and legal. The stakeholders were principally two Yorkshire families, the Tubhursts and Heckroys, represented by one person from each family.

George Tubhurst was dressed in an ill-fitting suit, a shirt that had seen better days with frayed collar and cuffs, inoffensive gold cuff links and a silk tie. He was close to retirement and was keen to see the castle project through both as a legacy and a useful boost to his pension. He'd worked with Edward Heckroy for years and had known him as they both lived in small estates outside of Richmond. Although George was very happy in rural Yorkshire, he liked his visits to London as a chance to meet up with friends in the evenings, and sometimes go for dinner or to the Opera.

Edward was a younger version of George by about twenty years and dressed in a very similar way, although he wore his regimental tie and had a silk square in the top pocket of his jacket. Like George he lived in Yorkshire and enjoyed his trips to London where he would meet with his friends from the regiment and rather than the Opera, he preferred going to either comedy nights or to smaller jazz clubs to listen to music.

The main topic of the board meeting was a project in Richmond Castle. The meeting kicked off with a report from Legal that the lease of 999 years had been secured for the castle. The obstacle of the incumbent tenant had been resolved through a break clause in their contract. The higher ground rent offer from Rufus was a major part of the deal, along with their ambitious project.

There had been extensive discussions with the landlord about the scheme they were planning to build and progress was being made with the various planning departments given the heritage status of the Norman castle.

The project architect, Cathrine Urquhart Jones, had been invited to the board meeting to present the latest version of the plans that they would be submitting, along with a 3D model which included a virtual walkthrough of the building. Cathrine asked for the blinds to be lowered as she prepared the presentation, connecting her laptop to the audiovisual system.

'The layout you see is the current structure of the castle. As you can see inside the outer walls there are few remains that would provide any obstacle to building the structure,' said Cathrine. The presentation then showed a big steel structure. 'The steel structure forms the core piece of the building that sits on top of the ground and is placed to be clear of the existing stonework, high enough to carry the services so we don't need to excavate into the historic fabric of the castle.' The presentation moved through the structure to show how it would look from different angles and was followed by the next version of the model. 'We can now see the floor areas added to the building and the access to the upper floors with the internal stairs and lifts. Here and here.' Cathrine shone a laser pen onto the screen. The presentation then moved to showing the steel structure covered with glass panes and living roof. 'This is the shell of the building. We are using a high specification glass that ensures the building is well-insulated and that it doesn't overheat in the summer. The living roof ensures that the flow of rainwater is slowed down, as well as meeting sustainability targets.' The final section of the presentation showed the complete model of the building, with high-end retail units and a specialist food court. It was animated by people circulating. 'This is what the completed building will look like. The food court will be a central piece to the building creating space to circulate, and the visitors will be drawn to the luxury shops.'

Cathrine paused to allow the board members to take in the model before saying, 'I hope this is clear. Any questions?'

George Tubhurst was the first to respond. 'That's a marvellous job you've done there, thank you very much. You mentioned the raised floor to allow the services to be built above ground and the living roof to slow the rain down. What happens with a downpour? Does the castle get flooded with all that glass funnelling the rain?'

'Good question,' said Cathrine. 'There's a system of guttering that feeds into a reservoir that sits underneath here, and forms part of the grey water system that feeds into the lavatories. We also pipe the excess here,' as Cathrine pointed the laser dot at the presentation 'which leaves the castle at these two points without causing any damage to the stone of the castle. I've shared a link with the detailed plans and would be more than happy to clarify anything.'

George asked, 'Are there any more questions? If not, I'd like to thank Cathrine once more and we'll have a short break while I show her out.' With that Cathrine packed up her laptop and was taken to reception by George, leaving the board members to discuss the model.

George returned to the room and said, 'I'll connect the video link with Luke from the estate agents who's been putting feelers out to gauge interest from prospective tenants of the units.' The video link projected to a screen at the end of the board room.

'Hi, Luke. Can you hear us okay?' asked George.

'I can, George. Hello everyone.'

'How've your discussions gone?'

'I've had informal, and confidential, discussions with high-end retailers as we discussed, and there's overall positive support and interest in the concept. Specifically one of the top luxury groups I spoke with was keen to learn more specifics as it's exactly what they're looking for as part of their expansion plans. I shared the key data, ensuring that the location details were confidential, including income, wealth data, and accessibility, and that was well received. I'm confident that once we're ready we can have the units signed up before you begin construction.'

'Did you discuss the outline rental with them?' asked Edward.

'Sure, obviously we were discussing in general terms. The more detailed discussions will happen once they have the full picture. The rent per square foot was towards the top end of the range we discussed in the previous meeting, and I think that a bit of pressure can be applied once I get the anchor client signed up to nudge a bit further.'

'What about the length of the tenancy? Did you get a feel for what they were prepared to commit to?'

'Again, that's looking positive. They were all looking for long-term commitments with the usual break clauses. The way they were looking at it was that it was a good concept and a longer commitment would justify the investment they would make.'

'Thanks, Luke. Any further questions from the board?' asked George. He was met with shaking heads. 'In that case, thank you for your work. We'll be in touch as we get updates.'

'You're welcome. One thing before I go. In my experience this type of development stimulates the boutique hotel market, and it may be worth considering investing in a couple of options in anticipation of the project as they take time to renovate and get the necessary licences. If you'd like me to do a survey and a report of suitable properties, please let me know.'

The call ended. George said, 'That was a very encouraging update, but we shouldn't celebrate until we have signatures for the leases. We'll move onto the deal for Section 106. As we've discussed we'll offer to renovate the Obelisk, which has been patched over the years and there's been some erosion on the carvings. We are also proposing a substantial contribution for the construction of an underground car park, built under the market place. The costs are set out in this report. I'm not expecting you to read it now or discuss, but take it away and consider it.' With that he handed out copies of the report to all the board members.

Edward Heckroy put his hand up. George asked, 'Edward, have you something you want to raise?'

'Yes,' replied Edward. 'A key strategy of ours has been to sell the heritage aspect of the project and we've robustly campaigned against any significant changes to the town centre that may be detrimental to the heritage setting. It's come to my attention that there are to be two applications to modernise a shop front which has been altered over the years, and one to build a modern house as infill in the historic town centre. We need to ensure that the shop front is put back to something near the original façade, and we have plenty of old photos we can use to make a case. The other one needs to be rejected out of hand, as it may set a dangerous precedent and could weaken our case for dealing sensitively with a heritage site. It goes without saying that there's a lot at stake here and I'd like a show of hands of support to do what it takes to achieve the best outcome for us and this key project.'

There was a unanimous show of hands.

The rest of the board meeting dealt with the obligatory reports of finance, including the status of funding of the castle project which was being done through several special-purpose vehicles based in Guernsey and Luxembourg. The financing involved some heavy financial engineering designed to leverage the investment from the partners and manage the risks to give the Rufus investors preferential treatment in case of liquidation.

The final matters being discussed included the selection process of bringing in the necessary teams to oversee the construction of the castle project, and the confidentiality and sensitivity of the tender process.

At the end of the meeting, George rang reception and

asked for Chablis and nibbles to be taken into the board room where they would have the informal discussions.

•

Verity was almost done with her renovations and needed a deadline to finish off the final pieces. She'd decided that if she hosted a house-warming in a month she'd have enough time to do all the small niggly things to get the flat looking nice.

 - *Hi Caitlin. How are you? I'm getting to the point of being able to host a house-warming party.*
 - *Good to hear from you. All well here. That's amazing news. You've been working your socks off.*
 - *I have, but to finish off all the niggly things I decided I needed a deadline, and thought if I set a date in about 4 to 6 weeks, I'll have enough time to do everything.*
 - *Good idea about a deadline. Do you need any help? I'm handy with a paint brush.*
 - *Are you any good at sewing? I might need a hand with some cushions.*
 - *Of course. I can come round and pick up the material/cushions? I have a sewing machine in the cupboard.*
 - *That'd be brilliant. Would you have time at the weekend?*
 - *Sure. Rob is taking the kids swimming on Saturday morning. I can pop in then?*
 - *Brilliant. How are your projects? Work? Kids?*
 - *The garden is coming along nicely. The kids are in good form at the moment. Work is hectic although I'm still managing my Friday lunches.*
 - *Good to hear. How's Mad James?*

- He seems to have gone off on one ever since he bought the book with the illustrations. He's rushing off at weekends, doing an Indiana Jones or a male Lara Croft.
- Sounds entertaining! That needs encouraging
- It does! See you on Saturday.

EIGHT

James and Luke set off early to get to the auction house with some time to spare before they closed at 12:00. They got to the collections area, which wasn't very busy. James gave his name, showing them his driving licence to verify his identity. The porter came back with a trolley loaded with the boxes of the lots he'd successfully bid for. Between the three of them they soon got the boxes into the car, and, as promised, James took Luke for lunch in a pub he'd found on a guide to the area.

'You're going to run out of space in your house if you keep buying all this old stuff. Do you know that you'll end up like one of those hoarders who can barely move around for stuff,' said Luke. 'It'll be a massive fire hazard. One little spark and your boxes of papers are exploding like fireworks.' Luke made a sound effect and a gesture of an explosion.

'Piss off. I've only bought these boxes, a couple of books from the second-hand shop, and a map from eBay,' replied James a bit too defensively. 'Once I've got to the end of my research, I'll give the documents I collect to the Yorkshire Museum if they want them, and if not I either put the rest online or see if Nesbitt's would buy them.'

'So, tell me,' said Luke. 'You bought these papers on a hunch that they may have just the information you're looking for. You said the other night that they seemed relevant but the description of the contents of the boxes was a bit general and the images not at all clear. Quite a punt?'

'If I'm right, which I think I may well be... and judging

from the style of handwriting they are from the right era, the punt I've taken is that they might contain some background on what happened to the walls and gates of Richmond. The present-day Richmond has a lot of Georgian buildings that suggest a period of wealth followed by a decline, or the buildings would've been replaced by more modern ones if there had been funds.

'What's a bit odd is that there's very little information about medieval Richmond other than a potted history of the castle, and the dissolution of Greyfriars, St Martin and Easby Abbey.'

'Where would you normally find that kind of information if it's not in the local history books?'

'Good question, it's a bit like hunting for a needle in a haystack, but there are resources like the British Library who have been digitising the medieval manuscripts to start with. There are a bunch of other institutions around Europe who have done similar things.

'Like all searches the hard bit is knowing the questions to ask. If nobody has written texts about medieval Richmond, there are two possibilities. Either there was very little to write about or the information has gone missing.

'At the moment I'm trying to figure this out. These papers may help me find out a bit more. Starting with what we do know is that Richmond's castle was built in the twelfth century complete with town walls. There was a friary, a gate at Finkle Street, and some references to a glass-making industry in the right era. So I'm going off the thesis that the information has got lost in time rather than there being nothing to write about.'

'It seems a logical conclusion, but you'll have to be

conscious that you're on track to becoming a hoarder. I'll go and ask what the pie of the day is. I'm getting hungry. Breakfast was ages ago,' said Luke, getting up to go to the bar.

James's optimism about the documents and letters could hit reality soon, as the process of working through them would need skills and knowledge that he lacked. The difficulty would come in interpreting the older texts as they would have references to events in the past, and the style very different to the modern texts. The sensible thing would've been to gather all the information he'd assembled, along with the books and boxes and taken it to the university for analysis. It would've been much less fun for James as he'd set himself off on a project that for some reason had giving up excluded as an option.

•

The collection that James had bought comprised a box of books containing an old book on the history of Richmond, a biography of a vicar from St Mary's Church in Richmond, a Victorian tome on the old customs of North Yorkshire, along with an assortment of books covering a range of subjects in various conditions.

There were two further boxes of papers spanning several hundred years, some loose, others carefully bundled and tied with ribbons. No doubt the late Henry knew the system and what belonged where, but that knowledge was not passed on or written down anywhere.

Beginning with the books. *The Old Customs of North Yorkshire* contained some sections on Richmond. A piece on the tradition of T'awd Oss, which is a custom featuring a person wearing a costume with a horse's head – incredibly made from a real horse's skull – accompanied by mummers in costume who sing songs written for the occasion. There was a chapter on the festivals of Richmond: May Day, Easter, Harvest Festival and the Goose Fair of Richmond held on St Martin's Day, running for three days. St Martin's Day was on 11th November and was also known as Old Halloween. St Martin's would have been the time of year when the harvest had been gathered in and the animals fattened. Time for one last get-together before the winter set in. Winter in past times was a period where travel became much more difficult. The fair was believed to have originated in the twelfth century when the castle and the accompanying town were built. The book described how the fair was thought to have to run continuously until the late sixteenth century.

The location of the Goose Fair was described as a field to the north of Richmond at the top of the hill. There were a collection of wooden buildings used for the running of the fair, where the trading and, importantly, some of the festivities took place.

The book referred to a long tradition of storytelling with storytellers from many parts of the country converging for the three-day festival. It was said that if the storytellers were not approved of by the crowd they would pelt them with whatever came to hand, which gave them a bit of incentive to bring the crowd along with them.

One tradition associated with the Goose Fair was the carving of turnips into lanterns that were lit as part of a procession led by a person in the costume of an old horse through the gates into the town centre of Richmond, where the guildhalls would provide food and drink for all. Each guildhall vied to supply the best beer. The guilds commissioned the breweries in the area to produce special beer. The section concluded with a paragraph explaining how the site of the Goose Fair was turned into a racecourse, and the stadium was built at the top of the hill to give the spectators a full view of the course. The racecourse and buildings survived into the modern era.

The papers contained more information about the demise of the Goose Fair. Letters addressed to Mr Heckroy usually began with pleasantries before getting down to business. It was very clear that there was a strong desire by a Mr Tubhurst to get rid of the fair as he disliked the festival, noise and the big influx of people into Richmond. There was a good deal of discussion around the increase in petty crimes, the cramped accommodation in town, and the three days of drinking and excess. One of the wilder ideas was to instruct the local militia, who would impose a strict curfew to tame the worst behaviour, but in the later letters this idea was dismissed as not only expensive but would not have the direct effect of stopping the fair, which seemed to be the main agenda. The approach they took was to appeal to members of Parliament and senior clergy to have the charter revoked. There were letters from members of Parliament that sought to claim the common land on which the fair was held. By means of a swap, they proposed to give some waterlogged moorland on the road out of town as compensation to the commoners. The approach to the claiming of the common land was done by wording in the documents to make it look more like some sensible clearing up of an ambiguous ownership, along with formally registering some land outside of the town. Notably there was no mention of the Goose Fair. The correspondence relating to the charter for the fair was also framed as tidying up legislation for something that was no longer relevant or necessary.

There was the thorny issue of the organisers of the fair. Having lost their charter, they no longer had a right to run the fair, even if they were to move to the new land they were offered. The correspondents discussed offering the organisers alternative venues in either Barnard Castle or Pateley Bridge which unsurprisingly was rejected as an idea. Finally, it seems that there was a compromise of sorts in which a field was made available to allow a one-day auction of geese a week before St Martin's Day. The offer came with restrictions that no food or drink was allowed to be sold at the venue. Entertainment of any kind was specifically prohibited.

Once the land where the fair was held was claimed by Mr Heckroy and his friends, they set about demolishing the buildings and built an enclosing wall around the area. There were some letters that discussed the building of a racecourse for horses.

A bundle contained a series of letters addressed to Mr Heckroy relating to the glassworks. The glassworks were sited outside of the town walls by the river, all detailed by the inventories, deeds and titles. The inventory of the glassworks detailed a sophisticated operation with the delivery of coal from the mines in Cockfield, copper from the mine nearby, lead from Swaledale, iron from the North York Moors, tin from Teesdale and sand from the river as it broadened in the Vale of Mowbray.

The glassworks inventories listed three furnaces that were coal-powered. The furnaces melted the potash, sand and the metals to make the coloured glass. A large warehouse, with a building where the workers lived complete with a communal dining hall, made up the complex.

The works were controlled through the guild, with additional support from one of the Benedictine monks on secondment from St Martin's. From the inventories it seemed they were very astute businessmen with good contacts all over Europe where the glass was sold.

There were a hundred people employed at the height of the business, but by the middle of the sixteenth century the production had declined, and it was only employing a fraction of the workforce.

The next series of correspondence took a darker turn, beginning with a letter that was organising the theft of glass being transported by mule train to the port at Yarm on the Tees River. The glass was destined to go by boat to Newcastle where it would be transferred to ships for export. The mule train, the author of the letters proposed, would be intercepted along a marshy part of the route which was uninhabited. The correspondence referred to a secret escape route through the marsh making it very difficult to be followed.

The correspondents planned to dump the eight crates of glass and the transport harnesses in one of the meres along the route where they would not be found. There was a proposal to take the mules to the market in Grassington where they would be sold to the many buyers who worked in the lead mining industry. There was a letter after the event confirming that the mule train had been robbed as planned, the crates safely dumped in the brackish mere where they sank, and the mules sold.

The mule train drivers had sacks thrown over their heads so they could not see where the mules had gone, and they were taken to a village and released. As agreed, the mule drivers were given some coins as compensation to keep them quiet.

There were letters that discussed the sabotage of the furnaces that made the glass by introducing impurities to crack the furnace or to bribe one of the operators to break them. A letter confirmed that two of the three furnaces were broken through an explosion made by the introduction of gunpowder into the sand, potash and metal mix.

One letter outlined how they planned to manufacture a crime to implicate the team of Bohemians and Venetians who were working alongside the glass experts and lodged in town at a hostelry. This was part of an ongoing campaign to create hostilities towards the team by the local population. The plan was to plant some valuables in their dormitory, claiming that they'd stolen them from a house in Richmond. The burglary was real, as it had been meticulously been organised. The thieves made sure they left evidence pointing to the Bohemians and Venetians.

This was clearly an orchestrated campaign to reduce the value of the glassworks business by lowering the revenue to make the purchase cheaper for Mr Heckroy. The thefts, sabotage, and creating bad will against the operation were clear incentives for the owners to sell. The final straw was an Act of Parliament designed to weaken the guilds, further reducing the value of the business.

Mr Heckroy, on completing the purchase of the glassworks, began corresponding with an architect in Edinburgh about demolishing them. He had expansive ideas about building a townhouse with a pleasure garden. There were letters relating to the disposal of the inventory, selling the equipment to other glassworks in the region, and reusing the building materials.

Mr Tubhurst wrote to Mr Heckroy complaining that he thought the castle tower looked shabby and run-down, with the roof of the tower sagging in places. He proposed that instead of a conical tower, it should be taken down and remodelled with a simple castellated top with a hidden roof. Mr Tubhurst also objected to the wooden structure around the tower which was there for defensive reasons. He thought the tower would be much improved by having plain stone, and the wood removed. The correspondence discussed the funding of the improvements and how it would benefit the town, aesthetically.

What the correspondence and books were describing was the systematic destruction of not just the medieval buildings of Richmond but also the customs and livelihoods of the people of the town by a small group of well-connected and determined people. This small group were led by the Tubhursts and Heckroys.

•

Dear James,

I hope you're well and your investigation is making progress?

I attach some copies of manuscripts you may be interested in. They are a bit tricky to read in places, but it seems to be in your territory. The first one is an inventory of glass that was being shipped by a merchant in Newcastle to another merchant in Hamburg. Of interest is that the document refers to the Richmond glassworks. The second one is another reference to the glassworks, specifically their specialisation in glass for religious houses and guildhalls.

Let's have a chat soon to catch up.
Best,
Angela

James clicked the attachments. Scrolling through to see for himself, it clearly referenced glass being made in Richmond. James was unsure where this fit in with his investigation but it was good background colour that showed how Richmond had a thriving industry along with the significant social event of St Martin's Day. He took down his history books on Richmond from his bookshelves to see if he could cross-reference the glassworks. He found references to copper mining, wool and mills. Nothing on glass making. He tried an internet search. After a while he drew a blank. There was glass making in North Yorkshire but no mention of Richmond.

James began pondering why copper mining was more significant than medieval industry and glass making. He put that thought aside as he wrote a longish reply to Angela's email, describing his progress. He outlined how his next task was researching the papers he'd bought at auction.

James then settled down on his sofa. He decided that, rather than messaging Grace, he'd call her to have a chat. Grace picked up after two rings. They spent a long time talking.

NINE

James and Caitlin went back to the dim sum fusion restaurant at Friday lunchtime. This time they were a bit more prepared with the tablet and the menu. It was less busy than last time so they had a big space on the trestle table. They enjoyed the quieter atmosphere. No need to shout this time.

'Mr Pickles had an interior designer in on Wednesday. According to the gossip there will be a whole set of meeting rooms with fancy whiteboards and projectors for video calls. We are all going to be grouped in huddles rather than us all being in one big office,' said Caitlin, after they'd placed their order using the tablet on the table.

'I'm in favour of that. I've never got used to the noise and distractions of an open plan office. Mind you, I'm surprised he wants to spend money on making the office nice,' replied James.

'Again, the rumour mill says that he has been to a seminar for business leaders which was all about the future of the office. Apparently having the right image is good for recruiting.'

'I guess it makes sense. It will no doubt be disruptive when they make the changes.'

'No idea. He might not go for it when he sees the quotes. Are you going to Sam's leaving do next Thursday?'

'I might be there for a bit, but I have band practice later. We are rehearsing for our first gig, which will be at the Black Lion in three weeks' time.'

The dishes they'd ordered all arrived on a big tray: a mix of dumplings, a salad of pickled cabbage, radish, spring onion and cucumber strips, and a plate of sticky pork ribs.

'This looks yummy,' said Caitlin, reaching for the plate of ribs. 'Your first gig with the new band. That will be exciting. Do you think I'll like the music?'

'It's very different to the last band I played in,' replied James. 'We have Helen with a big set of synths and gadgets, Grace is a master at improvising with her jazz background, and Rick does some heavy processing with his saxophone. The best description is experimental music. It might be your cup of tea.'

'Mmm, I'll have a think about that then. Mind you I've never been to see experimental music live. Let me see if we can get a babysitter. How is your project coming on? Is there much more to do?'

'I'm finding out more and more about medieval Richmond. One of the books I bought at auction was about the old customs of North Yorkshire that described the St Martin's Goose Fair, and I was sent some documents which referred to glass being exported to Hamburg from a workshop in Richmond.

'What is slightly odd is that neither of these come up in the history books of Richmond. To compound it neither of the new discoveries are directly related to the hunt for the two gates. On the plus side, it all points to a vibrant medieval town. That in itself is important as it would have made it worth defending. It would explain the fortified gates.

I have a load of letters, documents, and records to go through which I bought at the auction. That should keep me busy for a while.'

'You're on a mission. I suppose you'll get to a point

where you either run out of things to find or you'll get your answers. The big unknown is when.'

'Very true. Even though the scope is broadening, I'm still enjoying it.

'I'm still a bit peckish. Shall we order another couple of plates? More pork dumplings, and try the fish cakes?'

They finished their second course and walked back to the office with Caitlin telling James all about her gardening project.

•

Lucinda was cooking fish fingers and oven chips with peas as requested by the boys for their supper when her phone rang.

'Lucinda, Frankie here. Henry's cousin. How are you coping?'

'I'm holding together. Thanks. I can't talk long as I'm cooking the boys' supper.'

'I'll keep it to the point. I gather you had a bit of a clear out and got rid of the mountain of stuff Henry had accumulated. Did you by any chance come across some boxes of papers and letters?'

'Yes, I did, they were in an old armoire and the auctioneer suggested we boxed them up and pop them in the auction as some people are interested in that sort of thing. He was right as they sold for the reserve price.'

'Bugger. They were things that belong to the family. We will have to get them back. Can you call the auctioneers?'

'I must go, or their supper will burn. I'll call you later.'

Lucinda laid the table and shouted to the boys that it was supper time. She piled the fish fingers, chips and peas on the plates, and put the bottles of ketchup, brown sauce, mayonnaise, and Sriracha sauce on the table.

Once she'd washed up, tidied everything away, and fed the dog, she returned Frankie's call. He was very cagey about why the papers were important but was insistent that Lucinda called the auctioneers in the morning to find out who had bought them. What he really needed was a name, address and phone number.

Lucinda was a bit troubled. She knew Henry had kept some secrets from her about his family, but had always dismissed it as not very important. Why on earth were some old letters, documents and notebooks that had been shoved in a cupboard in the attic that precious? Surely if they had some value, they could've been stored in a safe or even better at the bank?

She was not at all convinced that the auction house would turn over the information on the buyer, but she would at least try. If nothing else, it would get Frankie off her back. She considered Frankie a pompous arse, a bit creepy with it, and generally to be avoided at family get-togethers, especially as he'd tried to grope her a couple of times in a very unsubtle way.

•

Lucinda called the auction house to ask for the name of the purchaser of the lots which included the papers. Not surprisingly the person she spoke with at the auction house cited data protection, and explained they were not at liberty to reveal the information to her. They offered to contact the purchaser to pass on her details with a message that she was looking to get in touch. Lucinda thanked them. She was more than a bit relieved to have that job done.

She mustered up the courage to call Frankie. She told him of the conversation with the auction house. He didn't seem too happy, muttering something about what would happen if the buyer didn't contact her. He added that he would call a friend who was a good friend of the chairman to see if he could get some traction that way.

Lucinda was happy that Frankie had picked it up himself. All she needed to do was forward any information if the buyer did decide to contact her.

There was clearly something fishy going on. It used to make her cross how Henry had his secrets, especially around family matters. The intervention of Frankie reignited those thoughts, bringing it all back how Henry would disappear into the attic or lock himself in his study for hours, occasionally going on some mysterious trip.

•

- Edward, how are you?

- Luke, good to hear from you. What can I do for you?

- I thought you might want to know that a friend of mine bought some lots at auction recently. They were from Richmond and relate to your family.

- I appreciate you letting me know. We were trying to find out who had bought them. Any chance you could pass on the contact details?

- Sure. I'll forward the contact details in the chat.

- Appreciate it. Thank you.

•

James noticed an email from the auction house letting him know that the vendor was interested in contacting him about a couple of lots he'd recently bought, offering to pass on his details. He didn't give it much more thought. He wasn't too interested in speaking with the vendor about the papers from what he understood was a clear-out. They may be trying to offload more items.

It was time to discuss his findings with Angela. James collected his notes together, settled down on his sofa with a cup of tea and he rang.

'Hi, Angela. How are you?'

'Nice to hear from you, James. I'm well. Thanks. You caught me at a good time. I'm going to a conference next week to present some of my latest papers. There's a whole set of events in the evenings. I read your email and wanted to give it some thought before I replied. I'm glad you called as it's probably simpler to talk rather than write a lengthy email.'

'Have you ever come across a series of letters, titles and inventories that are privately held, yet seem to be the only source of information about events in the past? It seems strange that there are no other sources or references in the books covering that period. The Acts of Parliament that were enacted are presumably documented, and available to be read?' asked James.

'It does seem very unusual from what you have shared. There were some significant events such as closing the Goose Fair. The glassworks seemed to be a significant enterprise with international connections which you'd have thought would've been documented elsewhere.

'To give it some perspective, the period of the late

medieval era saw a lot of major events such as the gunpowder plot and civil war. Plague was still ravaging the population and there was the battle between the Protestants and Catholics to hold power.

'While the events you have found are interesting, particularly in how the town was being changed by a small number of individuals, it could've been seen to be normal in this period of instability, conflict, and death.

'There were similar activities in the Georgian times when there was a fashion for romanticising the countryside. We see this with the creation of parklands that saw some major engineering works to create a rural idyll. A good example of engineering the landscape is the project that rebuilt part of Hadrian's Wall using the stones that had fallen down. The Roman built wall had collapsed years before,' said Angela.

'So, what I'm finding is a window to an era of the town of Richmond which shows how the town was shaped at a certain time in history? Even if the means were very underhand?' asked James.

'Right. I guess that's one way to look at it. There's probably more information that you could unearth which will complete the picture. Just think when you started on this, all you had were a couple of illustrations which piqued your interest. If you find much more, I suggest you share it with the university. We could make a bid to put some resources into researching it. That could be an interesting route to follow, especially if you could find a funding source. I'm making lots of notes. I still have more to do. Let's see where this ends up.'

'Thanks for your encouragement. And for listening. I have moments where I wonder what on earth I'm doing.

A little voice asks me whether I should be putting so much time into this,' said James

They finished the call, promising to speak again in a couple of weeks and making tentative plans for James to visit Angela in Birmingham.

TEN

'Is that James O'Connell? Frankie Heckroy. I believe you bought some lots including some papers at auction recently?'

'How did you get my number?'

'I have my sources. The lots you bought are needed back by the family as they were mistakenly sent to auction by my late cousin's widow. I'm going to send a courier to your house to collect them. We will, of course, refund you the money you paid. You will also include any copies you have made. You're to delete electronic copies on your computer.'

'Wait a minute. I've not agreed to return them. You can't just send a courier.'

'Look, those papers should not have been sold. You have no right to hold onto them as they don't belong to you.'

'I bought them at auction as they were as listed in the catalogues, and paid my money. They are now mine,' said James stubbornly. He really didn't like the way this conversation was going.

'Name your price then. I'll buy them back if that's what you're holding out for. Although I don't see why I should pay you any more than the price you paid, especially seeing as they belong to my family.'

'I'm keeping them as they are helpful in a research project I'm doing. I'm not prepared to give them back to you.'

'These are my family's papers. I insist that you return them to us. You know, if you've read the papers, that we're a respectable family who have long ties with Richmond. The whole lot belong to us.'

'What if I took copies? You can send a courier to collect the originals?' offered James, who had a moment of doubt that he was being unreasonably stubborn.

'You'll do no such thing. I told you we need them back. I also demand that you are not to make copies. These are family papers that should not have been sold in the first place.'

'I need to think about it.'

'There isn't much to consider. You will return the boxes of papers to me. As I've already told you, I'll book a courier to collect them.'

'I have your number. I'll call you back when I've considered your request.'

'Don't spend too much time thinking. I expect you to call me back soon.' And with that Frankie hung up.

On face value this was a clear case of returning the collection of papers that were sold by a grieving widow who didn't understand the significance of the material. It was made more complicated by Frankie and the way he'd asked James. Had he been less overbearing or had taken a more conciliatory approach, apologising for the mistake then James may have been much more understanding and willing to help. Antagonising James was not the best approach, although it was not a done deal yet. There were some get-outs for James. The worst thing was that Frankie had highlighted the importance of the papers in his zeal to have the papers returned. Had he played it low key, then James may have made some copies, but without the originals he would need to ask the Heckroy family for permission to publish or to cite the source.

•

James and Luke were driving to the new restaurant which Luke wanted to try: a Punjabi canteen on the edge of town in the unlikely setting of an old shopping parade, the restaurant, sandwiched between an old-fashioned haberdashery shop with a window display of rolls of colourful material, and on the other side a small betting shop with a battered steel door.

'I had a call from one of the family who sold the papers that I picked up at the auction. He was an obnoxious bloke. He demanded I returned everything, saying it belonged to his family. He claimed the lot was sold by mistake,' said James.

'How did he track you down? I didn't think that the auction house would be able to share that information unless they had your consent under data protection rules?'

'He was very blunt about that. He said, "I have my sources." He didn't volunteer how he'd found me. It seems he also knows where I live as he was ready to send a courier to pick up the boxes.'

'That sounds a bit fishy, especially as he hasn't got your details in a legit way.'

'I haven't even thought about that. My big dilemma is what should I do? People do make mistakes and it could be the right thing to do in returning the papers, but on the other hand he was being a real tosser about it.'

'From what you have read, are they personal letters that belong to the family or are they more to do with their business interests?'

'They aren't personal letters by any means. They are replies to letters sent to various people discussing some fairly underhand things to do with grabbing land. At a stretch, getting them back would help them maintain their reputation.'

'How old are the letters, titles, and documents?'

'That's the strange part. They date from the mid-1600s to the early 1700s. Nothing recent or anything that would be sensitive to living people.'

'If they're that sensitive then it seems odd that they were kept at all. It sounds like they might be incriminating. They aren't the sort of thing you would store away for centuries.'

'One thing I thought about was returning them, and taking pictures of the interesting papers. Or even returning the papers, and making sure I'd made notes of the key information. They are interesting for historians, but the documents don't change our understanding of history in the way a discovery of a pre-Roman settlement might do.'

'That's the big question then. Why do you want to keep them? If, as you say, there's evidence of misdemeanours, there's not much that can be done as there are limitations of statutes in how far you can go back and dispute things. What outcome are you expecting?'

Conveniently, they'd arrived at the restaurant. Luke found a parking space nearby. They got themselves settled at a table, and ordered drinks and a poppadom each with a pickle tray before resuming the conversation.

'You were asking why I'd want to keep them?' said James. 'I guess I took a punt in buying them at auction. As it turned out they were relevant to the period I'm looking into. They've given me a better idea about Richmond at that time, and importantly who was doing what. I approached the research as something interesting to do. I wanted to see how far it went rather than having a specific goal. The papers are part of that journey. I've only read through them once which means I could lose information if something new came up and I wanted to cross-reference. One thing was clear, he didn't want me keeping copies. I can imagine he'd not be open to me reading them once he has them back.'

'You could always take copies then sell him the originals back for, say, a 20 per cent premium to cover your time and the costs of collecting them.'

'That sounds like a good idea, as I'm sure he will hassle me. Even if I block his number, I can imagine he will just show up at the house. It wouldn't take me long to scan them. I can always extract the text from the images using one of those online tools.'

'You should call the auction house to complain about them giving your information out. You can mention the Information Commission, which is where you can complain if they aren't being helpful.'

They ordered, spending the rest of the evening talking about James's band, sport and Luke's complicated love life.

Luke dropped off James at home later in the evening. James decided to message Frankie with his offer of a 20 per cent surcharge and that Frankie could arrange collection. The response came quickly. Frankie thought James was being cheeky, but agreed and asked for his bank details. James suggested he drop the box off at a pickup point which would be at his local mini-market. Frankie agreed with this suggestion, and requested that James left the box by the following Wednesday.

Rick was very excited at the weekly band rehearsal. He'd sent some demo tracks to a couple of local venues, and both got back to him with a booking.

'James sent me a message apologising that he will be a few minutes late,' said Rick to Grace and Helen.

'It's becoming a bit of a habit,' said Helen, frowning. 'Let's start without him, like last time. I can always conjure up some basslines on my synths.'

'Sounds good to me,' said Grace.

'Rick, you might have a word with him about getting here on time,' suggested Helen. 'He's a lovely guy, and a decent bass player, but I've had bad experiences with unreliable band members in the past.'

'Fair enough, Helen. I'll have a discreet word. It seems to be working well but I don't want tensions to form. It might not even occur to him that he's being annoying,' replied Rick. 'As you say, worst case we can continue with sequenced basslines and don't necessarily need a bass player.'

They spent a bit of time talking through the set they would play before they began to practice. The first couple of tracks went nicely with the set building up with increasing depth, until Helen had a glitch with one of her modular synths that got into a muddle, starting to make some very atonal, random and fairly unpleasant noises. Helen apologised. After some fiddling, she got it sorted out. They started again. This time it went smoothly.

James appeared just over twenty minutes late, apologising profusely, and he quickly plugged in and began to play.

Rick and Helen were both aware of the chemistry between James and Grace, who seemed to instinctively know what the other was about to do, and hoped that if that chemistry evolved beyond the music, it didn't cause any tension in the band.

There was some experimentation with Rick routing his saxophone through one of Helen's mixers. It was connected to some filters and effects that gave the sound a real depth, with some interesting but unexpected effects. James was next to try something out with the bass, but it was less successful, so they concluded to leave it as it was.

The set they had planned was for an hour with a couple of tracks they could play to extend it if needed. The first gig was in two weeks and they agreed to do two more practice sets before the event. It was part of a mini festival of experimental artists, new and emerging bands and some DJ sets.

'I'm happy with that set,' said Grace. 'I was thinking about the gig. What do you all think about having a video loop projected as a backdrop?'

'Great idea,' said Helen. 'I've been playing around with some videos recently and looked into some live visualisers that work off the music feed. I'll bring in my mini projector and laptop at the next session so you can see it for yourselves. I'll also share some links in the group chat you can have a look at in the meantime.'

'Thanks, Helen,' said Grace. 'As we have a gig coming up, how about getting some merchandise printed? Maybe some T-shirts or beanies in small batches with a limited set of sizes? I know the guys at a shop that does printing and could bring some samples next week. If we like them, I can order a batch and have it delivered to the Union Bar.'

'I like that idea. It worked well in the last band I was in,' said James. 'There seems to be a certain type of person who wants the very niche T-shirts of up-and-coming bands.'

'I was thinking about mixing some of the tracks I've recorded at the sessions, and uploading them to Bandcamp, YouTube and Spotify, so people can listen to the tracks either before or after the gig,' said Rick.

'I'd rather take a bit of time to get the tracks right rather than rush something out. Not that I'm suggesting you can't mix!' replied Helen. 'A friend of mine, a sound engineer I know from a soundtrack project I worked on, would do the mixing for us. He owes me one.'

•

Despite both James and Grace having lots of experience playing live, they both seemed a bit nervous. James had gone to Grace's house to get ready for the gig. He helped Grace load the drum kit into her small van at the studio before making their way to the Union bar for set up and soundchecks.

They got the equipment set up and ran through a soundcheck, which didn't take too long. The acoustics in the room were good. The monitors were set up as they wanted.

There was a DJ set to open the evening, and another band before them, so they had time to go and grab some food. As they were eating, they ran through the set again... who was doing what and when, as well as the order of what they were playing.

The first band finished to big applause. Cosmic

Fragments got themselves ready while a DJ kept people in the room with a short set.

They came on stage to a nearly full room. They began playing. The opening was a roar of sound as they'd practiced. As they'd planned, it got the audience's attention. The next few pieces they played was to an enthusiastic audience who were enjoying the music. Helen fired up the projector for the next section with a swirl of colour in the background which matched the big drone sounds that Helen and Rick were playing. James brought in a dub element with his heavy bassline complemented by Grace's drumming. They played their full set, including a short encore, much to the pleasure of the crowd.

Backstage they were very happy with how it went, especially how the video worked in the background to add to the music. They loaded the kit into Grace's van then went to the front desk to see how the T-shirt sales had gone. To their surprise, there were only three left.

They all stayed to watch a couple of the bands, making an evening of it. Helen turned out to be a lot chattier than she normally was. James and Rick had a good catch up, gossiping about mutual friends in other bands.

James and Grace stayed for the first of the big DJ sets after the bands had finished, enjoying dancing together without being jostled too much.

They went back to Grace's house, after they'd unloaded the drum kit at the studio, and stayed up for a drink to chat about the evening before going to bed.

They had a nice leisurely morning with James popping out to get some fresh pastries while Grace made the coffees.

'The coffee smells good! I got some cinnamon buns

and Danish pastries,' called James as he walked into kitchen, putting the bag on the island, and giving Grace a hug and a kiss.

'Was the bakery busy? You were quick.'

'I got there just in time. There was a bit of a queue forming after I got there.'

'What are your plans today?'

'Nothing special. I thought we might go for a walk. Maybe have a rummage at the record shop?'

'I'd like that. I'm having my hair cut at 3 o'clock. I'm still buzzing after the gig. It went much better than I was expecting.'

'For a first gig, it couldn't have gone better. Helen and Rick were at another level. I was pleased how we totally nailed our stuff.'

They munched their pastries, sipped their coffees and began dissecting the set again.

ELEVEN

James made his way home with a couple of vinyls he'd found at their favourite record shop. He was looking forward to Grace coming to his house later as she'd promised to bring his guitar that he'd left at her house.

As he opened the front door, he could sense something wasn't right. He'd been burgled. The living room was a mess with books scattered everywhere. The bookshelves were emptied with the books all over the living-room floor. He picked his way through to check the window in the living room. There was no sign of entry there. Once in the corridor he could feel a draught that turned out to be from the backdoor being left ajar. A closer examination revealed that the burglars had crowbarred the backdoor to get in. James pushed the door open to see if there was anything they'd left behind in the yard, but there was no sign they'd been there. His back gate was intact.

He wandered back into the house. He sat down in the kitchen, wondering what he should do next. The first thing was a call to the police. He figured even if they could not find the perpetrators, at least he would have a report for the insurance. He figured it would be a statistic that may help when it came to budget time to make a case for more of whatever was needed to fight low-level crime.

James got through to the police who took his details, promising to send someone around to have a look. They suggested he take some pictures of the mess, clean up and figure out what was taken.

Before he set to and cleared up, he thought it a good

idea to buy a replacement lock and a couple of bolts from the hardware store. Worried that whoever had burgled him may return, he jammed the backdoor closed.

The man at the hardware shop was very sympathetic. He gave James some advice on the best lock to buy, and recommended some concealed security bolts that he could easily install himself.

James returned home with his kit. The mess didn't look any better, and he began the daunting task of tidying up. He took photos, as he'd been asked, of the room that had been ransacked. Once he was done, he did a tour of the house to see if there was anything else that had been disturbed. James could not be sure that everything was exactly as he'd left it, but it all looked fine. He returned to the living room, and began stacking the books on the shelves to clear some space and figure out what was missing.

It took him less time than he thought. From what he could figure out the only missing things were the papers he'd bought at auction, along with a couple of his books on medieval Yorkshire. The burglar had rummaged through his vinyl collection but hadn't taken anything. James took out some of the LPs to double-check. The records were in one piece. His desk had been thoroughly searched. One of his old USB sticks was missing, along with a notebook, but nothing else. Then it dawned on him that his laptop had gone.

He made a list on one the notepads he had to hand: the papers from the auction, one of his notebooks, laptop, and the USB stick.

It was time to take stock. His laptop wasn't too much of a loss as he was good about backing it up to the cloud, so he should be able to retrieve his data. It did prompt him to change his password just in case the thief tried to access his account. He could do that using his phone. He did the same with his email and social media accounts as a precaution.

The papers were a loss, as he'd discovered so much, but on the other hand he'd scrupulously made copies and had been writing up his notes which he could still access. James also had the problem that he had agreed to box up the papers and drop them off at the pickup point. That prompted him to check his messages to see if he had been sent a label to print for the box or an address. The conversation with Frankie now showed *deleted account* instead of his number. Looking though his search history he found the number and tried to call it. He heard *'the number you have called cannot be recognised'*. James checked his banking app to see if he had been sent the money on the off-chance, and unsurprisingly he had no receipts matching the amount they'd agreed.

James set to on the back door. He replaced the lock, and inserted the concealed bolts. Once he was done he felt more secure.

He did a quick dash to the supermarket to get the missing ingredients he needed, as well as stocking up on some beers and a couple bottles of wine. To partly take his mind off things, he began preparing dinner, with the added bonus that he wouldn't be in the kitchen all evening.

As he was in the middle of chopping up the vegetables, the doorbell rang. It was a police officer. James showed the pictures of the living room and the damage done to the back door, and gave them a list of things that were stolen. He explained about the papers that he'd bought from the auction, and the conversations with Frankie about returning them. The police officer seemed sympathetic but she managed James's expectations about the likelihood of the case being followed up. She gave him the incident number he could use when contacting the insurers.

•

It was Caitlin's first visit to Verity's new flat. It was reached through a small side door next to a large metal gate that led into what was once a parking or delivery area for the old light industrial building. Verity had warned her that the entrance to her flat was up the metal fire escape stairs to the side of the building. The ground floor entrance was locked and looked like it had not been open for a while. The glass was covered with thick dust and dead insects. There was a faded sign with some of the letters missing: 'ksire Precision Engin ring Ltd'.

The door to the flat looked newly painted and was finished with a robust door handle and plain keyguard. Caitlin pressed the buzzer to the side of the door and waited.

'Caitlin! Thanks so much for coming around. Come in,' said Verity. She enthusiastically opened the door.

'Wow, this space is amazing,' said Caitlin. 'So much light and a beautiful layout.'

'Thank you. I've really enjoyed starting with an empty space and having the freedom to knock it around.'

'Oh, I love that table. Where'd you get it from?'

'I made it. It was one of my first pieces of furniture. The first thing I did was to fit the kitchen, and then I knocked about what must have been a staff loo into a bathroom with a shower.'

'Amazing. That's really impressive. Especially as you have no idea how long you'll be here.'

'That's part of the challenge to make something quick, inexpensive and homely. Having a space like this allowed me to chop it up how I wanted, rather than having some massive airport lounge style living space with a lost sofa in one corner.'

'So you have put up the walls? I like the finish of the chipboard. I don't suppose the artwork is yours?'

'Yes, I did the walls and the paintings. Have a look around if you like. Would you like a coffee?'

'That would be fantastic. Can I have it short and black, please?'

Verity made her way to the kitchen area, made the coffees and brought them over to the table with a small plate of biscuits. Caitlin had enjoyed wandering around the flat looking at the details, such as the paintings, the various house plants, rugs and the collection of upcycled furniture.

'Where does that door go to?' asked Caitlin, pointing to a door at the right of the bedroom door.

'Oh, I put a door into the wall when I made the room a bit smaller. It goes into a big empty space at the moment, which I will do something with one day. I don't need it at the moment and it's a big space to heat. We need to talk about plants! I got the bigger plants from a nearby office that was clearing out. I re-potted them and given them a bit of a feed. Is there anything else I need to do?'

'It sounds like you have done just the right thing. One tip I have is to use a layer of gravel or something to keep the moisture in. So tell me, what's the sewing project you have for me?' asked Caitlin.

'I need a hand with these cushions on the sofa. I bought some nice material and some big buttons, and I'm running out of time. As you have seen, I need to finish off the bathroom, and want to paper those walls,' said Verity, pointing towards the walls across from the kitchen area. With that, Verity got up and retrieved a roll of material to show Caitlin.

'How many cushions are there to do?' asked Caitlin.

'Those five uncovered ones on the sofa.'

'What about me cutting the material now and tacking it, rather than trying to get the material and cushions home with me and back?'

'Good idea. I have some scissors somewhere and I think I know where my sewing box is.' Verity got up again and rummaged around in one of the drawers of an elegant piece of furniture. She asked, 'How is the family? Work? Garden?'

'Rob and the kids are off doing sporty stuff this morning and are all in good moods at the moment. Work is entertaining as always. Mr Pickles is talking about an office refit and there has been a spectacular fight which will not end well. Mad James is getting deeper into his historical mission. He seems fixated on Richmond in the Dales and medieval history for some unknown reason. I am nearly done with the garden layout and am making good progress with the planting.'

'What does Mad James think he will achieve that the great and good from academia haven't already found out?'

'It beats me. He seems to be very scattered in his approach and doesn't really know what he's looking for. It started with a book and now he's randomly following threads from the last thing he reads. The latest thing was something about an old Goose Fair, which is a royal sidetrack. He's taking it all very seriously.'

'I hope you're encouraging him?' said Verity, and laughed.

'Just enough as the stories are entertaining, and it's pretty harmless stuff he's doing.'

Caitlin and Verity worked together in cutting out the material around the cushions and tacking it to form rough covers. Caitlin carefully folded them up and put them in a bag to take home along with a paper bag of large, brightly coloured buttons.

•

Grace arrived a little late which was handy as James was a bit behind things in the kitchen. It gave him time to clear up a bit before she arrived. She brought his guitar as they'd arranged, a bottle of white Rioja, and a box of truffles from the artisan chocolate maker they'd discovered in town.

'Your hair looks great. I like the blue,' said James as they made their way through to the kitchen.

'Thanks. I dithered, but I was talked into the shade. It's smelling good in the kitchen. Have you been busy all afternoon creating?'

'It has been a bit of a dramatic afternoon. I got back to find the house had been burgled, but thankfully they haven't taken much or trashed it.'

'Oh god, that must be horrible. Poor you.'

'It's all sorted now. I changed the lock, tidied up, and had the police pop by.'

'Did the police have any wisdom about it?'

'The police officer was very nice, managing my expectations. She said that there were not that many domestic burglaries and was surprised how little was taken. It could've been that they were disturbed. What was slightly creepy is that they picked last night, which may have been a coincidence or they know who I am and that we were playing last night. I suspect it was a targeted burglary knowing what they took. Before I launch into the full tale, I'll pour us drinks, and put the chilli in the oven to warm up. White wine, or a beer?'

'A beer would be nice.'

They took their drinks and a bowl of mixed nuts to the living room. James put one of his new LPs on, turning the volume down from earlier when he'd been cleaning.

James told the tale of his hunt for medieval gateways to Grace, weaving his way through the various episodes, including his bookshop hunting, the weekend visits, and his quest.

'I had no idea that you were so into history, but then we did meet through music.'

'I thought it was a bit of fun to do some digging as I had this thing about the medieval era. Partly from my time at uni and partly from the talks I've been going to. I didn't imagine that it would take me on the path it has.'

'So what has this got to do with the break-in?'

James continued his tale, embellishing the story and injecting his conjectures, which made it all a little hard to follow. He ended on his theories about who had broken in and why.

'Wow, that seems a bit extreme to break into someone's house to get the papers when you'd already agreed to return them.'

'It's very odd, especially as the papers were mainly old letters from hundreds of years ago. There was nothing racy in them. I really don't know why they would be important enough for someone to go to the lengths of breaking into a house to get them back.'

'What's next? Are you going to carry on or put it down to experience?'

'Do you know, I'm not sure. I didn't find out what I set out to discover but learned a lot about Richmond at the end of the medieval period. I'm half tempted to see what else I find out. Another beer? I need to go to the kitchen to put the rice on. I could bring one through on the way back.'

'Another beer would be lovely. Can I help with anything?'

'Everything is under control! I'll be right back.'

TWELVE

Caitlin and James were back in the little café they used to go to regularly on their Friday lunch break. Not much had changed. The same plants and cacti, the same clientele and the same bustle and aromas. In short a winning formula. They sat near the window and ordered from the specials menu, which was a choice between homemade ravioli stuffed with sweet potato, sage, and rabbit and penne arrabbiata.

James launched into his tale of sleuthing and the dramatic burglary with gusto, interrupted when the food arrived. They were asked if they wanted some parmesan sprinkling on. They both nodded and watched the parmesan being sprinkled with a flourish before James continued his story.

'What now?' asked Caitlin. 'You won't have time to carry on, what with Grace, the band and work?'

'I'll squeeze in some time to do it. This has spurred me on to keep digging. It's interesting what I am finding and I don't like being told not to do something. The band doesn't take up masses of time. We have got some good stuff written already. It seems to happen by itself. We have a couple more gigs lined up that Rick seems to magic out of nowhere! Work? It pays the bills and Mr Pickles seems to like us all leaving on time. He has changed with the new office plans. He's now keen that people don't overwork.'

'I know we thought the budgets would scare him off but we were both wrong on that count, unless he has driven a hard bargain. Have you heard the rumour that he's getting a proper table football and that there will be a modern kitchen area which will be all Scandi and reclaimed wood?'

'Now that does surprise me. Have you heard the rumour about the takeover of the publishing house which does *Dentistry Monthly* and *Catering Weekly*? I heard that the people running it were retiring. There was an offer to take on the titles and bring some of the team in.'

'New one to me. I hope there are some sales people. We are running short at the moment. It would be good to have a couple more people to help.'

'Antique shop on the way back?'

'Good plan. Let's get the bill.'

•

The burglary unsettled James more than he thought, and although he had a very interesting collection of papers from the auction, he lacked the skills to piece it all together into a coherent picture. His approach was haphazard enough to learn snippets of information and connect them in a way that suited his various hypotheses and theories.

Despite James being scatty, he had awareness of his limits and sought the help of Angela. Luckily for James, Angela was interested in what he'd come across, although she was under no illusion that he had the ability to piece it together and was planning to steer him into giving the materials to the university.

James asked Angela if he could come and visit her in Birmingham to discuss his findings in person. He suggested to Grace that they make a weekend of it with the promise that he would show her the fun parts of Birmingham, but that he needed a couple of hours with Angela.

They took the train to Birmingham on Saturday morning, setting off early to make the most of the day. The train wasn't very full. They had a nice time chatting and munching on the breakfast they'd brought to eat on the train. They'd got it from James's favourite artisan baker and coffee shop. They talked about the band, James's research project, work and about each other's past lives without being too intrusive.

Once they got to Birmingham, they made their way to the small hotel that they'd found trawling the internet for a nice place to stay that was not too pricey. They left their bags in the store room as they were not able to check in until mid-afternoon.

James was meeting Angela at two o'clock at the university, so they had plenty of time to go and explore. The first stop was the Custard Factory where they had a look around the shops, and had the mandatory rummage through the record shops.

James made his way to the university while Grace had plans to visit some galleries and explore other parts of Birmingham. They agreed to meet back at the hotel around four.

James called Angela as he was approaching the university, she arranged to meet him at reception.

'James! Good to see you,' said Angela enthusiastically.

'Nice to see you again, and it's good to be back in Birmingham!'

They walked through the lobby to the lifts, making their way to Angela's office. James ran through his well-rehearsed synopsis of what had taken place, and what he'd discovered.

Angela's office had a couple of medieval maps on the wall, a few well-looked-after plants, a range of books, a filing cabinet, a surprisingly clutter-free desk with a monitor and connected laptop.

'There are a couple of things that are still puzzling,' said James. 'Firstly, why are there significant events missing from the history books of Richmond?'

'Your discoveries have been about the Goose Fair and the glassworks so far,' said Angela. 'While it might seem strange to you that something as big as the Goose Fair was not very well known, it did come up in the book you found. To give it some context, you have to bear in mind that the fair was run during a period of plague, war, the dissolution of the monasteries and other major historical events. The glassworks aren't mentioned in the history books as they would have been seen as a small business compared to the trade in wool or later on the advent of larger-scale lead mining. That said, the campaign to undermine the business with a view to buying it for less than it was worth is worthy of a mention in the history books.'

'Okay,' said James, 'I probably lost some perspective somewhere in my research. What's interesting is forming a picture of what Richmond would've been like in the medieval times and the extent they traded.'

'That's important given how Richmond was subsequently transformed in the eighteenth century with the medieval era more or less forgotten. If the fortunes of Richmond had remained robust in the nineteenth century, it would've been remodelled to fit the taste of the times.'

'Okay, so what if I wrote a piece about the medieval times of Richmond and how it functioned as a town? I've made copies of some of the letters, titles and inventories, but how do I reference these as the originals are now missing? I'd planned to hand them all to the Yorkshire Archive.'

'That could be a challenge, but now you have a better idea what you're looking for. There could be other letters and documents in the North Yorkshire county archives. I'll keep digging for connections to my work on the Hanseatic League, especially the ongoing work in Newcastle and Groningen. There was certainly trade with the glass produced in Richmond and I imagine that it was not the only trade if the merchants were already connected.'

'Okay, I've made a lot of notes which I can do something with. I'll keep digging. I think my approach is to look for charters, Acts of Parliament and archives of the active guilds of Richmond.'

'I might be able to help there. There's some research going on with the medieval guilds of northern England in the department, and I'll make some enquiries. The guilds were important in medieval times, gradually losing their power before they were eventually abolished by an Act of Parliament. Are you finding enough time to do this with work and life?'

'Funnily it has really fired me up. I enjoy doing the research, fitting the pieces together and writing it all up. Even if my day job is writing, I don't really associate the two. I've also got back into music. I've joined a new band, Cosmic Fragments, which has been really good. We have written lots already and done our first gig.'

'Oh, I'm pleased to hear that. It sounds like you're in a good place with lots going on.'

'I do seem to be on a roll at the moment and it feels good. How are things going with your research on the Hanseatic League?'

'It's going well. It has been good to work with the archaeologists doing the dig in Newcastle and the researchers in Groningen. I published some papers, and gave some talks at a couple of conferences. I'm putting a funding proposal together to build on what we have found out. Perhaps I should include a piece about the glassworks, given that they were prolific exporters to important religious houses across the continent.

'Shall we have a wander into the library to do a search for information connected to Richmond? It would be good to give you some pointers at what to look for and how to cross-reference the information. Do you have some time?'

'I'm okay until about four when I told Grace I'd be back at the hotel.'

'It's just before three now. Let's go and spend an hour there. It will give you plenty of time to get back.'

•

Angela showed James what search terms she used and how to cross-reference the links and citations. Angela had made some notes while James was talking and began with the topic of the St Martin's Goose Fair in Richmond.

The first reference that she found was a report in a collection of papers from one of the town's militia. There was a detailed description of rioting and unrest in Richmond following the passing of the charter that effectively banned the Goose Fair. There were three people who were accused of being the leaders of the riot and were put into the gaol in the militia's complex. What had triggered the riot was the public reading of the charter banning the fair by the town crier at the butter cross in the market place. The residents of Richmond were very angry that they'd not been consulted. The Act of Parliament was seen as malicious and cynical by the rioters. In a later document there was a description of further riots, and general upset in Richmond as the traditional time of the Goose Fair approached. It was triggered by the usual movement of people from the surrounding area converging on the fields where the fair was traditionally held. When they arrived, they found a collection of soldiers from the local militia who told them the fair was no longer permitted and they should go home. Instead of going home they teamed up with the still angry residents, and it resulted in more unrest, protest and rioting. Angela pointed out to James what was important, such as the dates of the documents which would help narrow the time frame for finding the relevant Acts of Parliament. The names of the instigators of the riots were also a good starting point for the parish records. There was a reference to further records from the militia at the time, which were held in the county archives in Northallerton, not too far from York.

Angela continued with records of the militia, and showed James the way they were written and how to interpret the information. Of interest to James was that the head of the militia was a Mr Heckroy. There were documents in the auction lot that James had missed, from the box which was stolen, that had listed the buildings associated with the Goose Fair: a large banqueting hall, stabling for horses, accommodation built over the stables for the travellers, a kitchen and an enclosure made up of pens to accommodate the geese. It was not clear whether the buildings were used outside of the fair, or if they were specifically used for the three days in November. This information was not in the documents from the militia and not something James could ask Angela how to find.

It was an instructive session for James, and Angela seemed happy that he'd been making copious notes and had asked sensible questions, although she was not confident that he had the patience and rigour to trawl through the archives to find the information he was looking for.

They gathered up their things, making their way to the ground floor, summing up what they'd discovered and what to look at next. James promised to share his notes with Angela so she could follow progress. She in turn would share things as she came across them, especially now that she had a better idea of what was being unearthed. They both agreed it was an interesting period of history that wasn't that well known. Having the information gathered into a nice document connecting everything together was a worthwhile exercise.

James made his way back to the hotel where he'd agreed to meet Grace, walking through the familiar streets, taking his favourite shortcuts. It felt like yesterday that he was a student, yet it had changed with new shops and bars popping up. The old haunts had gone, and that reminded him that it was a while since he'd lived in Birmingham.

As he approached the hotel, Grace sent him a message saying she would be there soon, so he made his way to the bar adjacent to the reception desk to wait.

•

James and Grace lounged around in the hotel room, planning their evening out and talking about what they'd both been up to. Eventually they got themselves ready to go out.

They went to a cocktail bar near the hotel to kick the evening off. It was busy with an early evening crowd. The cocktails didn't disappoint. Having enjoyed a couple of drinks and now feeling peckish, they set off to a restaurant they'd found on one of the many websites about dining in Birmingham. They'd managed to book a table. It was a short walk along one of the canals. Walking towards them was a familiar face.

'Luke! Small world, what brings you to Brum?' shouted James.

'Bloody hell! I could say the same to you.'

'Luke, meet Grace. Grace, meet Luke.'

'Hi, Grace, good to meet you,' said Luke, turning to Grace.

'Hi, Luke,' replied Grace.

'Where are you heading to?' asked Luke.

'We are off to a restaurant around the corner, then plan to go clubbing. What are you up to?'

'I'm meeting my cousin and some of his mates at a bar down the way. I'm not sure what's happening after that. I'd better be heading to the bar. Catch up soon? See you.'

With that, they went their separate ways. James filled

in Grace on how he knew Luke, and before they knew it, they'd arrived at their restaurant.

•

The insurance claim had been paid quickly. James wasted no time in buying a new laptop. He spent some time setting it up, and installing the apps he was used to. For good measure, he encrypted his hard drive in case the burglars returned.

He then went through all the security settings on his cloud apps to make sure he had two factor authentication turned on, strengthened his passwords and subscribed to a secure backup service.

James felt more comfortable once he was done, knowing that if the burglars struck again at least his data would be safe.

He opened up the online drive where he started going through the copies of the correspondence, titles and inventories once more. He was looking for information about the militia, especially given what he'd discovered in Birmingham with the Heckroy connection. Thanks to the coaching from Angela, he had a better idea of how to approach the documents. There were long inventories, tax demands, and even the odd invoice dating from the early-1600s. Pieced together, these documents created an interesting snapshot of history. The interests of the militia, which had a cavalry section, aligned with the interests of the Heckroys and Tubhursts in repurposing the common land where the annual Goose Fair was held as a racecourse and a place to exercise their horses. James was able to make sense of some of the documents, although not all of them, and he was being too selective in what he wanted to see to fit his theories. The approach he took was to collate it into a document that he could share with Angela.

THIRTEEN

The county archives in Northallerton contained a lot of information about Richmond. There were a surprising number of records from the 1500s that documented the guilds of Richmond that were a powerful group at the time. The main guilds were based on the main trades of the town: glassmakers, haberdashers, and fellmongers. The largest guild was the glassmakers. The guilds had monopolies and control of the trade and had a big influence on the social fabric of Richmond. One of the key buildings was the guildhall, which was well documented. Early maps showed it to be in the location of the present Kings Head Hotel, which was the former town house of Mr Tubhurst. It had been built with a ballroom and an extensive set of rooms for guests and entertainment. There were detailed records about the demolition of the guildhall and the building of the Georgian townhouse, including reclaiming some of the gilt furniture and fittings, and the disposal of the stained glass. The demise of the guilds was a slow process of Acts of Parliament which ended with the abolition of their privileges, and this was reflected in Richmond where there was a transition from the guilds to the local merchantmen.

James had booked himself some time at the county archives in Northallerton on Tuesday morning. He'd wanted to go on Monday but they were closed. He found some on-street parking nearby. He went in with his notebook and his laptop, ready to find out more about the militia.

He began with the records held on microfilm from the

early 1600s. The first step was to make some copies of the records on the militia, made up of mainly inventories and accounts of the barracks.

One of the more interesting finds was in the financial records… apparently the Heckroy family were significant contributors to the militia. This spanned the period leading up to the abolition of the Goose Fair through to the building of the racecourse, which in itself was significant as this spanned nearly a hundred years in a turbulent century.

A record of horse races showed that the militia's cavalry were active participants in the horse racing. The militia riders were frequent winners of the Richmond Cup.

The picture was becoming clear about the events around the closure of the fair, the establishment of the races and the involvement of the Heckroy family. The remaining information he uncovered was the Act of Parliament relating to the removal of the charters that were granted to the Goose Fair.

The next line of enquiry would be how the guilds were weakened and Mr Tubhurst's involvement in business that could've conflicted with the guilds. He wanted to find out if Mr Tubhurst was acting alone or with others.

The guilds and interest in the Tubhurst family represented another tangent that James had embarked on. It was a distraction from what he'd set out to find. It was also clear that, while he'd learned from the session with Angela how to approach the records, he was not focused enough to collect all the information he needed before trying to interpret it. That said, his unfocused approach was leading him to an interesting epoch of history.

It was approaching closing time. James collected his

notes together, carefully putting them in his bag along with his laptop and charger. He signed out, thanked the people working on reception then made his way to the car before deciding, as it was a nice day, to have a short walk into the town centre to see if he could find somewhere nice to stop for a coffee and a bite to eat.

As was his habit, James could not help going into an antique shop as he passed, just in case there was anything interesting. He nodded to the person sat behind a cluttered desk with a phone, a laptop, a printer, a delft vase with a nicely arranged bouquet and a collection of magazines, papers and a couple of copies of printed catalogues from a local auction house.

'Hello, are you looking for anything particular? Would you like some help?'

'I'm interested in books and old maps principally, but I also enjoy a bit of a browse as you never know what you may come across,' replied James.

'The maps and books are in the room to your left as you go through. I do have some rare books in the glass cabinet which I'm happy to open for you.'

'Thanks. I'll take a look'

There was a history section with a selection of old books that James made a beeline for, with a significant part being military history, some books on archaeology, and a small section which looked like they could be relevant under the general history subsection.

James reached for a book on medieval guilds from 1200 to 1600. It covered the period when guilds were in their heyday. It seemed like a good primer, with the added bonus that it wasn't an expensive book. There was another older book on the guilds with some copied text from older manuscripts that James also decided was worth buying to help his investigation. Deep down he knew it was a bit of a sidetrack to the original mission of uncovering the location of the gates he'd discovered, but he was in total denial. The story of events in Richmond during the turbulent seventeenth century with the twilight of medieval times and the emergence of a new order was something that was intriguing, especially as the changes were huge and had not met with much resistance from the ordinary people.

James took the books to the counter and put them down on the table. 'These two please.'

'Did you find everything you came for?'

'Yes, I'm doing some reading up on medieval England. I want to know more about the guild system, and I find old books interesting in how they interpret the events.'

'I have a book from the late 1600s, which is in the cabinet, that's about the guilds of the north. Would you like to have a look at it?'

'That would be very helpful, but I'm afraid I don't have very deep pockets,' said James.

'It might surprise you. I'm sure we can work out a price. Let me pop and get it for you.' With that, the shop owner got up, took a bunch of keys from the drawer, walked around the desk to the locked display cabinet and returned with the book which they handed to James. 'Take your time, have a look through it, and see for yourself if it is something you might find useful or interesting.'

James opened the book. He carefully turned the pages. The print was nice and clear, and for an old book, it was easy to read. It showed a publishing date using Roman numerals on the title page. To James's untrained eye it did look as if it belonged to the right era. There were descriptions on the origins of guilds, with chapters on specific guilds. Then James froze. There was a chapter on the great guildhall of Richmond. He very slowly turned the pages as the text described the guildhall's humble beginnings and how it became a grand building. James was entranced as this was exactly what he'd been looking to find.

'This is a very interesting book in a good condition, but I doubt it's in my price range,' said James.

'I could let you have it for a nice discount, say 40% off?'

'It's way more than I could pay. I was looking at no more than half the price,' replied James, who had already committed further than he should sensibly have done.

'I could do that. You look like someone who's interested in the book. Rather than somebody looking for a collectible edition… or worse looking to flip it online.'

James left the shop elated that he'd made the discovery. He was a little anxious that he'd paid way too much for a book. He forgot all about stopping for a coffee and something to eat, returning to his car in a haze.

•

Following the burglary James was wary about keeping valuable things in the house. On his return from Northallerton, he made copies of the pages about the Richmond guilds and their magnificent hall. The rest of the book was certainly interesting to read, but he wanted to keep some focus on the turbulent years of Richmond. Rather than keep the book on the bookshelves with his other books, James began thinking of a safe place to hide it in case the burglars came back.

There were some obvious places. He had a stack of cookbooks in the kitchen, and he could hide it there. He even thought about buying a cookbook of roughly the same size so he could wrap the cover around the book. There was one good place he could think of. His bedroom had exposed, polished floorboards covered in rugs. He knew there was a cavity under the floorboards, which was ideal as it was dry. He set to and cut one of the boards, and put the book, which he wrapped in paper, into the cavity, before screwing down the board and covering it with one of his tribal rugs.

He ate a light supper, cleaned up and poured himself an IPA before sitting down at his laptop to examine the copies he'd made. After reading through the first paragraph he decided it would be better to print them off so he could make notes and annotate. He loaded the printer and printed off the images until he had a stack of copies to work his way through.

The text was easy enough to read, even with the old English showing the letter *s* as an *f*. The first section was about the demolition of some humble houses and a barn or storage area with the land acquired by the guild. The acquisition of the land was made in 1420. The construction work happened two years later as the text described in detail with the layout of the guildhall to accommodate a large amount of people assembled, a banqueting hall, and a place to do business. At this point the text only described the function of the building and not what it looked like.

Sixty years later the guildhall was substantially

refurbished. This is where the finery was described in detail. The refurbishment included remodelling the façade to include gilded figures representing the key guilds, a golden horse at the very top of an arch and a vast expanse of windows edged with figurines and gold inlay. The text referred to the building being five storeys with each storey's façade being mostly windows. It was clear that the local expertise from the guild of glaziers had had a significant hand in the construction. The hall was designed to impress, and rivalled that of the great Flemish guildhalls in Ghent, Antwerp and Bruges. The interiors also had no expense spared with vast rooms that were fully decorated and a large collection of embroidered wall hangings depicting scenes of the various guilds present in Richmond. The expense of the refurbishment was eye-watering, which suggested that the guilds were very wealthy and powerful force in Richmond.

There was a final refurbishment that added further decoration to the façade. This time the document referred to painting to gild the carvings of figures and animals. This was instigated by the guilds of glaziers, mercers and haberdashers.

The text described the banqueting events that were held during the year, how the various guilds operated and maintained the building through taxation and control of trade. From what he read, the business was extensive.

James made copious notes, inserting sections of the relevant text from the photos he'd made. He had the beginning and the end, but was missing the piece on when and who demolished the guildhall, which, as described, must have been one of the most impressive buildings in England. What he knew was that Mr Tubhurst had built his townhouse on the site of the guildhall. Given his track record, there would no doubt be an interesting tale on how that transition was made.

From what he'd learned about the demise of the St Martin's Goose Fair, it was likely that there was a similar mechanism used of abolishing the charters and privileges of the guilds using Acts of Parliament. There was also a good chance that the usual suspects were involved in the destruction of the guilds and their fabulous hall. He made notes, determined that he would continue the research into the Acts of Parliament from the late 1600s and the early 1700s. This period would have been a time when the powers of the guilds were fading, as was seen with the demise of the glassworks around that time.

As a precaution, James shredded the printouts and scribbles he'd made and put them in the paper collection for recycling.

•

Thursday's band get together was brimming with energy… and no negativity as James had turned up early for a change.

Rick assembled them around the collection of slightly battered chairs. 'I wanted to give you an update on the gigs,' he said, barely able to conceal his excitement. He told them, 'I have three gigs confirmed, and, wait for it, I'm quite far down the line with negotiations for a slot at a summer festival. Someone who came to our first gig thought we would be a good fit for the festival line-up and it took them a bit of time to track down our contact details.'

'Brilliant. I don't suppose you can tell us which festival?' asked Helen.

'I don't want to jinx it, and normally I wouldn't say anything until we have everything signed up as there are always plenty of discussions that go nowhere,' replied Rick. Changing the subject, he said, 'Given that we are hard to find, I was thinking about setting up social media channels. The big question is who will do it and how often do we keep the channels updated, as we all know a page with few updates is worse than not having a page.'

'I'm happy to post video clips and photos, regularly,' said Helen.

'Great. I'll do the events and diary part,' said Rick.

'Given that I write for a living, I could do some longer pieces such as press releases or a blog,' said James.

'That would be good to have in place,' said Grace. 'Do you have enough time to do the writing?'

'Sure, I can slot it in. Press releases are timed events and we will know well in advance when we will release things, and blogs tend to be more in depth and less about events.'

Helen had been working on some sound recordings that she wanted to incorporate. They spent a while playing under her supervision as she had a clear idea of what she wanted. She had James play bass which she routed through her modular set through all sorts of filters, effects and oscillators. It was slightly unnerving as there were a few delays that she'd put in, but it really worked well. Grace had a couple of digital pads set up with her drumkit. They too had Helen's magic applied.

The band were really beginning to form a distinctive sound with their own approach, and their gigs were proving popular. They were also making good progress with their debut album.

After practice they all went for a drink at the pub around the corner. The main theme was the discussions about their up-and-coming gigs, the video streaming they would use as the backdrop, stage lighting, and whether to use smoke machines or not.

It was a nice evening, a nearly full moon illuminating the streets with diffuse light. Grace and James decided to take the scenic route back to James's house.

'How did your trip to Northallerton go?' asked Grace.

James gave Grace an abridged summary of what he'd found in the archives and his haul at the antique shop. He shared his excitement about the expensive book, without revealing how much he'd spent.

'Sounds like you were lucky to find that book. You're taking interesting directions, away from your original quest to find a gate, but it looks like you have found an interesting period of history.'

'That's always in the back of my mind,' said James. 'My long quest to find Finkle Bar and Frenchgate Bar. I know where they were, I have one illustration of what they looked like, and I'm sure I'll find something to corroborate them. I need to look back into the time they were built to learn how they were made. I hope to find the plans or drawings. I also need to find out when they were knocked down, which would not have been a trivial task given they were defensive structures.'

'There's a lot more to do?'

'Yeah, the fun bit is not knowing what else I'll find along the journey!'

They walked in silence for a while along the path by

the river. A gentle breeze came down the river, and the moonlight danced on the water. In the distance they could hear the bells chime half past the hour.

'I'm loving where the band is heading. Helen is doing some amazing things,' said James. 'The routing of my bass was wild but really good. It sounded a bit strange to begin with but I got used to it quickly.'

'Yeah, and those pads she has programmed up are fun to play with the normal kit. Again she does some spooky things with the sounds and effects.'

'I'm looking forward to seeing what she has lined up for the next gig. She has been working on some new fancy visuals.'

'Me too,' said Grace. 'It'll really help make our gigs stand out as an experience. It'll also make nice images for the social media channels, which'll help build our fanbase.'

'What do you think of Rick's idea to release a vinyl album as well as streaming?'

'It makes sense. It depends a bit on cost, but it'd be nice to have a mix of some coloured limited editions alongside ordinary black ones.'

'That'd be great. I guess between Rick and Helen we'd have some real talent to master the tracks.'

'You'd think so, although we could threaten to do the mastering!'

•

- Hi Rick. Good news about the gigs and I can't wait to find out what festival you have lined up. Hx

- Helen! I'll let you all know as soon as I get the agreement signed.

- I was thinking about last night's session. It went really well

getting the drums and bass routed through the synths and effects. Better than I expected.

- Yeah, it was unusual and really worked.

- The only niggle I have is that the bass doesn't really add much more than I can produce using my sequencers. James isn't bringing a lot to the writing or compositions. He's a competent bass player, but I don't know if that's enough?

- I think you're right. Like you say, he's a competent player and works well with Grace, but I agree there are questions as to what he's bringing to the band. We could have a session musician on stage when we need them.

- I guess we don't do anything too rash as we don't want Grace leaving in a huff if she feels we haven't been fair. I really love her style and quickness in improvising.

- Okay, let's keep an eye on things and see how he fits in. If he's not contributing, we should have that difficult conversation.

•

George crunched along the gravel in front of the house and parked near the old stable block before making his way to the back door. He walked past the boot room, and the larder, into the kitchen.

'Morning, Eddy. Grand day out there.'

'George. Good to see you. I was thinking a cup of coffee, and we then go for a walk around the lake?'

'Splendid. Black coffee for me as usual, please,' said George as Edward rummaged in the cupboards for the stove top coffee maker, carefully pouring water into the bottom and filling the right amount of ground coffee before tightening the pot and putting it on the range. George said, 'The deal is getting into the critical phase, and we could do without the bloody complications to distract us at the moment. I asked that idiot Frankie to sort out those papers of Henry's that Lucinda had put up for auction in her clear-out. He couldn't have fucked things up more if he'd tried. Firstly he seemed to have got the young man's back up, no doubt being pompous and overbearing, and instead of being happy to get the papers back, he organises some dodgy contacts to break in and steal them. Apparently Freddie was annoyed that he was asked to pay more than the chap had paid at auction. Not that I blame him. There's the buyer's fee, collection and faff. I'd have done the same. It was not as if he was taking the mickey and asking for double.'

'I'm assuming you asked Freddie so you were not directly involved?' asked Edward.

'Absolutely. Now isn't the time to hit the headlines for all the wrong reasons. Investors are flighty enough without giving them an excuse.

'Freddie's fuck up seems to have made our chap even more determined to keep digging, and according to Luke, he has Richmond in his sights and is pouring over the archives. I was not too worried that an amateur sleuth would find much, but he seems to be building a connection with a professor at Birmingham University which might up his odds in finding out things we would rather stayed dormant.'

'What a mess. Here is your coffee. Help yourself to sugar and biscuits,' replied Edward. 'Is there anything specific that's buried that you're worried about?'

'There were clearly some shenanigans by our ancestors centuries ago when they knocked down most of Richmond and rebuilt it as they wanted as a modern town. There are no legal issues, as the limitations of statutes are clear, and it would be unheard of to drag issues that happened so long ago into the courts. It's more the reputational damage that a salacious tale of our families knocking Richmond around could do at this vital point in the process. We know that once we submit our application there will be a big response, and we want to set our position as the guardians of Richmond with the preservation of the historic buildings as our central theme. If a story starts flying around that our ancestors flattened the town centuries ago, it could undermine our credibility and put the scheme at risk. If we don't get this across line, we will end up with the liability of a long lease until the break clause in ten years, not to mention the money we have already invested in plans, consultations, and expert reports.'

The two of them finished their coffees and got their coats, wellingtons and hats on. George in the boot room, and Edward had his kit in the back of his car. George disappeared into the stables and came back with two retrievers, who in their excitement were running around apparently deaf to George's shouts and piercing whistles. They set off through the formal gardens, through a gate to the walled vegetable gardens at the far end where they went through a rickety door leading to the woods.

'What are we going to do with this chap to head him off from digging too deep into the past or getting ideas that he needs to publish a tale?' asked Edward. 'Seeing that Frankie made a mess so far, I'd like to keep him away from things as there is real danger he could make things worse than they are.'

'We get a bit of information from Luke, who's keeping him close, but I think we need to up our game. There are some people I've used in the past for corporate espionage that are very professional. We could put some bugs into his house so we can keep a track of what he's up to.'

'That's a bit risky. I assume there would be no trace back to us?'

'Good God, no, these are professionals.'

'How about if I went to see him and warned him off? I would be polite, but firm, and tell him to stop what he's doing without being an idiot like Frankie?'

'Let's keep an eye on the situation and see how it unfolds. If you do decide to see him, make sure you don't give him any clues to who you are, and above all don't threaten him as I suspect he would do the opposite of what we want.'

'Sounds like we have a plan and should have the situation in control. We only need a couple more months until the scheme is submitted and we can begin the consultations with the town folk.'

The stakes were high for Rufus Investments. They'd invested considerable amounts of money drafting the detailed plans, on experts advising them on the structural pieces, the complexities of the water management in the absence of drains, historical building conservation experts, and in PR campaigns to promote the historical heritage of the town. Their investments were partly their own funds, and they'd formed a syndicate of international property funds who had pledged considerable amounts of cash. The investments were packaged to make it attractive to borrow further funds and leverage the investment. If there were issues with the planning application or there were major delays, the syndicate members had options to withdraw and thus put the whole scheme at risk.

•

'Hi, Angela. How are you?'

'James, good to hear from you. How are you getting on?'

'I'm well, thanks. You should have got an email from me with a link to the files I wanted to share.'

'Yes, I saw the email, but I was on a trip and have just got back. Sorry I haven't had a chance to have a look yet.'

'Been anywhere nice?'

'I was in Copenhagen for a conference. There were some interesting papers being discussed about the Hanseatic League and their trade routes which have come to light recently. So, tell me what have you discovered. Why the secrecy with password protected files?'

'Since the burglary I've been a bit cautious about keeping my research secure. I haven't been able to prove a connection, but given what was taken, it was connected with the papers I got at the auction. I'm fairly certain they got what they were looking for. They have no reason to come back, but I want to be cautious.'

'That sounds reasonable. Like you say it could've been only to do with the papers you bought, and if it was them, now they have them back there's nothing more to worry about.'

'I did what you suggested and put all the material I had into a paper. I used a lot of images I made of the documents to show the sources.

'I also had a session at the county archives, where I found out more about the militia as we discussed. It confirmed what we found in Birmingham. As I was searching, I found some references to the guildhall which

I was not too surprised about. What I did come across in an antique shop was a book from the late seventeenth century which was a history of guilds. I paid way more than I wanted, but it had some good material on the guildhall. When it was built, the subsequent renovations and which guilds were involved.'

'That sounds like a good discovery.'

'According to this book the guildhall was one of the most fabulous buildings in England. There's no trace of it left, and from what I can work out, it was situated on what was a former Georgian townhouse and is now a hotel.'

'I haven't come across any mentions of it before. Strange. I'd probably have stumbled across it as part of my research. I'm sure there's a rational explanation as it's almost as if there has been an attempt to bury that part of the history of Richmond? But conspiracy theories aren't a territory that I like to spend time in!'

'I have a couple of loose ends to tie up. I want to find out who got hold of the guildhall and whether it was the decline of the guilds that precipitated it's demise or whether something more murky went on. Given what went on with the Goose Fair, I'd assume some Acts of Parliament were used to strip the guilds of their rights and powers. Especially in the taxation and the monopolies they held.'

'Good point. That would be a good place to search. It is likely to be among the private Acts which are all online. As I previously mentioned, there was a lot of turmoil in that chapter of English history. Power structures changed considerably, but you already know that. I promise to read your paper and give you some feedback soon. I'm in the country now for a couple of months until the next conference.'

'I really appreciate your help as a sounding board, and look forward to hearing what you think.'

FOURTEEN

The doorbell rang, followed by a very authoritative knocking. James had got home from work some quarter of an hour earlier. He'd just changed from his work gear to a more casual T-shirt, his usual checked shirt and cargo trousers.

At the door stood a man with a tweed jacket, a striped shirt open at the neck, bottle green moleskin trousers, and highly polished brogue shoes. James had never seen him before and was wary, thinking he was either a salesman or a person with religion.

'Hello. I'll get to the point,' said the very well-spoken man. 'You're poking your nose into things that you shouldn't. I'm warning you that you should leave things to history. Stop raking about and stirring things up.'

'I'm sorry what are you referring to?' asked James innocently. 'More than that, who are you? How do you know what I'm doing? How do you know where I live?'

'Don't pretend you don't know what I'm talking about. I know you bloody well do know what I'm talking about. It has to stop right now,' barked the man.

'You haven't answered my question of who you are and how you know where I live.'

'You don't need to know who I'm or how I got your address. Don't close the door. What I have to say is important. I know you're on some crusade poking into the archives and history books. I have no idea what you hope to achieve or what's driving you. What I will say is that no good will come of it. The information should stay in the books and archives. It definitely doesn't need some amateur historian to bring it all to light for no particular reason.'

'How do you know what I'm doing?' said James. 'What I do in my spare time using public information is none of your business.'

'Let's say I've become aware of what you're doing. I insist that you stop.'

'Was it you who broke into my house?'

'Absolutely not. I'm a law-abiding citizen. I don't go around breaking and entering,' said the man with a guffaw, as if he found the idea amusing.

'I still don't know who you are. You haven't given me a very good explanation of how you came about the information you claim to have on me. You certainly have given me no good reason, if I *am* doing the things you claim, to stop.'

'I'm politely but firmly asking you to desist, delete your files, and stop searching the archives. Leave any books you find in the antiques or second-hand bookshops where they belong. The next time I will not be so polite. I obviously know where you live, and where you work. I also know about Grace. Pretty little thing, although blue hair isn't my thing.'

'How dare you bring her into it? I'm minded to call the police if you continue threatening me,' James said forcefully, and he was getting some colour to his face. He was getting upset about where this conversation was going.

'As I said, I'm politely asking you to stop what you're doing. I'm sure you will, and we will not have to meet again.'

'I think you're mistaken, Mister…' James paused hoping the man would give him his name, but despite the pause the man looked back with an expressionless face. 'You don't know what I do. I can't see how you know what I've been doing with my time.'

'I know a lot about you. Believe you me. I also know you're poking around in things that you shouldn't. It would be better for all if you stopped immediately. Well, I hope my message has been clear. I trust you take heed of what I've said. Goodbye.' And with that the man turned around and walked down the road with a sense of purpose without looking back once.

•

The visit from the man had shaken James up, and what had upset him the most was that someone knew what he was doing and had somehow been tracking his activities. After taking some time to think, James concluded that, to have the level of information the man hinted at, he may have been bugged, and while it might seem paranoid, it would do no harm to eliminate possibilities. For his new laptop, he'd ensured that the hard drive was encrypted, and he'd set the security software to scan regularly. The security settings were at the highest level, and he'd even gone to the lengths of setting up two factor authentication. He'd reasoned it was not likely to be his laptop that was bugged, and for peace of mind, ran an in-depth scan. The next possibility was his phone, it was possible that spyware could've been installed, and it could listen to his calls, read his messages, or do screen captures. If it was a really bad one, it could do key logging which potentially meant his passwords may not be as secure as he would like. To check his phone for spyware, he looked at the apps running in the background, and sure enough there was one which didn't look right. After installing a well-known malware detection and removal app, a full scan revealed a possible threat.

The priority was to make his laptop secure. Given that whoever was behind this may have also bugged his house, he decided the safest room was the downstairs cloakroom, that had a toilet and sink with nowhere to hide anything such as a camera. As the scan had finished, he changed his passwords to some very long ones he generated using an online tool. He made frequent trips back and forth to the kitchen, where his phone was, to get the authentication codes he needed to make sure that he wasn't being watched somehow.

Once he'd changed the passwords, he did a scan for Bluetooth and WiFi from his laptop, to see if there was anything unusual. The WiFi showed his neighbours' networks, which all had the prefixes of their broadband suppliers followed by some random numbers and letters. There was an odd Bluetooth device he didn't recognise.

The big dilemma was what to do with the phone. There were two options. He could get rid of the spyware by removing the application and then doing a factory reset on the phone, or he could buy a new handset. If he bought a new handset, he could switch off the infected one or he could continue using the phone, feeding it misleading or false information. If he got rid of the spyware or replaced his phone, he could imagine that whoever put the spyware there would simply try to hack his new phone, or find some other way to spy on him until they were convinced he was no longer a threat.

He decided to keep the phone as it was. He would buy a cheap second phone. He would then make calls on his new phone away from the house to tell people he would be sending them messages on his old phone saying he'd given up his project. He would have to be careful not to raise suspicions. If they were tracking him, they would know his patterns from the phone location, so he would need to carry both phones.

With that decision, he put his plan into action by buying a pay-as-you-go phone. He then called Angela to tell her that he had suspicions that his phone had been hacked. He told her that he would be sending her a WhatsApp message to say that he'd got stuck with the history project and was giving up. He did the same with Grace and Luke, telling each of them that he would call later to explain. Once he'd finished the calls, he walked home, sending out the WhatsApp messages from his old phone.

He did some searching online for gadgets that detect bugs and ordered one that had good reviews, figuring it was worth trying.

James hoped that whoever was spying on him would think that he'd responded to the warning and stopped his project. It had had the exact opposite effect. It spurred him on to find out more. He needed to find out what was so explosive that people wanted to protect themselves from the story getting out.

He texted Grace on his new phone to tell her he would call on the old one. He asked her not to talk about his project, saying he would explain later. He then called her on his old phone. They chatted briefly, arranging for James to go to her house. He said he would call in to the mini-supermarket to get a bottle of wine on the way.

•

As James got to Grace's, he took his coat off and switched his old mobile off, leaving it in his coat pocket in the hallway.

Grace got two glasses out as James opened the screw-top bottle.

He began with an apology. 'I'm so sorry about the muddle with the phones and the messages today. I got a visit today from a man who wouldn't give his name… he was very determined to stop me with the history project. He gave me the distinct impression that I was being watched. He made it very clear that he was not happy with what I'm doing.'

'What? How could they know about your research? You haven't been posting anything. From what you told me, only a few people know about it.'

'That's what worries me. It's also why I played the game with the phones. I suspect they have put spyware on my phone, so my thinking was that if I sent messages to you, Angela and Luke saying I've stopped the project, they would think that their message was well received. I hope they now think I've given up.'

'You're mad, you know,' said Grace. 'From what you have found so far, concerning events centuries ago, I can't see how it has any bearing on today. It started as being a bit of fun to do some historical research. Now it seems to have taken a dark turn with spyware, unannounced visits, the break-in? Don't you think it would be sensible to stop? I am worried what you're getting into.'

'It did really shake me up, especially as he seemed to know all about what I was doing. The effort he and presumably his people have gone to seems to be significant. What puzzles me is how they found out. Something must have triggered their interest in what I'm doing. I can only guess it began with the papers I bought at auction. There must be something I missed, an important piece I wasn't looking for. I was busy hunting for evidence of the barbican gates. I found the correspondence about the glassworks, but nothing explosive. It was important enough for someone to break into my house to get them back.'

'That sounds like you want to carry on,' said Grace. 'You don't know how nasty these people can be. You know nothing about them. They may go to great lengths to stop you. It can't be worth that risk. What would they do next if you carried on? What happens if they find out?'

'If I'm careful, covering my tracks, they won't find out. I'm close to finding something important. It's likely to be in the papers or something I've yet to uncover. The other two bits of unfinished research are the gates, my original mission, and I want to finish off looking at the events of the demise of the guildhall. Neither of these are controversial. Even if there was something dodgy all those years ago, the perpetrators are long dead. There's a limitation of statutes meaning that, even if there was something, no charges could be brought.'

'Why are you so determined to continue? You have an okay job, the band, me? Why do you need stir things up? You're putting yourself in danger over events from centuries ago.'

'I feel as if I'm so near to finding out what I began. If I'm careful, whoever has been spying won't find out. There's also the fact that someone has told me not to do something, which tells me there's something worth looking for. Once I find it, I can decide what to do with the information. If it is something dangerous, I can delete all my notes and papers and leave it to history.'

'Seeing as you're not going to stop, make sure it doesn't become an obsession. Don't give up everything else. Especially the band as we need you to be fully involved. It will be an important summer for us. Helen has put a lot into the music and the visuals, and Rick is lining up a good set of gigs and a potential record label. We need you to be totally committed to playing your best.'

'Don't worry,' said James, 'I'm all in with the band. It's been amazing what we've done in such a short time. There's a lot to look forward to, like you say, with the gigs and the debut LP. I want to see this project through though. This warning will make me more careful in what I do, and where I go in case I'm being followed.'

Grace topped up their glasses, and walked over to her record player, putting on one of her latest acquisitions that she'd ordered through their favourite record shop. It was a bass heavy experimental album by a band she'd been following for a while, and she began enthusing about it to James.

•

'Man, it seems ages since we bumped into each other in Brum,' said Luke. 'And what's with the burner phone? Are you diversifying into something more dodgy than historical sleuthing?'

James had made sure his bugged phone was deep inside his bag, wrapped in a beanie hat to make sure nothing could be recorded.

'That was a nice surprise seeing you,' he said. 'We had a great weekend. We went to that club which was amazing. The second phone thing is a bit of a long story, are you ready?'

'Yeah, this had better be good!'

James told Luke the full story of his visitor and his concerns about being spied on which had prompted him to get the second phone. He finished with his strategy of leaving the bugged phone to deceive the listeners into thinking he'd given up.

'That sounds like a work of fiction,' said Luke. 'Bugging and visits from someone threatening you. All over a bit of history. Come on. You're bullshitting me. On a more serious note, have you any idea who your visitor could be? Is he a mad individual, connected with the family whose papers you bought. The ones you suspected of the burglary? And, please, no wild conspiracy theories.'

'I have very little to go on, other than what I've uncovered. While it's tempting to connect the burglary with the visitor, I have no proof. I also have no idea who the man is. He wouldn't give his name. For now he holds all the cards. That's why I thought I could turn the bugged phone into an advantage to feed them misleading information. If they think I've stopped, I can quietly carry on in the background. My thinking is that they'll leave me alone. Strangely, I'm more motivated to dig now as there's clearly something that people are going to lengths to hide. If they hadn't threatened me, I may have quietly gone on until I found out a bit more about Finkle Bar and Frenchgate Bar, and published my findings. That would've been that, and I'd have been done with it.'

'You need to be very careful if you continue,' said Luke. 'Laying a false trail might be a short diversion tactic, but if they find you're carrying on and hiding it from them, they may up their game and things could get nasty.'

'That's a big risk that things could escalate. What really bugs me is that I don't know what they are protecting and why. Perhaps once I find the answer to that, I can decide what to do next. It seems unfinished business to stop on the say-so of a stranger coming to my door. What is so precious that they don't want me to find out about?'

'Fair point about knowing the reasons behind it, but do take extra care. If it starts getting really dangerous, go to the police. You can't do this on your own if it turns really nasty. As a friend, I really think you should put it behind you. Sell your antique books, delete your documents and images and focus on the fun but harmless, like the band, Grace and going out with your friends. I know you have put a lot into your research. It has been fun, especially those trips at the weekend, but look at the bigger picture. Do you want to risk getting caught up with something that could turn dangerous?'

'I'll be very careful,' said James. He was as reassuring as he could muster, but he could see on Luke's face that he was not fully convinced. There was nothing Luke could say that would influence James. They changed the subject continuing their conversation.

•

- George, whoever visited James has spooked him and he's paranoid that he has been bugged. Luke

- Luke, thanks for letting me know. Do you think he will stop his digging around?

- I'm not sure. It has made him more determined. Partly because he has no clue who's behind it and he hasn't been given a good reason to stop.

- Thanks for letting me know. If you have any brainwaves on how we might nudge him off course or divert him to something else do let me know.

- I wouldn't worry too much. He's charging around, flitting from one thing to another and isn't doing anything too deep or serious.

- Good to know. Thanks for your help. How are you doing with the units? Did you get the commitments from the last ones?

- Almost there! I'll let you know as soon as they sign. Not long now.

•

Friday lunch saw Caitlin and James at the window table at the fusion place, and as was becoming traditional, they ordered from the specials menu. They'd eaten there a few times and were getting familiar with the offering, and yet James didn't tire of photographing the food for his feed.

'I was called into Mr Pickles's office this morning which in itself is a bit unusual. I was getting a bit worried when he left a message this morning... I was fearing the worst, but it turned out to be something very different.

He asked me to stop doing my historical research project as I was upsetting some important customers. He told me if I continued, he would have no choice but to terminate my employment,' said James. He watched Caitlin's face carefully for her reaction.

'I don't see that your historical research has anything to do with the publications?' she said. 'Did he give you any clues to who it was that complained?'

'No, he wouldn't elaborate. He just stuck to the line that I should stop my research. Without getting too carried away, I wonder if it's a big advertiser. Or the other possibility is that Mr Pickles is a mason, and perhaps someone from his lodge has had a word?'

'I don't want to be funny, but that sounds like pure speculation. I doubt you're going to get any information from him, knowing how he is. I wouldn't waste time figuring out if he's a mason or who the advertisers are.'

'I agree. I was trying to rationalise it. I guess I got a bit carried away,' said James disappointedly. He told Caitlin all about his visitor, the aftermath of it, and what he'd been doing with his bugged phone. That's really upping the stakes. You have had a visitor threatening you, bugged phones, a break-in. Now the boss threatens to sack you. You'll have to stop?'

'Luke said exactly the same. As I explained to him, what bothers me is that I don't know what I'm supposed to have discovered that makes it so important. I want to find out what they want to keep a secret. I can then make a decision based on facts. I can carry on being very careful so as not to raise any suspicions until I get a glimpse of what people don't want me to find.'

'James, be serious. Is it worth risking your job for?' asked

Caitlin. 'I know we moan about work and all that, but it's a nice steady job that pays reasonably well. Besides, you're not ready to change careers, or go back to university. We discussed that not so long ago, remember. You were a bit lost at work. You liked the idea of doing something else, but didn't see any opportunities?'

'The stakes have certainly got higher,' said James. 'I'm well aware this isn't some game. I know I've been a bit adrift for a while, following the easy path to just go along with things, but this project has sparked something in me. It was a bit of fun to start with to track down the missing gates, but it's got way more interesting the more I dig. I'm not being reckless, ploughing on regardless. It's made me think more carefully. I'll be a lot more discreet in where I go and what I do to minimise my trail. Like I say, until I know what I'm dealing with, it feels wrong to stop now. Worst case, if Mr Pickles boots me out, it might well be the kick I need to settle on something I really want to do. But for the moment I want to keep the job as it isn't too demanding. I have enough excitement going on.'

'I know something has changed in you. I've not seen this determination in you before. You've always been very laid back. Be very careful, and I say this as a friend. We should be heading back to the office soon. No time to pop into the antiques and second-hand bookshops today, as that gets you into trouble,' said Caitlin, trying to make the conversation a little less deep and reflective. She was beginning to think that she should've been more firm with James and persuaded him to drop his quest or whatever it had become. It had been a bit of fun encouraging him, but she was having real reservations now. She resolved to find a way to persuade him to stop.

FIFTEEN

'I can't believe it's wine-o'clock-already. My day has flown by,' said Caitlin. She raised her glass to Verity. 'Cheers! You'll be pleased to know that I'm nearly done with the cushions. I'm just finishing off the buttons at the moment.'

'Cheers!' replied Verity. 'Oh, you're brilliant. I don't know how you find the time juggling the family, job and your hobbies.'

'I've really enjoyed making them. A nice change from watching nonsense on the TV in the evening. It's got me thinking that I should do more making and creating.'

'Good idea. What are you thinking? Textiles? Painting?'

'I'm not sure yet. I'd like to have a go at painting, but we don't have a lot of room to set up.'

'That's something I have. I can always make a small studio for you by dividing the big empty space.'

'Do you know, I might take you up on that! Now I have a bit of a dilemma…' said Caitlin.

'Go on, what's bothering you?'

'You know how I've been egging Mad James on with his history quest? While it was fun with him haring off all over the place looking for his medieval walls and gateways, and hearing how he was getting royally distracted as he read things, it's turned a bit darker. It started when he bought a couple of lots at auction which were boxes of old papers. He was burgled, had a bloke come to his house to tell him to stop digging around the archives, he found spyware on his phone and to cap it all Mr Pickles hauled him into his office and told him to stop what he was doing.'

'That sounds a bit weird. What's he got himself into?'

'Well, given all that happened,' said Caitlin, 'he has no real idea who he has upset or why, and he's now determined to find out what it is that people are worried he might find. I tried to discourage him and he seemed to listen, but dismissed it saying he would be more careful. Should I have been a bit more forceful?'

'I guess he's an adult, and you did advise him to stop. Does this all relate to that book he bought with the illustrations?'

'Fair enough, although I might have another go at telling him to stop. It began with the book, but he has gone down so many paths as he comes across something new, it's difficult to keep a sense of what he's up to. One constant is his obsession with medieval Richmond. Maybe there's something dark that people want to keep hidden, but I can't see Mad James as being such a threat.'

'I agree that he's a chaotic amateur who's not really a threat to anyone. If there are dark secrets that are hiding in plain sight, someone would've found it by now and written about it. Who is an expert in the field? You could persuade him to just read up on the subject, not go on his visits and certainly not publish. That way he stays out of harm's way.'

'Yeah, that could be a good compromise,' said Caitlin. 'I still feel a bit guilty encouraging him, but it seemed innocent fun.'

'Don't beat yourself up too much. You couldn't have known where it was all going.'

Caitlin felt much better after talking to Verity about her dilemma. It wasn't something she wanted to bother Rob with as he would dismiss it and rightly remind her that James was a work friend who didn't need too much of her time. Annoyingly it would be a good point. She enjoyed her lunches with James, as an escape from the office and the daily routine, but it was also one of those friendships that had an enclosure around it, and they would never dream of meeting at the weekend or going out in the evenings. Verity, too, was mulling over what she'd heard from Caitlin. That the innocence of James getting excited by a subject, and getting inappropriately deep, could develop into something so dark so quickly was perplexing. How could information in the public domain open to anyone be so dangerous?

•

James had reason to brood on recent events. He reflected on all of the conversations he'd had with his friends. They were right to be worried, especially as he'd had warnings from the unknown person who made it very clear there would be consequences, and then the out of the blue warning at work. As everyone had rightly pointed out, he didn't need to continue. He had the band, his friends, and Grace. He could jeopardise all of that. What if his visitor contacted Grace or threatened her. He hadn't told her about it as she was angry enough about the visitor and the threat at work. He knew exactly what she, and indeed what any rational person, would say.

The obvious solution would be to donate his history books to the Yorkshire Archive, if they wanted them. In addition, he could delete all the information he'd gathered. After all, it didn't matter where the gates were. What was clear was that the gates were demolished when the town entered a more peaceful time, as they would be no longer be important to protect the town with such strong defences. There had been a practical decision made that the entrances should be made wider to accommodate traffic of horses and carts. So why continue with the researching?

James had clearly stumbled on something that people wanted hidden, and even if he discovered whatever this big secret was, he would be making some people very unhappy by exposing it. Could the revealing of a historical story even make a big impact? It could make very little difference to modern-day Richmond or indeed to his life.

What if he gave up the research, and instead put all his energy into the band? They were building a good following, selling out gigs, working on an album, all heading in the right direction. And, thanks to Rick, all in a very manageable way. This was in contrast to the previous band with all the drama that went with it.

He needed to have a real think about what was important. He needed to decide whether he needed to go poking around in history to discover something he didn't know what he was looking for. Whatever it was, he also didn't know why people were going to great lengths to deter him from doing his researching.

James's head was spinning with all these thoughts, without any clear or logical answers emerging. He paced up and down for a while before opening an IPA, and immersing himself in a lowbrow action film to stop thinking about things for an hour or so.

The questions would not go away despite knowing that the sensible course of action was very obvious. Yet he was being drawn in by some irrational reasons: driven by a desire for knowledge to do the exact opposite of what the man had told him. For no other reason than he didn't like the person or the tone he took.

•

Discovering spyware on a phone is annoying, can make you angry and is relatively straightforward to address. Hidden cameras are the horror stories of rented holiday places, and are luridly exposed in the tabloids and online blogs that write extensively on how to detect them. Suspecting bugs in your home is another level altogether, and this was exactly where James had got to. In ordering the gadget online, he was wanting peace of mind that he was not being monitored or, if he was, he wanted to find and remove the appliances. Working his way through the house, it didn't take him long to find an adapter which had his printer and desk lamp plugged in. The device flagged it up as suspicious. On closer examination, it was slightly larger than a normal adapter, which he imagined would house the bugging device and transmitter. Continuing to scan the house, he found another one, this time in the form of a lightbulb that looked like a normal bulb, but on closer examination there was a tiny camera with a small component attached to it that was presumably designed to transmit the images. He took them both to his back yard where he crushed them with his lump hammer, before wrapping them up in paper and putting them into the bin.

To reassure himself he then did a second sweep. This time there were no alerts, and he satisfied himself that his house was now clean of listening bugs. There was, of course, his old phone that he continued to use as normal, ensuring he made no hint of continuing his research, and feeding misinformation, such as telling people on his messaging apps that he'd hit a wall and was stopping the project.

He was confident that his laptop was secure. The final step had been to install an authenticator app on his new phone, so he didn't need to use his old phone when accessing his cloud accounts. He then signed up for a reputable, paid-for VPN to further secure his internet connection. He'd taken all the steps he could think of to make sure he wasn't being tracked. Satisfied, he finally he sat down on his sofa, confident that there were no hidden cameras or microphones that could monitor him.

It was time for James to get back to work. There were two areas that he needed to focus on. He urgently needed to find out what people thought he'd discovered, and why it was so important to them. Secondly, he really wanted closure on the gates. What he needed was to find something to corroborate the illustrations from the book.

The collection of scanned papers contained some of the answers that James was looking for. There were letters describing how the part-demolished gates of Finkle Bar, Frenchgate Bar and Bargate were to be tidied up. A sale agreement that the stone removed was destined for building materials. There was correspondence describing how the gates had been widened in the past, but that they had left some of the structure in place. One of the correspondents complained that not only were the remnants ugly but there some stones had fallen down in a storm. They didn't sound as grand as the illustrations but functional defensive gates. Could the illustrator have embellished, and used lavish artistic licence to make them way grander than they were? The correspondence confirmed that sometime later they were demolished for good as they'd become derelict and a danger to passers-by, as well as offending the local gentry, who wanted the entrances to town tidying up. There was also a reference to the remainder of the defensive walls being dismantled as they, according to the correspondent, made the town look dingy and old-fashioned, having such relics from the past.

James found some of letters related to his search, and skipped some others, as the relevant paragraphs were part of a broader range of subjects written between the correspondents about the rebuilding and modernisation of Richmond. He did have enough of a picture from the documents he'd read. That was it then? The extravagant barbican gates he saw on the illustrations didn't match reality. How much had been generous artistic interpretation? There was a lingering doubt, despite the evidence being in front of him, that the gates were in Richmond and not York, they were demolished, and that they were part of a heavily fortified structure around the town. It was disappointing. Indeed he was a bit angry with himself that he hadn't read these papers earlier, as it would've saved him a lot of time and effort. It could've brought his project to a close. What did he have? An illustrator who may never have actually been to Richmond? An editor who didn't follow up or check whether the illustrations were accurate? James decided that he should write the story down, including all the events and research he'd done, with the cautionary note about checking sources and not always taking them at face value. He didn't really know why he was writing the story down, other than to organise his thoughts.

There was one unfinished piece of business. Find out

what the secret was that he was supposed to know, the secret that people wanted him to stop digging further about. It occurred to James that one section he'd not paid much attention to was the inventories. Maybe the answers were in those?

He gritted his teeth, beginning the work of reading through the inventories, not knowing what he was looking for. He figured he would know it when he saw it. The inventories in the hands of academics would've been valuable as they would be able to interpret them. In the hands of an enthusiast they were less exciting. No smoking gun in the inventories.

Taking a step back, it was clear that the papers were a smaller part of James's interest and activities, and it suggested the interest in Richmond was more of an issue. Richmond was a sleepy Yorkshire market town, rich with history, a fine Norman castle, the ruins of a friary and a big cobbled square lined with old buildings. There was nothing that could possibly provoke the reaction that James was experiencing.

Parking the inventories out of despair and frustration, James needed to try something to make sense of it all. He began a very unstructured search online for medieval documents relating to Richmond. There were extracts, copies of original documents and very specific resources that he skipped through, not really knowing what he wanted to find. He felt more in control when he was searching than when he was dwelling on why people were going to great lengths to stop him.

A combination of random clicking on links that looked interesting and stumbling on a page that held lots of links to scanned documents led him to a partial list of valuables containing gold cups, silver platters and plates, and a long list of glassware. There was a very hard section to read. It took a while before James could make out a chest of gold. Whatever it was represented vast riches, which was plain to see even with an incomplete inventory. From the time period James interpreted these goods as belonging to the guilds of Richmond, and this opened up many questions, such as what happened to the guilds and their treasures? The medieval system of guilds fell into decline as they gradually lost their charters and rights to collect taxes in favour of the government. Did the guilds slowly dispose of their wealth as they disbanded? Was there a slow decline or did someone move in to take it? The very strong symbolic moment was the demolition of the grand guildhall of Richmond and a house being built in its place. It would've been a transfer of power from the enfeebled guilds to an individual. Given that these transitions are rarely peaceful, could the owner of the new townhouse, Mr Tubhurst, have also got his hands on the wealth of the guilds which, according to the list, were substantial?

It began to dawn on James that perhaps the treasure of the guilds was hidden, and those who knew where it was did not or could not pass on the knowledge. Could it be that the treasure of the guilds was still hidden in or near Richmond? It was a possibility that people had been looking for the treasure ever since? It would certainly explain why he was being warned off doing further research if people thought he was close to discovering the location of the treasure? It was beginning to make sense. It was a plain and simple treasure hunt with a very big prize. There were people who were keen to make sure that even the existence of the treasure was kept a secret, so that they were the only ones looking for it.

•

The Rufus Investment board met in the customary room in their London office. There was a full agenda, and the members preferred to discuss in person rather than on video calls or through email.

George chaired the meeting, and began with the formalities of the attendance, declarations of conflicts of interest and approval of the minutes of the last meeting. Getting into the substance of the meeting, he gave a summary of his meeting with the culture secretary, as the development was centred in the castle, which was registered as a nationally important heritage monument. The scheme was met with support from the culture secretary, who was in favour of bringing heritage assets to life as a means of keeping them relevant and preserving them. There was even a suggestion that they enter the scheme into a prestigious architectural competition as an example of maintaining and developing a historical monument. The culture secretary agreed to summarise the meeting in a letter, and importantly stating the support for the scheme. The significance of this was that it would greatly improve the chances of approval at the planning stage.

George continued to the finances item. The agreements were all in place with the investment syndicate, and were guaranteed by the bank that was arranging the financing. They now had the means to build the scheme, and the final hurdle was the planning application. George was confident that the process would go smoothly as he'd spent a lot of time with the planners in consultation and indeed with the highways department. The formal application would be ready to be submitted in the next few weeks.

Next up was Edward, who reported on the various planning applications submitted for the town centre that they'd objected to had either been withdrawn pending some major reworkings or had been abandoned. The strategy of maintaining the heritage fabric of the town was paying off. The central theme of their application was that they were guardians of the heritage of Richmond, and their project would enhance and maintain the historic core of Richmond.

'On to more unpleasant matters. I went to see the individual who has been poking about the archives, and firmly told him to stop. He seemed a bit shaken, but I think the message got through,' said Edward. He reached for a bound report on the table in front of him. 'Please don't minute this next section. This is the report from the private investigators that we hired to see what the individual has been doing. They reported that he has been telling his friends that he's stopping his research, but from the surveillance in the house it suggests that he's still doing some online digging. He has since discovered that he has been bugged, removed the spyware from his phone and destroyed the surveillance devices in his house. The report suggests that this will either mean he will stop as the stakes are rising or he will go underground. Either way, he won't be involving his friends, and will be wary of publishing. The investigators offered a team to follow him, but I didn't think he warrants such a threat, especially as Luke is keeping tabs on him, and will report back to us if there is anything to worry about.'

The meeting concluded with finances and the final discussion on the planning application.

•

The old book that James had bought in Northallerton contained a wealth of information about the guilds of Richmond in the context of the wider network of guilds from Newcastle down to York. Richmond had a special place through the activities of the glassworks, and the guild of glaziers in Richmond had close connections to Bohemia, which was at the forefront of glassmaking in medieval Europe. There was a system in place where the apprentices or journeymen from the Richmond guild were sent to the glassworks in Bohemia to learn the trade alongside the masters, and it was not a one-way process. The Bohemian masters came to Richmond as part of a secondment arrangement. In addition, there were some references to Murano in the Venetian republic where it seemed that there was some extensive knowledge sharing that went on along with the exchange of apprentices.

There was a section that described the important buildings of the guilds in Richmond. Not only the grand guildhall that had got James excited. There was a description of a smaller but no less extravagant merchant's hall on the site of the current townhall. There were extensive cellars and storage areas where the merchants' goods were stored during the trading processes over the period of a week at a time.

James wanted to revisit the book. He carefully undid

the screws and lifted the floorboard of his hiding place. Unwrapping the guilds of the North book and taking it downstairs, he spent a couple of hours reading, and making lots of notes. James rewrapped the book carefully, put it back in the hiding hole and secured the floorboard again with the screws. His final act was covering it with a rug.

What was clear from the book was that the guilds, and particularly the glaziers, were very wealthy and well-connected organisations with extensive trade. Although there was no specific mention of treasure, it would be reasonable to deduce that the wealth of the guilds would've been significant, and there was nothing obvious to contradict James's thesis. What did pique his attention was the description of the merchant's hall, which mentioned tunnels. That set him off to see if there was anything remaining, despite the demolition of the hall and the construction of the townhall. James tried looking at the area with LIDAR to see if there was anything obvious to his amateur eye, but there was nothing to suggest any hidden areas of tunnels coming out of the property. He also did some online research for tales of tunnels, coming across a legend that King Arthur and his knights lay sleeping in a cave beneath the castle compound. He learned of the tale of the drummer boy who was sent down a tunnel playing his drum so people could hear where he was. According to the tale, the noise stopped between Richmond and Easby Abbey. Legend had it that the drummer boy was never seen again. Could this have been an early search for the guild treasure? Perhaps it was not about finding the route of a tunnel to Easby? There were also tunnels near the river connected to the mining of copper. These could've been used to hide the treasure.

The mines opened in the fifteenth century, which was in the right period, and continued being used on and off until the early 1900s. Presumably the later tunnels didn't knock into the old ones which may have hidden the treasure, or it would've been documented.

This was going to prove interesting. How could he begin a treasure hunt in stealth mode? James had convinced himself that if he went back up to Richmond, and started digging around, he would alert people to the fact he'd not given up. Furthermore, as he'd found the lightbulb bug, he was very careful how he used his bugged phone, so that the surveillance effort on him would be very much hindered. The only niggle he had was that he could easily be followed by a team of people. He lacked the skills, expertise and know-how to be able to spot them.

There was only one person that would be up for the treasure hunt. He would call Luke to brief him on the new mission.

•

Caitlin arrived at Verity's flat with a bag full of carefully folded cushion covers that she'd finished sewing.

'You're amazing. So quick. Thank you for helping and bringing them over. I could've come to pick them up,' said Verity enthusiastically, as she let her into the flat.

'I really enjoyed making them, and it's good to come over for a change of scenery,' replied Caitlin. 'I'm a bit nervous in case they don't fit, and have brought some thread, needles and scissors in case I need to make some adjustments.'

'Would you like a coffee? We can fit them after.'

'I'd love my usual, please. Short and black. I will make a start while you make the coffee.' And with that Caitlin began putting the covers onto the cushions, finishing just as the coffee was ready.

'Oh, that looks great,' said Verity. 'Another thing off the list! I'm almost done with the bathroom too, which is a good job as the flat warming is coming up very quickly.'

'You know we talked about painting last time, and you offered some studio space? I'd like to take you up on it, unless you have changed your mind?'

'Absolutely. Of course you're welcome to set up a studio here. There's always the caveat that, when the landlord gets his scheme approved, I get a month's notice to leave, and the building will be demolished. Come on. I'll show you the space.'

Verity led Caitlin through a door off the living space into a large open room, which was unfurnished other than a bench, some canvases, and an easel. At the end of the room was a dividing wall with a single door to the left-hand side that Verity explained as a dumping/storage room.

'You paint as well?' asked Caitlin. 'Perhaps you could throw in some lessons too!?'

'I find it relaxing. The opposite to being on the computer doing graphics,' said Verity. She laughed. 'Let me show you some of the paintings. You might also have noticed some on the living room wall?'

'Those are yours? Amazing.'

Verity's paintings were in the style of the old Dutch Masters, with domestic scenes and a clever use of light. There were some that were of the era, and others that had a much more modern setting. The modern scene was of a kitchen, complete with an island. A coffee machine was the backdrop, and a woman was sat on a chair, smiling, looking at a mobile phone, with the sun streaming in through a window. The woman was dressed in a laced top, not in the old Dutch style, but given a modern makeover, her hair tied back and a delicate pearl earring catching the sun. The composition was exactly in the style of the Dutch Masters.

Verity took some time to explain to Caitlin how she approached the paintings, beginning with sketches and some smaller versions, before building up to the larger paintings. She showed Caitlin how she built up the layers of paint, the mixing of paints and the array of brushes and palette knifes she used.

Caitlin was hooked. She really wanted to try her hand at painting, and was encouraged that Verity had offered her not only some space but to give her some tutoring.

SIXTEEN

After much dithering on what he should do with his bugged phone, James made a decision that was surprisingly easy. He transferred his old number to the SIM on the new phone that he'd been using as his secret phone, and did a factory reset on the old one. He found a website that would buy the handset. They said they would check it over, recondition it and resell it. All he had to do was put it in an envelope with a printed label, and drop it off at the mini-market, which is exactly what he did. He called Luke on his way back from the mini-market, which was a ten-minute walk along some quiet streets, a well-trodden route he normally did on autopilot.

'James, good to hear from you. Are you enjoying your free time now you're not sleuthing with your historical research,' asked Luke as he answered the call.

'Ah, yes! I have a bit of an update for you.'

'You're a nightmare.'

'I've ditched the bugged phone I was telling you about. I found a hidden camera in a lightbulb in my living room along with a socket that had a bug in it. Proper James Bond stuff.'

'No way. That sounds very serious. I hope that scared you enough and you're now giving up?'

'Not exactly. I'm going to be a lot more careful from now on.'

James ran through his recent endeavours with Luke and his change of tactics.

'No way. That would be massive. A classic treasure

hunt with baddies on your tail. The stuff of films. And you playing Indiana Jones.'

'The thing is, and this is a bit awkward, it would be a lot more fun to have someone to join me on the treasure hunt. Are you in?'

'I wouldn't miss it for the world. It sounds like we need to have a planning session.'

'Brilliant. How are you fixed in the next week?'

James and Luke organised to meet up later in the week at Luke's flat after concluding that a pub or restaurant would be a bad place to discuss a treasure hunt. There was an outside chance that there were undetected bugs in James's house.

•

- George, it turns out our intrepid friend has not been put off by the various attempts to make him stop. It certainly spooked him, but he carried on. He's now on the trail of what he thinks is treasure that the guilds hid in the 1600s. Luke

- FFS. Why on earth does he think there's buried treasure that has laid undiscovered for 400 years in Richmond of all places?

- It's complicated. On the plus side, he has been distracted from his mission to find the gates, and the story about your family knocking down medieval Richmond and rebuilding it all those years ago.

- It sounds like it will keep him busy and away from causing us trouble. Keep me posted on what he's up to, especially if he has another sudden change in direction.

•

The band gathered around a scruffy table in the corner of the studio with the sort of stackable chairs that you find in village halls around the country, steel-framed with wooden laminate backs and seats. Rick opened his laptop as he'd prepared a list of the tracks, and he wanted to discuss the ordering on their up-and-coming album.

'We need to refine the track names, to reflect the music. The names we have for them are more like shorthand so we know what to play,' said Rick. 'For example, "Explosion in E" is something we all know how to play, but it needs a bit of polish. We could call it "Stellar Collision" or "Fission". It doesn't need the key in the title.'

'Yeah, I see what you mean,' replied Grace. 'I like the space theme. Perhaps we could call it "Gravitational Collapse", the thing that happens when black holes explode, or is that too nerdy?'

'The space theme does work, but rather than using scientific terms and straying into Kraftwerk territory, how about we reference it instead? Something like "Pulasarmatic"?' asked Helen.

'Got it,' said Rick. 'How about "When a Pulsar Explodes"?' to which they all murmured agreement and nodded. 'You have been very quiet, James. You are normally the wordsmith.'

'I'm liking the process, but space isn't really stuff I know much about. Don't worry. I'll be chipping in.'

They continued to go through the track names, and turned to the ordering with everyone contributing and building on their enthusiasm.

Rick hooked up his laptop to the studio monitors, and played a couple of the mastered tracks to make sure everyone was happy with the result. Again, there was a healthy discussion and the conclusion that the mastered versions were good.

The next steps were finalising the sleeve design for the vinyl and CD. It would then go to pressing. Helen volunteered to coordinate the social media campaign around the promotion of the release. She asked for James's help with the copy, both as a longer press release and shorter snippets for the social media channels. Helen planned to make some video footage ready for a couple of tracks that would be released as snippets.

The final topic was a touring schedule for the summer. Rick had a bunch of local gigs lined up, and there were some dates for a couple of festivals that Rick had been in conversations with the promoters. The local gigs were a solid foundation as they were getting some good income from them. The festivals were another boost. The way things were going, they could take the band to the next level. With the right traction, they could all think about part-time work knowing that the income they could make would make up the shortfall.

James was very reassured with this. It made him much less dependent on his day job. It opened up other possibilities. The recent conversation with Mr Pickles had unsettled him more than he thought. He was only working there as it was a steady job, and reasonably interesting, but it was definitely not his life's ambition to write and edit stories for trade magazines. This could be the prod he needed to make some changes. The band was high on his list of things he wanted to do.

They all agreed on the gigs and festival dates. Rick committed to putting them all into the shared calendar.

Following a short break, they set up their instruments.

They began with playing the album, followed by the set they were rehearsing for the upcoming gig at the weekend. They did it without Helen's video feed. Instead they focused on getting the sound right, and finding the right level of improvisation in their sets.

The band finished practicing with smiles on their faces. They'd played a fantastic set. They could not wait to play in front of an audience. They finished up with a very animated chat as they were putting their gear away. To end the session, they dropped into the pub for a quick drink together.

James and Grace went back to James's house still on a high from their evening at band practice.

James waited until they got back to the house and they'd settled in before broaching the subject of his research. Grace was still worried about James, what he'd got himself into, and how he wasn't taking the situation seriously enough.

'I have a confession to make,' said James. 'I wanted to tidy up my history project, and put it in a place so I could make sense of it if I ever picked it up years later.'

Grace didn't look too impressed. She moved to look at James more carefully. She'd hoped, given all that went on, especially with the band going so well, that James would've packed it all in, and put his all into the band, and spending time with his friends.

James gave Grace a very abbreviated summary of what he'd been doing and how he'd come across the information that led him to form the theory about the treasure and how nobody had found it in all that time.

'I've spoken with Luke about it. He's up for helping me. Don't worry. Whatever I do, I'll be ultra-cautious so as not to make people aware of what we are up to. I figured you wouldn't be too interested in getting involved. I'd be very happy if you did, but also understand if it isn't your thing.'

'Sweet of you to ask me,' said Grace, 'but treasure hunting isn't on my top list of things I want to do.'

James was slightly disappointed that Grace wasn't keen to be involved, but it wasn't a big shock. He was both relieved and glad that he'd told her about it. The main thing he wanted was to make sure that he wasn't keeping secrets from her.

•

This was a special Friday lunchtime, and to celebrate they went to a new place that Caitlin had been recommended by her friend Verity. There was nothing special about the décor. No exposed brick and steel ducting overhead, the wallpaper was not too contrived, nor was the artwork, or neon signs. The tables had a chunky look of recycled wood. The benches were sturdy.

They were not really there for the food. It had been a dramatic day in the office… James had handed in his resignation, and with it, they knew their long tradition of Friday lunches were drawing to an end.

'How did Mr Pickles take it?' asked Caitlin.

'Well, he didn't seem too chuffed about it. He asked me why, which was a bit tricky. I didn't want to bring the warning up, which clearly was a trigger, nor did I want to tell him about the band. I kept it a bit vague, saying I'd enjoyed my time but was ready for a change. I told him I've found another job.'

'Did he accept that or question you?'

'He told me to work out my notice and holidays with HR. He gruffly thanked me for my time at the company. That was more or less it.'

'Have you got another job?'

'I have a couple of interviews lined up for some part-time roles at a couple of marketing agencies who need people to write copy. One of them specialises in the music and film business, which is the one I'm keen on. I was also looking into some freelance writing work you can get online, and I was thinking it might also be an idea to sign up to that co-working space near the river.'

'Have you stopped your research since we last spoke?'

'I tidied up the loose ends, and called it a day,' James lied. Although Caitlin was a friend, he wanted to minimise people who knew what he was up to. If the people who threatened him were as ruthless as they appeared, he wanted them well away from Caitlin.

'Good,' said Caitlin, looking relieved. 'It all started to sound a bit menacing. Definitely not something you should be involved with. Especially as it was supposed to just be a bit of fun, and seeing where it led. Will you miss *Earth Moving Weekly* and all the other great publications?'

'Funny, now you mention it, not really. I'll miss the people, and the writing part as it suited me nicely when I needed work, but as you know it was only going to be for a period of time. I'm not sure it was to be a lifelong calling, even though at this point I don't know what that is. The warning shook me up more than I thought. The band is starting to get a steady stream of well-paid gigs, and we have an LP coming out, which should help us grow our fanbase, so I figured a part-time job would be a good move for now. The band may not go very far, but as I work things out, I can juggle the part-time work and the commitments to the band.'

'Sounds like you have things sorted out, which is good to hear. I'll miss these Friday lunches. It's always been fun to gossip about work, eat somewhere nice and have a good natter.'

'Me too,' said James, 'although we have a few left. We will have to use them well, and revisit the ones we liked. I'm staying in York, so we should still be able to meet for lunch, although I guess it won't be quite the same.'

'I'd like that,' said Caitlin. 'I imagine over time the gossip from work will become less interesting!'

'You're probably right, although we have plenty of other things to talk about.'

•

James arrived promptly at Luke's flat, which was tastefully fitted out with vintage furniture, complete with an interesting collection of house plants that Luke seemed to keep in rude health. The décor was less hipster than James's style, more of a nod to fashion, and had an emphasis on practicality and comfort.

'I've ordered a takeaway,' said Luke. 'They said it should be here in the next twenty minutes. Do you fancy a beer while we wait?'

'Good plan,' said James. 'I brought some with me. They would be best put in the fridge to settle. Where did you order? I'm getting hungry!'

'I ordered from the Thai place around the corner. They're pretty reliable and the food is good,' replied Luke as he was opening the beers and getting his glasses from the cupboard. 'This is so cool. Planning a treasure hunt, with real-life baddies in the mix.'

'It'll be new for both of us. I've never done anything like this before. I still have no idea how many people are involved in wanting to keep the existence of the treasure secret.'

The Treasures Act of 1996 was a key piece of legislation as it sets out what constitutes a treasure. Given that they were assuming the treasure was over three hundred years old, made of precious metals, and was deliberately hidden, they were firmly in the realms of treasure under the law. In addition, the legislation set out a mechanism for the distribution of the rewards between the finders and the landowner.

The hypothesis that there was treasure hidden in Richmond was laid on the foundation that the guilds were very wealthy, and there was a period of great turmoil in the seventeenth century which made hiding the valuable pieces of the guild's collection plausible. There was no written evidence that the items were hidden, and if there was, the records were long lost. Using some imagination, it was entirely possible that there was some secret knowledge about the treasure and shadowy groups that protected the secret. And while it was an exciting prospect, such a theory quickly transformed into a conspiracy in the absence of hard facts. James had fallen into the conspiracy trap, believing that the guardians of the treasure wanted to stop him finding it, and he didn't ask himself the question of why people would guard the secret of a treasure and not take it for themselves.

What the co-conspirators could safely conclude was that, if there was a hidden treasure, it had remained hidden for over three hundred years as there were no written accounts of it being either hidden or indeed found.

'Can we find out more about the guilds, more specifically who managed the wealth? If we know that we can maybe narrow it down to where they lived,' said Luke.

'Let's start with a timeline. We should try to find out when it was hidden? We know that at the turn of the eighteenth century the guildhall was demolished to make way for a town house. The guilds were in decline throughout the seventeenth century. The glassworks were in trouble around that time, though they were one of the bigger and richer guilds,' said James. He drew a banner with some arrows at either end – writing 1600 and 1700 respectively – on an A4 notebook he'd brought with him. 'We can add the dates of the plague, civil war and the restoration of King Charles II, which will give us an idea of what was going on at the time.'

'From what you have outlined, we focus on the last twenty to thirty years of the century?'

'Yes, that would be my educated guess. I'd think that Richmond, being where it was in relation to the big trading cities, would have held on to the guild system a bit longer than most.'

They were interrupted by the doorbell and the takeaway being delivered. Luke got some plates, cutlery, a big bottle of sweet chilli sauce and a smaller one of dark soy sauce. James helped set the table. The dishes were in the middle of the table so they could both dig in.

With their beer glasses refreshed, they tucked into the food, continuing their conversation about the treasure hunt.

'This is tasty,' said James. 'Now where were we? We were narrowing down the time frame. If I focus on that period, there are a couple of directions I could go. Either figure out who was who in the guild with the hope that it might lead us to the right place, or figure out what the town looked like then to figure out what has changed? Do you have any other ideas?'

James and Luke continued building their case for where the treasure could be located. They sensibly excluded the old town as it had changed beyond recognition from the late medieval times, through the extensive rebuilding programme undertaken by the Georgians and incremental changes in the ensuing centuries. If there had been hiding places, they concluded they would've been discovered. They pored over the maps of the area, dismissing some places while putting others on their shortlist like an elaborate game of pin the tail on a donkey while wearing a blindfold. The shortlist was the old copper mines, which had an extensive network of abandoned tunnels, and the drummer boy route, which is based on a legend. Although they dismissed the story of King Arthur with his knights asleep under the castle.

'I'm thinking one of the ways we can be very anonymous once we get to that stage is to have a white van, wear high-vis jackets and have a couple of those plastic barriers set up. I bet nobody would bat an eyelid,' said Luke as he cleared away the plates, getting some more beers from the fridge. 'This would work well if we needed to start digging somewhere. I think we might have to work out some alternatives to mini-diggers or pneumatic drills if we need to get to underground places. Do you reckon we can rent those geophysics machines they use in Time Team to find the entrances to the tunnels we are looking for?'

'I love the idea of pitching up in a white van with us wearing high-vis,' said James. 'You're right we would not raise any suspicions at all. We wouldn't need to have any logos on the van as many companies subcontract these days. Let's worry about geophysics if we get close but have trouble finding the tunnel entrances. Again one of us walking around with one of those. Maybe the other with some kind of surveying kit would not look out of place. If we get busybodies asking, we can always say we are trying to find the location of sewage pipes we suspect are leaking or something like that.'

'It feels like we are starting to get a plan together,' said Luke. 'This is going to be fun. I'm going to need a deadline or I'll procrastinate. Shall we give ourselves, say, a week to get the background information together? Meet here again, same time? Different takeaway?'

'Yes, that would make sense,' said James. 'Again if either us gets really stuck or needs a bit more time, we can always message each other. What about a Mexican next time?'

'Mexican sounds good to me! Sorry to kick you out, but it's a school night and I have a couple more things to do before I turn in.'

'Yeah, I should be heading off. Even though I'm working my notice, the ever-vigilant Mr Pickles is making sure he gets his pound of flesh. I need to be fresh in the morning.'

•

The process of planning and researching became more intense the deeper they got, pushing themselves with artificial deadlines in order to stay focused, and maintaining a sense of urgency, even if the dormant treasure had lain undiscovered for centuries, and glossing over the fact that it may not even exist. Armed with nothing but maps, and selected books and papers they found online, they developed a comprehensive plan.

A week later as had been agreed, James returned to Luke's flat, armed with some cold beers, his laptop and a sheaf of papers. They put together a case for the tunnel from Richmond to Easby, based on the story of the drummer boy. The story goes that there's a tunnel that went from the castle in Richmond to Easby Abbey. The tunnel was in a poor state with the entrance partly collapsed, so they sent the drummer boy who could squeeze in. They packed him off with his drums and a lantern, ordering him to play the drums so they could follow him from above. There's a plaque marking the spot that he disappeared on a path by the river on the outskirts of Richmond heading towards Easby. Using what they had, they concluded that if it existed then it would follow the contour lines beginning at the castle, across the market place through Frenchgate, before passing through St Mary's Church, and after that it continued along the small road or footpath towards Easby Abbey. They also developed an idea that, if such a tunnel existed, it could be accessible from the church, and despite the fact that the church was extensively remodelled in the nineteenth century, they didn't discover any tunnel or treasure, come to think of it.

•

George, Edward representing Rufus Investments and Cathrine from the architects went for the final meeting with the planning department. There had been informal discussions going on for a while to ensure that the application was prepared, and that any concerns could be addressed before submitting the application.

George relayed the conversations that he'd had with the culture secretary, and Cathrine had a few more technical topics that she wanted to be sure that she and the planners both had the same understanding of.

There was a lengthy discussion on the proposals for the renovation of the obelisk in the town centre and what the underground parking scheme would look like. This was a key part of the application as it needed to demonstrate benefit to the setting of the town, as well as meeting the wider objectives of generating jobs, bringing in visitors, and making the most of the historic monument in a way to benefit the community.

The planners would not be drawn as to whether they would approve the application as they would need to see the details, but equally they couldn't envisage any major objections to the scheme as outlined. The main topic where they did make suggestions was to have a public consultation before submitting the plans. It'd be seen that Rufus Investments were interested in the public feedback, and that any material objections could be addressed in the application before it was submitted.

Edward was concerned that the plan could be objected to in the court of public opinion, but was reassured both by Cathrine and the planners that the purpose of the consultation was to present the scheme to the community, and that there could be valuable feedback.

Clearly objections on the grounds that it was new, or not to an individual's taste, could be registered but wouldn't have material consideration on the plans. If the public could be won over and support given to the plans, it'd help in the overall consideration.

George, Edward and Cathrine left the meeting, happy that there were no major obstacles from the planners, and that they had one challenge remaining. They went to a nearby café to have a debrief from the meeting and sketch out what needed to happen for a public consultation.

SEVENTEEN

The gig had gone well… tickets had sold out, which wasn't surprising as that was becoming normal. They were getting good reviews on social media, boding well for the upcoming album launch.

Grace stayed with James, and was looking forward to a long sleep in the morning, and then the anticipation of a leisurely day while James went off on his adventures. Although Grace knew what he was up to, she didn't ask too many questions. She was happy for him go and do his own thing.

James thought it was wise to travel light and try to blend in so as not to raise any suspicions or stand out. He put his walking gear on, which was a standard blue waterproof, technical trousers made of lightweight material with extra pockets and his trusted pair of walking boots which were nicely worn in. He deliberated on wearing a beanie hat or an old baseball hat he had lying around, and opted for the simple beanie hat. To finish, he slung a camera over his shoulder.

He left the house quietly so as not to wake Grace, and waited outside after getting a message from Luke saying he would be five minutes.

The trip to Richmond had a sense of déjà vu. They chatted about the previous trip, remarking on all that had happened in between. Luke had been at the gig the evening before, which gave them another meaty topic that they dissected in detail.

A small road to Easby Abbey ended near an old church dominated by the ruins of the abbey. Making their way into a small car park, they found a space under the trees at the far end. Easby Abbey was an impressive ruin, and picturing what the buildings would've looked like before the dissolution of the monasteries all those years ago was not too difficult. The small church between the car park and the abbey had some medieval paintings, which were discovered during a renovation programme. The frescos would've been interesting for those who liked churches and the chance to see some rare medieval ecclesiastical art. The frescos had no references to the guilds of Richmond nor any hint of treasures.

They emerged into the sunlight, leaves rustling in the wind, and walked around to the entrance of Easby Abbey with the soft rush of the river in the background. The ruins of the abbey were interesting to look at as tourists, even if they were not connected to their research. They both enjoyed walking around the remains of the buildings, and reading the boards along the way to understand what they are looking at.

Once they were done, they followed a small road around a house tucked away behind the abbey to join a field with a well-trodden footpath, which had a grazing flock of sheep that totally ignored the walkers. The footpath turned into the woods. At the fork they opted to go down a set of steps towards the river. They followed a path that weaved through the trees on a mixture of silty sand – which had been deposited by the overflowing river – and patches of mud. The path went along a long field that was filled with grazing rabbits on one side and the river on the other, under a canopy of old trees of mixed species. They arrived at the plaque that commemorated the drummer boy, which was set in the ground next to a gate that led to a playing field. Not much to see once they'd read the plaque other than the roughly made roads leading to the playing fields. They continued along the small track. James speculated that the tunnel could well be below the road, but there was no way to find out without digging. At this point they decided against it as it would attract unwanted attention.

The track joined a road that went up sharply, which they thankfully didn't need to climb. Instead they turned into the grounds of St Mary's Church, through a small gate nestling under a luxuriant yew tree. As James and Luke walked along the path, looking at the old gravestones gave them a glimpse of history. The older ones dated back to the eighteenth century. They looked ancient with the erosion by time obscuring the lettering and decorations.

The church door was unlocked. They opened the heavy doors that yielded with a creak into silence. They picked up a guide to the church, and then made their way around the building, meticulously looking for anything that could be a concealed entrance to a tunnel. Given the renovations, it was unlikely to be obvious in the walls or in the side chapels, which looked as though they dated from the renovations, dedicated to the local regiments.

The choir stalls, according to the guide, were taken from Easby Abbey on the dissolution of the monasteries in Henry VIII's time. James had a careful look to see if there were any hidden catches or obvious mechanisms that might lead to a tunnel. Towards the altar end of the stalls, James found what he was looking for. One of the benches was hinged, designed so that the choristers, and presumably the monks before them, could perch during longer services. What he noticed was that the bench was very slightly different to the others. Excitedly he called Luke over. They needed to act fast as there was nobody in the church.

'This seat is different to the others. You see how it looks like the others, and works exactly the same way if you lift it up and down, but there's a small difference. If I push here on this decoration, it goes all the way in. The next bit is exciting. When I move the seat down, watch what happens,' said James. A section of the wooden screen behind the seat moved to reveal a mechanism that looked a little like a door handle. 'We had better stop in case someone walks in. We will have to come back later to explore this properly. I reckon that the church is locked at night, so we will have to figure out how to get in. Meanwhile, let's see if I can close this.'

'Why don't you try just pushing the panel shut?' asked Luke. James nodded, and gave the open screen a firm push. Sure enough it clicked back into place. Luke took a couple of pictures of the mechanism and the seat as well as a shot from further back so they could find it next time.

They walked around the church again looking at the doors. This time they checked for alarms and CCTV cameras, as well as figuring out how best to get into the church later. The north door looked promising. It had a couple of bolts which they easily moved up and down, and was the only antique door.

James asked, 'Any idea how to pick a lock?'

'I have an idea. I think this one will open with a coat hanger without too much bother.' Luke chuckled. He had some expertise in this area, gained in his early days as an estate agent with a portfolio of difficult tenants.

With that they left the church, following the steps, and

walked out of the churchyard onto a road leading to town. Checking the map, they walked along the Batts, a wide open stretch of grass edged by the river, framed by the castle walls and tower at one end. The bridge leading to the old railway station was at the other end. There was a stream of walkers, some with dogs, a dad playing football with his children, and a couple of picnicking groups.

Following the river around, they came to the roaring waterfalls where they stopped at the platform next to the falls on the site of the former gas works. They blended in with the families admiring the falls and enjoying their ice creams. They continued along a road which was pinched between the castle walls and the river. Crossing the bridge at the end of the road, they had time to stop to look down the river towards the castle with their ever-keen eyes checking for any possible places which might once have been used to hide treasure. There was nothing obvious, which is what they expected. For a moment they were distracted by the flash of blue of a kingfisher on its way up the river.

Leading off the bridge, they followed a path that had begun in Billy Bank Wood. Mature beach and oak trees formed a dense canopy. After a few hundred metres walking under the tall canopy, while a pungent smell of the wild garlic which decked the banks filled the air, they found the lower path along the river. The path became narrower, with trees becoming obstacles, before it widened again with some very large rocks, which formed a path. James had read that rock slabs were connected with the copper mine. The rocks were put there with a tramline to move the buckets of copper ore, and over the years the force of the river had dislodged the rocks in places, making them look like a discarded pile of giant Jenga. Around a bend in the river, they found the entrance to the mines, which was much smaller than they'd imagined, and was secured by a metal door and padlock.

'I know what you're thinking. Snip off the padlock, and send a drone down,' said James. There were specialist drones that could be used for mapping mines that required a high level of skill in flying and navigation, not to mention the cost of such specialist kit. James was getting ahead of himself thinking that they could simply fly a drone around the tunnels to find a treasure that had been concealed for centuries.

'Partly,' said Luke. 'As I'm standing near to this river, I'm thinking that it might not be a good place to hide precious things. I guarantee that it would flood regularly.'

'Good thinking. I guess the more tunnels you make, the more the river can pour in, which doesn't matter if you're digging rocks out, but would if you were keeping things safe.'

'I'd need to check the geological maps, but I have a hunch that the copper veins would not just be a thin strip following a line from this entrance. If what we are looking for was hidden three hundred and fifty years ago, the tunnels could have been dug at different heights chasing the copper ore seams. Shall we see if we can find anything interesting a bit higher up?'

James checked his app. He saw that there was a footpath that ran parallel in the woods, which they could reach by following the field at the end of the path through a gate.

'This way,' said James, showing Luke his phone, pointing down the path.

They climbed up the steps through the trees, stopping a couple of times when they noticed that there were sink holes in some places, which were marked on the map. Taking photos and putting pins on the map was all they could do for the moment as they had no kit to investigate further.

'This could be promising,' said Luke. 'Do you think there are maps of the mines dating back before 1650?'

'I would think there would be some as mining rights were complicated in medieval times. There's a chance that the guilds were involved, especially the glaziers who would have been buyers of copper for colouring their glass.'

'I guess, not much more to do here? Have you got your app handy? Does this path continue round?'

'Let me check,' said James. 'Yep, it takes us back to where we came from, and from that we go over the bridge again. We follow the road round to the green at the end of which is the Heckroy Square car park.'

'You're kidding me. We are off to a car park?'

'Yes, I told you it was on the site of the glassworks that were demolished when Heckroy House was built. That in turn was knocked down, and ended up in what's now a car park.'

'Weird. Guess there isn't much to see there?'

'On paper no, but I want to have a look. It looks like there's a footpath that starts there.' James pointed at the app again.

'Lead the way.'

Retracing their steps, they followed the footpath around the green towards the car park that James had been keen to have a look at.

'There really isn't much to see here,' said Luke. 'What are you looking for?'

'I was wondering if there were tunnels or caves nearby as they would've been obvious places for the guild of glaziers. On the other hand, the glassworks were demolished along with the house that replaced it. To finish it off, the area has been tarmacked over. Let's try along the footpath to see if we can find any clues? You're right. Not much to see here.'

With that, they went along a road before turning into the entrance of Temple Grounds, all that remained from Heckroy House, below an elaborate folly, and traced the footpath which headed towards the river, more or less opposite the copper mine entrance that they'd stopped to look at.

'Do you think we could put high-vis jackets on to do a scan of the grounds here?' asked James.

'I think that we would be less likely to get away with it here. Unless you have really strong evidence of tunnels or chambers, it would be a bit risky. We are trying to not draw attention to ourselves? Remember? I think we would get away with it if it were on a street as it would look more normal.'

'Do you always have to be right?' James laughed.

They ended up near the river, and had a quick look in a cave they'd found, which, judging from the empty bottles and sweet packets, was a popular spot for youths.

There was no chance of a secret passage here as the walls were smooth. They decided that they'd done what they could in their initial reconnaissance trip. They had two possible contenders: the church to find the drummer boy tunnel, and the sink holes above the copper mine.

The route they took back to the car was on the opposite side of the river, following an old railway line, but before they walked back, they stopped for a needed cup of tea and a cake, on Luke's insistence, at the old railway station café.

The journey back gave them plenty of time to discuss their plan of action and what they would need to bring next time, and to have a lengthy debate on what time of night they would attempt to get into the church.

•

Verity had gone to town on her flat, getting it ready for the party. She'd put tea candles in old glass yoghurt pots on either side of each step leading up to the entrance, and had woven some small LED lights through the balustrades below the handrails.

Inside she'd moved the furniture and plants around, set up a bar on a table next to the kitchen area and continued the lighting theme, with tea candles in pots on all the window sills and strings of LED lights across the ceiling.

The speakers were set in the corners of the main living area where they would not be knocked over or become impromptu surfaces to put drinks on. Caitlin arrived early as arranged. Rob would join them later once the kids were in bed and the babysitter had arrived.

'Wow, this looks lovely. I'd have come and given you a hand if I knew you were doing all this!' exclaimed Caitlin.

'I enjoyed pottering around and figuring out what I wanted to do as I went along,' replied Verity, making her way over to the bar. 'Glass of fizz?'

'That would be brilliant. I have brought you a couple of bottles.'

'Lovely. Do you want to pop them into the bin there? I filled it with ice.'

Caitlin dutifully put the bottles into the bin with ice, and took the glass from Verity.

'I bought a sketchpad as you suggested,' said Caitlin, 'and had a go at copying the pictures you recommended. It was good to try it out. Like you say, it helps appreciate the perspectives and composition.'

'I'm glad you made a start. I've made a bench in the room out of some wood that was going spare, and I had an old easel that I fixed, so it was ready for you.'

'That's so kind of you. I can't wait to get started.'

'Come on. I'll show you the set-up before people arrive.'

Verity opened the door with a key, and showed Caitlin what she'd done. There was a bench with the pots, brushes and paints, which is where Verity was working. On the easel was a board that Verity had begun to paint, beginning with a red wash and traces of a window.

'This looks interesting,' said Caitlin. 'What are you going to do with this one?'

'I'm experimenting with old paints they'd have used in the 1500s, and have used a board that I've treated. It'll be as close as I can get to the old Dutch Masters.'

'I like the sound of that. Making the colours they used will be fun to do. And getting the brush strokes right will make it look right?' asked Caitlin.

'Yes, that's part of it, and I'll use some varnishes, and find a way of ageing them. Then I'll finish off with an old frame.'

'This sounds a lot of fun to do. The Dutch Masters are collectable because they are great pictures, and from what I read the painters were very prolific.'

They continued their discussion, and moved back to the living area. Verity made sure she'd locked the door. What was not exactly clear was what Caitlin and Verity were going to do with the finished pictures, and whether they would be pieces to hang in their homes. Caitlin was picking up that Verity was planning some mischief, but was not entirely sure. Anyway, Caitlin was sold on painting in the style of the Dutch Masters, and would see what she could accomplish.

The guests began arriving at the party and the drink flowed. Verity made a natural host. She had the knack of being in the right place to introduce people, get conversations going and make people mingle. She deftly made sure that the music wasn't hijacked, by keeping her phone firmly parked in her pocket and not sharing the new Wi-Fi code.

Caitlin and Verity talked some more about their Dutch Masters project when they had a quiet moment, and they thought nobody was listening. Although they didn't discuss passing them off as originals, the question was left hanging in the air as an ethereal mischief that they both seemed to be amused by.

There was a big difference between making perfect copies or originals in the style of the old masters and forgery. The route to forgeries would take them into the criminal world, and have major consequences if they were caught. The two of them were, no doubt, exploring the grey area where they sold their paintings on the clear understanding that they were not originals, and a less scrupulous person could then invent a plausible provenance and create demand, perhaps as painting from the studio or school of a well-known artist. For the moment they would enjoy the process of creating the paintings, even if the goal was less clear.

The party went on into the small hours as Verity had no neighbours to disturb, being in a small industrial zone.

•

Rick bounced into the rehearsal room carrying a bulky bag, excitedly announcing, 'I have a whole bag full of vinyl, and these lovelies are the first of many!' With a flourish he took a couple of the albums out of his bag to share with the others.

'Wow,' said Helen. 'It looks so good.' She carefully removed the vinyl from the cover to get a closer look. 'It feels real now that I have it in my hands. The artwork looks better in real life than on screen.'

'The label has printed an initial run of five thousand to see how they shift,' said Rick. 'They have sent a load to the various journos, influencers and radio stations for review. Fingers crossed that we will get some kind words said about it. I'm so happy to have one of these in my grubby fingers.'

'I can't wait to see how they sell,' said Grace. 'If we sell them all, can we get another run printed?'

'Yes, we can do as many runs as we like, subject to a minimum of one thousand copies,' replied Rick.

'Any idea where James is?' asked Helen. 'He's late again.'

'He said he would be here on time,' replied Grace. 'It's a bit strange. He's always on time for everything else. I don't know why he's late when we meet for the band.'

'It's getting a bit annoying,' replied Helen. 'We need to

have a word with him. Don't worry. I'm not making a big deal of it or getting angry, but it's important to tell him.'

'Thanks, Helen. I agree he needs telling,' said Rick. 'Big gig this Saturday. I'm sure we'll nail it. I just wanted to have a run through the set if you're all up for that? We can do it like last time, if you don't mind, Helen?'

'Yes, I can do the basslines like last time. I saved the sequences,' said Helen.

They all moved around with energy, getting set up, and then began the set they would be playing at the weekend. The set was played with passion. It was clear that the upcoming gig was going to be a success. They were really working well together, finding a path to bring in the right amount of improvisation without totally deviating from the music they'd written.

As they finished the last piece, Rick let out a big shout. 'Oh yes! Now that was brilliant. We can give ourselves a big round of applause.' He started clapping for theatrical effect. Helen and Grace joined in.

'It was brilliant,' said Grace. 'Just imagine, it will be even better in front of an audience. Rick, were you recording it? We might be able to do something with it for the next album?'

Rick winked and replied, 'You bet I was, although I tend to do that anyway. There are loads of recordings from our sessions. I need to sort them out.'

'Grace, can we have a quick go at the last bit again? I want to try something out with the drum pad,' asked Helen.

'Sure,' replied Grace. 'The same as last time or do you want me to have a go at something different?'

'Keep it the same. Let's see if I tweak the pad settings whether it makes it better or worse!'

Helen counted down before beginning to play, and on cue, Grace joined in. As Grace played, Helen changed the settings of the drum pad that Grace was using to adjust the reverb and make some tweaks to the filters.

'How was that? Did you hear the difference?' asked Helen.

'It added some depth which made it a bit more interesting. I liked the delay,' replied Grace.

'Brilliant. That's what I was looking for without getting too nerdy about it,' said Helen, and laughed.

'I'm confident that if we ever have issues with James not turning up for a gig, we can carry on, and do a decent job. Well done, Helen. Those basslines aren't half as mechanical as I thought. They worked really well,' said Rick. Almost on cue, James made a loud entrance, making it more than a little awkward for them to continue the discussion.

'I'm so sorry. I totally got the time wrong. Have you all had a good practice? What did I miss out on?' asked James.

Rick showed James the LPs and gave him a summary of their discussions. They played a couple of tracks with James, but didn't have the appetite to do a repeat of the full set. James could sense that they were not happy with him for being late, and tried to compensate for it with his playing. He turned on his full charm afterwards, which did rescue things somewhat, and they all went to the pub in a good mood.

•

- *George. Just to let you know I'm going to Richmond this weekend with James. James is convinced there's treasure hidden somewhere in Richmond by the guilds. Luke*

- *It's hard keeping up with the direction of travel of this mad mission.*

- *The plan is that we'll be in the woods in the early hours. I'll send an update when we're in position.*

- *We are close to public consultation on the application, and really do not need stories from the past getting out that could put our scheme in a bad light.*

- *Understood. There's nothing concrete emerging and I'll let you know if he strays in the wrong direction.*

EIGHTEEN

The nocturnal trip to Richmond was meticulously planned, and they timed their arrival for 11 p.m., figuring that there would not be many people around, but neither would it be deserted as there would be a trickle of people leaving the pubs.

James parked at the lower end of the main square, and to his relief, there were a few people around so they blended in a little. They put their coats and beanies on, took the backpacks out of the boot, locked the car and made their way to St Mary's Church. They went around the side of the church, which was less well lit, and stayed away from the main road, so they would not be seen by passing traffic. It was the best spot that they'd scouted on the earlier trip, and had identified as the place where they were planning to pick the lock to get into the church.

Luke got to work on the lock. After a short time, there was a reassuring click as the lock opened, and he turned the handle opening the door. They both quickly went in, closing the door behind them.

'Let's keep the torches switched off,' whispered Luke. 'People might see lights in the church and get suspicious.'

There was enough light from the outside lights to see where they were walking. They knew exactly where they were going as they made their way as quietly as possible to the choir stalls and the secret door they'd found during their previous visit.

'Ready?' asked Luke, as he repeated the sequence of pressing the decoration, lifting the seat, pulling the handle. This time, once the panel clicked, Luke opened the door.

He put his head torch onto the lowest setting so he could see into the dark void. The light revealed a set of steps that went down a narrow passage.

'Come on. Let's get in here quickly, and pull the panel door to,' said Luke.

They both went down the passage until they reached a small chamber that had two round, unadorned arches opposite each other. A musty smell of damp stones filled the air, but they could feel a slight breeze. Apart from a faint sound of dripping water, it was silent.

'Given we have come more or less straight down, I would suggest we take the right-hand entrance as that would lead us towards Easby. The left one will go back towards town,' said James. He took some pictures of the chamber with the flash setting to get a better depth of picture.

'That's what I was thinking too. After you.' Luke adjusted his torch to a brighter setting to get a better view of the entrance, and what lay beyond.

The tunnel appeared to have been carved out of the rock, with small chisel marks along the walls. In places there were sections where there must have been holes that had been repaired by filling them in with cut stones. Stalactites had formed where the water seeped in. They made eerie shadows as James and Luke walked down the tunnel with their head torches making the light dance as they lit the way.

The tunnels dated from around the time of the construction of the castle, and were developed to connect with Easby Abbey. The tunnels were initially used for the safe movement of troops, and later on to facilitate the movement between the two buildings, especially in the transport of valuables rather than risking theft from either opportunists or more organised attempts to steal. James and Luke had constructed their hypothesis from the drummer boy legend, and had not been thorough enough in their research to discover the purpose of the tunnels. James and Luke were only concerned with the discovery of a hiding place and in their hypothesis it was plausible that the guilds would've known of the tunnels and taken advantage.

The ground was dry, as there was a floor made of slabs of rock, which were set so as to drain the water into the small gullies to either side running parallel to the walls. They could only see so far with their torches. Beyond their arc of light, they had no real idea where the tunnel was heading.

After they'd been walking in silence for a few minutes, the tunnel gradually turned to the right, which they'd been expecting as it followed the contours. All the while, they were scanning the walls for any anomalies that could suggest a hidden door. They had a good hunch that the treasure of the guilds had yet to be discovered. Given the legend of the drummer boy, they knew that people had been in the tunnels, certainly in the eighteenth century.

The tunnel opened out into a chamber with another unadorned arch. To the left, there was a short tunnel that ended in a roughly cut wall, suggesting that the attempt to tunnel further had been abandoned. James examined the walls carefully, looking for hidden mechanisms, holes or anything that might be a hidden entrance. He took some photos along with a video, so he could study in more detail at home, but was fairly satisfied that there wasn't anything other than an abandoned tunnel. They missed an engraving with the initials AF and the date of 1238 in the rock towards the end of the tunnel and an old chisel lying on the floor. Not important for their quest but it could've helped them make sense of what they were looking for.

'It looks like it was started, but they gave up on it quickly,' said James.

'Yes, I think we continue along the tunnel through that way.' Luke pointed to the tunnel at the opposite side of the chamber from where they'd come. 'What do think this chamber was for? It's a lot of effort to cut out the rock. Never mind the work to remove it.'

'Not sure, unless they had plans to continue. Perhaps they needed the space before they could begin tunnelling?'

'You could be right. Shall we continue?'

James nodded as they entered the tunnel on the opposite side of the chamber. The size, construction type, height and width were identical to the one they'd come down, which was to be expected, considering the tunnels were completed at the same time. They walked a further ten minutes before the tunnel began descending very slightly. The walls had the same finish all the way along the tunnel, until they came across a carved figure in the wall.

'That's one ugly brute!' said Luke. 'I'd love to know who that was modelled after? And why they put it here.'

'Let's have a closer look. Is it some talisman or could it be a mechanism?'

James dug into his bag, took out a torch, and looked at the figure and the surrounding stone. He brushed the stone with his hand.

Luke pushed the figure. It moved into the rock as he did. Encouraged by this, he applied a bit more force to make the figure retreat further. As it did, there was a low rumbling noise, and a section of the wall, which looked like all the rest of the tunnel had before Luke had pushed the figure, moved to reveal a passageway into a chamber.

'It's just like Tomb Raider!' said Luke excitedly. 'I hope this is where our treasure is. Wait. Before we go in, should we be looking for booby traps or is that only on PlayStation?'

'Good point. We should be careful as I have no idea what the mechanism is that opened the door. We certainly don't want to somehow trigger the closing of it when we are inside. If we get trapped, nobody knows we are here, and we can forget about shouting as we would never be heard.'

'In the games, it's always pressure pads on the floors,' said Luke. 'Although I doubt it would trigger saw blades or something ghoulish like that.'

'What about if we go in one at a time, so one us can push the figure. Just in case it's reset or closes.'

'Good idea. Do you want to go in?'

'Okay then,' replied James. As he shone his torch into the chamber, he cautiously moved in.

The chamber was the size of a small room, and was carved out of the rock like the tunnel, although there seemed to have been more care taken to give the walls a finer finish. There was a stale smell, though not a damp or mouldy fragrance... more of air that had not circulated for a very long time. What stood out was how dry it was compared to the tunnel. There was no water running here. The floor was covered with a light layer of dust. At the far end of the chamber, there was an inscription in what James presumed was Latin, which he captured on video and in stills. He would translate it later.

The room was empty apart from a small wooden box in the corner of the room. The box had an elaborate iron band around the top. It looked like it had a lock. James made his way over to the box. He lifted the lid as the box was not locked, and shone his torch inside. All it contained was a scrap of parchment. Not what he expected, and an anticlimax. James picked it up carefully, wrapped it in a plastic bag and put it into a small pocket in his backpack.

'There's no treasure here, apart from a small box,' James called out to Luke. 'From what I can see, I don't think there are any traps.'

'I'll stay here, just in case. I don't want to be entombed,' replied Luke, with an uncharacteristic nervousness to his voice.

'Okay, I'll be out shortly.'

James had a closer look at the box to see if there might be a secret drawer. The bottom of the box could not have concealed anything as he could see a crack. His torch shone through it, casting shadows on the wall. Looking at the top of the box, the lid looked solid yet had no depth to it. He turned his attention to the metal band. He saw the engraved words 'Guilde of Glaziers', surrounded by symbols and patterns.

James deliberated whether he should take the box, or leave it. It was fitting that it stayed where he'd found it. There was nothing to be gained by removing it, especially as it was empty. He came to the conclusion that it would slow them down. On top of that, carrying such a box, late at night, might raise suspicions.

Finishing up by taking photos of the box, with a last scan of the chamber, James rejoined Luke in the tunnel.

'Do you want to go and have a look, and I'll stay here with the switch?' asked James.

'Okay then,' replied Luke. As he went through the entrance, he began walking around the room. The rumbling began again, and Luke raced out of the chamber as the entrance started closing again.

'I think I must have trodden on the trigger. I didn't hang around to take pictures,' said Luke.

The figure emerged out of the recess as the entrance closed, until it was in the same position as before.

'We know how to open it. I guess we can figure out from where you walked how it closes,' said James. 'I think it has a connection. The box was empty, but I found a clue. Look at this engraving.' He showed Luke the picture he'd taken.

'So we're in the right place, but they'd moved the treasure to a safer place,' said Luke.

'Exactly my thoughts. I said the box was empty, but there was a scrap of parchment I've taken with me to read later. Could give us some clues.

'Let's continue down the tunnel to see where it brings us.

'How are we doing for time? Being down here has totally disorientated me. Weird.'

James checked his phone. 'We've been down here for forty minutes so far. Another twenty mins max before we retrace our steps?'

'Lead on,' said Luke.

They continued along the tunnel, scanning the walls for other possible mechanisms, and after around ten minutes, they could see that the tunnel was blocked by rocks where it had collapsed. They could feel the air moving, which suggested that there was a connection to the surface.

'Do you think the drummer boy is under that?' asked Luke.

'He might well be if the story is right. Anyway, I think this is the end for us, as we aren't well prepared to unblock the tunnel.

'We still need to walk back through the tunnel, get out of the church while everyone is asleep, and get ourselves to the mine to do a bit of digging.'

'It does feel a bit precarious that a tunnel carved out the rock has collapsed. But it could also be like that chamber back there with the tunnel they started. Maybe the digging caused something to bring the roof down?'

'Might be that. If you look at the tunnel roof, it's curved, which is a stronger structure than a flat one.'

'Let's get out of here.'

They retraced their steps past the figure and the hidden door, through the chamber with the abandoned tunnel and back to the stairs leading up to the cloister in the church.

'Do you think it's worth having a quick look up the tunnel?' asked Luke, pointing to the tunnel they'd not explored.

'We have been down here for just over an hour, so I guess we would not get behind schedule if we had a quick walk up.'

They walked up the tunnel which was just as the other side had been. Again they scanned for anything unusual. It turned very quickly into a dead end with the tunnel being blocked by a very substantial wall with large stones filled with mortar. Scanning the wall with the stone, they spotted a small inscription on one of the lower stones of the date 1714 in Roman numerals with the initials CT.

'The carving of the date 1714 suggests that this was built well after the tunnel was first made. It coincides with a building phase of Richmond when a lot of newer houses sprung up,' said James. 'I wonder if CT refers to Charles Tubhurst?'

'No clue,' replied Luke. 'Given how we have learned that the medieval town was knocked down to be rebuilt in the early eighteenth century, this would fit in with that. I'm also guessing if they blocked it off here, they would also have explored it on the other side. Any treasures would be long gone.'

'Let's head back up the steps to the church.'

With that they walked back to the steps. As a precaution, before pushing open the panel, they switched off their head lamps, and used one torch on the lowest setting to light their way.

The church was quiet as they emerged. They closed the panel door to the stairs, switching off the torch before making their way back to the door they'd come in.

Once they were out of the church, Luke quickly locked the door with his adapted coat hanger key. The street lights were partially switched off, giving them better cover, and a light drizzle had set in. They heard the odd car driving along the road with big gaps between.

They made their way along the river to the woods above the copper mine entrance on the south bank of the river Swale. The drizzle meant that they had a good reason to have their hoods up. Not that they needed to worry as they encountered nobody along the way.

It took a little while in the dark tramping through the damp wood to find the spot on the map that they'd identified as a good candidate. The overcast night meant that strange shadows loomed as they walked through the forest. It was a bit too dark to see clearly. The noise from the flowing river formed a backdrop to a rustle of leaves rising and falling with the wind, punctuated with the odd groan from a branch creaking. There was a risk that if they switched on their torches and head lamps, they could be seen, although it was the early hours of the morning, and there was nobody about. Faced with not being able to see at all, Luke switched his head lamp to the lowest setting to be sure they were in the right place. James followed.

'Let's dig in this depression as it's either a collapsed tunnel or an entrance,' said Luke, beginning to dig with one of the foldable spades they'd brought. The soil was rich in organic matter and easy to dig. 'Do you want to start that side? We can meet in the middle?'

'Okay. Let's see what we can find.'

They dug in a companionable silence for around half an hour, removing a good deal of the loamy soil before encountering the odd stone.

'That was easy so far,' said James. 'I guess the next bit will be where we either find an entrance or a dead end?!'

'Yeah, should we have a bet on it? Feeling confident?' asked Luke. He continued to dig, moving the soil onto a small mound they'd created.

A further twenty minutes elapsed before they got to the bedrock. They began lifting the rocks in what looked like a promising place. By this time the drizzle had stopped and the wind had picked up, causing the trees to creak and the leaves to rustle. The background noise of the water passing over the rocks in the river below remained a constant. The old copper mines contained a labyrinth of tunnels that was well documented and spanned the centuries, the mining activity coinciding with periods of the high prices of copper. Unfortunately, many of the attempts to mine copper only found measly seams that rapidly petered out or got complicated, requiring a lot of expensive extraction and pumping of water.

'Look. These rocks look like they have been put there!' said James, pointing to what looked like part of a wall. 'Can you see they are layered as part of a structure or something?'

'That looks promising,' said Luke, who interrupted his lifting of rocks to walk over to where James was. Out of the corner of his eye, he thought he saw movement, and a torch further down the path. He turned to see the bobbing of a couple of lights.

'Time to get out of here. There are some people coming this way through the woods.' He pointed down the path while switching off his head torch. 'We have a head start if we go now. I don't want to hang around to find out who they are.' While swiftly putting his bag on his shoulders, he picked up his foldable spade before making his way up the path.

James followed, folding up his spade, so it was ready to put in his bag when they'd got a bit of distance between them and the people approaching.

They crossed a wooden bridge over a narrow stream, heading up a path on a flight of wooden steps, and paused at the top to look back. The torches were flashing around where they'd been. One was making its way towards them. They put their folded spades into their bags, slung the bags on their backs and broke into a jog on the downhill section to get as much distance as they could.

'Let's cross the road. They are less likely to see us from

the footpath,' said James quietly as they reached a road near the Green Bridge. They hurried across the bridge, turning into a road leading to the waterfall. Once they'd passed the last house, they took a sharp left and climbed the steep steps that zigzagged through the trees up towards Castle Walk. As they were towards the top, they could see a pickup stopping at the bridge, and they could hear the noise of car doors closing.

'If we follow the walls, we'll come out onto a road that leads into the bottom end of the square where the car is,' said Luke. 'They are definitely looking for us. Hopefully they'll drive around the roads before getting to the main square.' Even though it was overcast, they could see enough of the path nestled underneath the castle walls to confidently run until they met the road, slowing to a brisk walk, fearing that running might arouse light sleepers in the houses lining the street. Pausing before entering the market place, Luke gave a thumbs up as an all-clear sign. They walked to their car, quietly putting their bags and coats into the boot before collapsing into the seats.

'So far, so good,' said James as he switched on the engine.

Luke put his postcode into the satnav, and followed the instructions out of Richmond, through Catterick Garrison before joining the A1 South. Neither of them felt like talking for a while.

'I've no idea how they knew we were there. We had minimal lighting with our head torches. There was definitely nobody about when we walked into the woods. They seem to have come from the other end of the path, which is where the Round Howe car park is,' said Luke while scrolling through the map.

'I suspect someone may have seen our lights somehow and alerted the others? There's no other explanation other than some kind of sophisticated monitoring set-up, which doesn't seem that plausible.'

'It was good that they didn't find us in the tunnel, or that they didn't have people on both ends of the path. We may have got ourselves into a bit of difficulty!' said Luke.

'So true. It has been a good trip getting into the tunnel, and finding the hidden chamber. I wonder what they, whoever they are, will do with the bit we were digging. Do you think they'll continue? Beat us to it?'

'They might do. Thinking about it, we have a good idea the Guild of Glaziers were in that tunnel, which they considered unsafe, and moved whatever they'd stored there. I do wonder about the old copper mines now that we have spent a bit of time there,' said Luke. 'The lower passages would've been at risk of flooding so we ruled those out. We were taking a longshot that there were some abandoned passages that were not connected to the lower ones. There was always a risk with old mine shafts that mining could continue if the price of the minerals made it worth the while to resume digging.'

'I can see where you're going with that, but what if the guild thought they were only hiding their treasure for a few months or a year tops?'

'The tunnel at the church would be a better place to hide their treasure as it was bone dry, unless it was widely known about amongst the guild members.'

'I think it's time to do a bit more digging in archives and online, and to look for other leads. It might worth giving it a bit of time before going back to the old copper mines.'

'Yes, I guess they would be more organised next time. They might get people either end of the paths. Thinking about it, what would they actually do if they did catch us? Beat us up?'

'I hope we never find out. It's also good that they didn't identify us, as I wouldn't be keen to repeat the mystery caller experience!'

The journey back to York was uneventful with a thin stream of cars on the motorway, and the odd person out and about on the roads leading to the city.

NINETEEN

The decision to host the public consultation in the historic townhall was a calculated attempt to reinforce the heritage credentials of Rufus Investments. They'd also decided, following some consultation, that the application should be made through a wholly owned subsidiary called Rufus 'Regeneration', as people responded more negatively to the word 'Investments'.

A public relations firm had been hired to create a story around the project to make Rufus Regeneration appear to be guardians of Richmond's heritage, who were bringing a precious monument back into everyday life. Taking charge of the event, the PR team had set up the room with a series of information panels, with high quality images showing what the finished project would look like, and a couple of large LED stands with short videos playing on a loop showcasing the building.

The format was that the exhibition was open all day, and people were encouraged to visit and discuss any concerns they may have. The PR company brought a team of specialists, trained in public consultation and experts in handling difficult situations, who manned a desk where the public could ask questions.

There were three scheduled presentations, each finishing with an open discussion. Edward began with a short introduction about Rufus Regeneration and the scheme, then a heritage consultant, Toby, gave a short talk of the history of the castle and how bringing buildings into use helped preserve them by giving them a second life. The final presentation was from Cathrine. She presented the design of the building, and played a video showing a 3D model of the building seen from above, outside and inside.

The afternoon session was well attended by a mixture of local business people, a cohort of retirees and a couple of reporters for local papers. The presentations were well received and the questions answered professionally, and to the satisfaction of the audience. The concerns raised revolved around the construction traffic, where the visitors would park and how it would be managed, the impact on the local businesses, and questions around the benefits, such as the number of jobs created.

The second session was scheduled for early evening with a glass of wine and nibbles to follow. The session had the same line-up as before, and the addition of the minister of culture, who was a local MP. As with the earlier session, the questions were polite and the answers reassured the packed room.

The informal drinks and nibbles were where the real discussions took place. The crowd was more weighted to the business community and the interest groups that had been invited.

The full spectrum of opinions was being expressed, ranging from praise for the bold project, which would bring a heritage building into modern day use balanced with preserving the structure, to unease that the fabric of the old castle could be irreparably damaged.

The PR team had done a good job of steering the conversation to that of heritage and building on the past. The message was that Richmond was a town that had inherited a rich architecture that had been preserved. It didn't labour the point that the castle was the oldest structure in the town by far, and the townscape was mainly from the last three centuries, apart from the odd religious building. It re-enforced the narrative of Georgian Richmond, despite the castle being medieval, and spun the narrative around preservation and continuity. The project was praised by the crowd for marrying the modern with the old, and the consensus was that it had achieved the right balance of preserving the old with a modern use.

•

James had started a new part-time job at a media company, writing copy for the social media campaigns they did for a variety of businesses up and down the country. It was a very different place to Davidson and Sons and he'd yet to find an equivalent to Caitlin. Although he did meet Caitlin at Friday lunchtime from time to time, which was still enjoyable as he knew enough of the characters to relish the gossip.

James went out of the office to the noodle bar nearby for a takeaway, and as he was waiting in the queue to be served, he checked his phone. He'd got into the habit of setting it to Flight Mode while he was at work, and switching it off, his phone sprung to life, a surge of alerts began popping up.

Grace had messaged James during a work break with exciting news of the album, sharing a link to a rave review. James replied suggesting they meet after work in a bar around the corner from where Grace worked. He got a heart emoji reply to his message.

James collected his bowl of noodles and a cup of

green tea, heading out to the nearby square with benches, popular with the lunchtime crowd. He sat on one of the benches next to a jumbled rack of bicycles, in front of a vintage clothing shop. Clicking on the link which Grace had shared, he ate his noodles while reading the article. The article was written by a well-respected music reviewer on one of the more prestigious music blogs. The album was rated 10 out of 10 and it had been put on a list of bands to watch for. The album review had been widely shared across the social media platforms, prompting a stream of comments and likes.

James messaged Grace to tell her he'd read the article and how fantastic it was before checking the website selling the LP to see how it was doing… only to find that it had actually sold out.

He messaged the band in the group chat to let them know about the article, the news of the LP sales and reactions on social media. Rick was first to reply that he'd already had a message. The website selling the LPs was keen for a further run, and they also suggested issuing a limited edition for collectors. Helen was next, adding that the traffic on the video sites had really grown in the last twenty-four hours.

They all agreed that they should do more events to capitalise on the publicity, that in turn would grow the fanbase. Rick volunteered to go through his contacts to do a push for bookings. This prompted a discussion whether they should get an agent to take care of all the admin for them as it was getting to a volume of work that it was not fair to burden Rick with. The chat concluded that they should discuss this at the next scheduled practice.

James had long finished his noodles and tea, and putting his phone back onto Flight Mode, he went back to the office with a spring in his step.

•

James arrived early at the pub, ordered a drink, sat down at a table in the corner and waited for Grace. She'd messaged to say that she would be fifteen minutes late as something had come up at work.

To kill time, he scrolled through the band's pages on social media. He was taken aback by the volume of messages and comments as people discussed their LP. It was being picked up, not only by their local fanbase, but by people all over the world who had been able to stream the album. There was disappointment that the LP had already sold out, discussions and speculation on whether a further edition would be made.

As she crossed towards James's table, Grace called out, 'Sorry, have you been waiting long?'

James stood up and they hugged.

'I've idled my time away on social media looking at the band pages. It's amazing. First things first, drink?'

'Yes, I need a glass of white wine. I've had a shocker of a day,' said Grace as she took her coat off, arranging her things before sitting down.

James returned from the bar with the glass of wine and a refill for himself, along with a bag of dry roasted nuts.

'How exciting that the LP has already sold out. What about that fab review we had?' said Grace. 'From what Rick was saying, the label is keen to release another batch. They also liked the suggestion of a limited edition set.'

'Totally amazing. I've a feeling that we will be in for a busy summer with the festivals. It wouldn't surprise me if a proper tour was on the cards.'

'It's exactly what we were all hoping for, although it seems to have happened a bit quicker than we expected.'

'I like the idea of an agent, as it's becoming a bit of a burden for Rick managing everything. If we can pack our day jobs in then we can spend a lot more time writing, touring, playing. I don't think it will be too far away if things continue as they are.'

Grace leaned forward with a concerned look on her face, and began what could be an awkward conversation. 'James, don't take this the wrong way. I want to understand what's going on. You're regularly late for band practice to the point where everyone has noticed. We have even played some sets without you, where Helen sequenced the basslines.'

James looked crestfallen and replied, 'I don't know what's wrong with me. I'm not late for anything else, and for some reason I seem to mess up and either get the times wrong, totally forget or don't realise the time.' He paused, sighing and scratching his head. 'I'm really enjoying playing in the band, and love the direction it's going, but there seems to be a block. I don't know if it's imposter syndrome as I seem to contribute way less than the rest of you. Like you say, Helen can replace me easily with the synths and sequencers.'

'You can definitely play bass as Rick wouldn't have asked you otherwise, and we play well together, so I'd stop feeling sorry for yourself. The only other thing I can think of is your time is totally taken up with your quest?'

'It could be a factor as I seem to have gone deep into it, but on the other hand, wouldn't I be late for everything else too if it was that? I really don't know, and I'm beginning to wonder if I should continue with the band? If I left, as you say, Helen could step in,' said James. Then he said, in a more anguished tone, 'It changes nothing between us if I'm in the band or not, other than I'll miss you madly when you're on tour.'

'I don't want you to think that we can only be together if we are in the band. I really want to be with you, and I'm sure we can make things work, even if I'm away for long tours,' said Grace as she leaned over to kiss James.

•

The scrap of parchment that James and Luke had found was written on vellum and contained a partial list of glass, silver plates, candle sticks and platters, all suggesting high-value goods in a neat script written in Latin. On translating the list from the Latin, which in itself was a slow process using online tools, James concluded that the treasure was real, and must have been in the chamber where he found the parchment, and that it had been moved to a yet-to-be-discovered place. Having the list of valuables was no proof that they were collected together and hidden. It could've been a simple inventory, and there was nothing on the parchment to suggest that they were placed in the chamber, or indeed anywhere else.

The photos and video footage taken from the tunnels were a good record of the carving and mechanism that opened the door. The details of the carving in the photos showed a person with a big nose, bulging eyes and a strange upturned mouth with teeth protruding. Nothing was made by accident in the medieval times, and it was likely to represent someone or something that would've been well known at the time. The figure could've been made much earlier, possibly a gargoyle carved for Easby Abbey, which may have been removed during the dissolution of the monasteries in the 1500s. As to the mechanism, there was nothing in the photos which revealed how the mechanism worked, other than the figure being protruded when the door was closed, inset when the door was open. The mechanism would require expert analysis from an archaeology team to understand how it worked and was able to move such a heavy stone door.

James left Luke a long voice message explaining how he'd been examining the photos and videos, his conclusions and where Luke could find the notes.

- Thanks for the message. It sounds like the treasure must be somewhere nearby and secure enough not to have been found. I've been thinking about the old copper mine, and have strong reservations. They seem too leaky to store valuables and have been extensively mined since the medieval times for the treasure not to have been found.

- I get that, but why were there people with torches at that time of night unless they were safeguarding something valuable?

- The only rational explanation is that the people with torches must have thought that we know more than they do. Or a coincidence. Maybe they were looking out for poachers.

•

Luke had invited James around as he'd come up with an idea of where they could look next, suggesting the usual format of a takeaway to discuss plans.

They settled down with a beer while they chose what they wanted to eat from the app. Luke put some Balti mix into a bowl for them to nibble at while they waited.

'It should be thirty to forty minutes according to the app,' said Luke. According to their custom, they split the bill equally, with James paying through bank transfer.

'So what have you been up to? I'm intrigued to hear what you have come up with.'

'The copper mines bothered me as they're too close to the river. They are very likely to have flooded on a regular basis. I did a bit of research on the history of the mining operation. There have been many phases of mining, largely driven by the price of copper over the centuries. I concluded that, due to the location, especially with the flood risk, it was not a good place store treasures. Even if they'd been smart, storing it in an upper passage, the mines were being worked at the time and it would've been risky for them, even if it were a short-term solution. Not only that, it stood a fair chance of being discovered in the many years that have passed through mining activity. Beginning with the question of where you would hide your treasures, what's the criteria? We know that the chamber we found was a storage place they used, given the chest along with the fragment of parchment. Something must have spooked them as they moved it to another, safer, place. The chamber was well hidden, bone dry, carved out of the rock. That got me thinking, where else could they make a safe hiding place in the rock, away from risks of water or fire that could destroy the treasure?'

'I can't fault your logic. So what candidates have you come up with?'

'I started by looking for candidates that were near the site of the guildhall. Starting with the geology, that clearly has the section of town that sits on bedrock. We can dismiss this section here,' said Luke, showing James an area on the aerial view of the market place, 'as it was developed by the Georgians who used it as a reservoir, and put up their obelisk as a fancy water dispenser on the site of the former butter cross used in the medieval times.'

'This area was the Shambles, or meat market, in medieval times. I think it was very unlikely to have been considered a safe spot, even less likely that they could excavate such a busy area. So I moved my attention to this area behind the town hall and castle. The townhall as it stands is clearly a Georgian building, replacing a medieval structure that could've been a minor guildhall given its footprint. But that's less important. You see here that the ground slopes. It follows the rock strata you can see below the castle walls that rise above the river.' Luke pointed at to the aerial view. 'If you look at the cottages here, these ones have been replaced with more recent buildings, and this, these houses look like they have been there for a while.'

'Do you think they date to the right era? There's no trace of timber-framed medieval houses in Richmond.'

'I took the liberty of booking one of these cottages the weekend after next. I have a hunch that there are tunnels leading off these places. They could well be houses that the guild members lived in. It sleeps four, plenty of room if you want to bring Grace?' said Luke.

'I promised I'd keep her out of our project, as I don't want her getting tangled up with the people who seem to be angry at us for digging into Richmond's history. We have a gig on the Friday evening, so the earliest would be Saturday morning.' said James.

'Fair enough. I guess we don't need to make a weekend of it,' said Luke. 'What got me interested in this particular place was the floor plan, which you can see on the booking site. It's an upside-down house with the bedrooms on the lower floor, and the kitchen living space on top. Looking at the bedrooms, do you see something odd here?'

'Not really. They look like two rooms and a staircase?'

'Look a bit closer. This looks like something boxed in or walled up. The photo gallery shows the rooms here,' Luke pointed at the image, 'and this bit looks like it should be a cupboard or wardrobe, but it's actually a wall.'

'So you think there's a tunnel or a secret chamber behind it?'

'That was my conclusion. The only way to find out is to go there. Before we get there, we need to figure out how to explore without totally smashing the cottage up. I have some ideas about a drill combined with a long inspection camera.'

'Good thinking. I guess there's a lot you can do with those. If we do find evidence of the treasure there, we can figure out how to go about extracting it.'

They were interrupted by the arrival of the food, as was also becoming tradition.

'I've been busy too with an angle of research,' said James. 'I wanted to know more about what would prompt the guild to hide their treasures, how someone got their hands on the guildhall, and importantly when it was demolished.

'We know that the political landscape was turbulent at that time. To make matters worse we know from the records that there were periodic outbreaks of the plague until the late seventeenth century. What got me interested was how it affected Richmond. The politics could've been significant from a London viewpoint, but it didn't mean it had the same impact through the country as life may have continued uninterrupted in Richmond. The nature of the plague outbreaks could be very localised.

'The starting point was the church records. From that I could figure out, when the plague outbreaks occurred, there was a surge in recorded deaths, even though they may have been buried in a plague pit with a good smothering of quick lime.

'I counted two outbreaks in the date range that we are investigating. At the same time, there were Acts of Parliament that weakened the hold of the guilds in favour of liberalising trade.' James began drawing a line with the key dates on his notebook. 'You can see in this gap here between the plague outbreaks and the Acts of Parliament when someone or a group could go after the guilds.'

'So what you're saying here is that the plagues and the turbulence in Parliament created the right environment for people to take full advantage?'

'Exactly. I began tying this back to the activities of the Heckroys and the Tubhursts around the Goose Fair, along with what led up to the demolition of the glassworks. I would say that they also had a fat prize they must have had their eyes on. My hypothesis is that this all went on just before the second plague outbreak, when the guilds may have been fatally hit. It's also plausible that the people who held the secret of where the treasure was all perished in the outbreak.'

'That would suggest that whoever is taking a keen interest in what we are doing must have some knowledge. A secret handed down the generations. Or perhaps they have part of a document, but not enough of it to tell them where it is.'

'It's looking very likely, unless the secret got out somehow. There's also the possibility that descendants of the guild, who knew of the treasure but were not entrusted to hide it, are our people with a strong claim on its ownership.'

'I'm not sure I'm too keen on finding out!'

'I'll keep researching to see if I can pinpoint the dates when the guildhall was sold, and to whom, and then add this to the timeline.'

'Brilliant. Shall I come and pick you up on the Saturday afternoon? We can stay overnight. Come back on Sunday after lunch? I fancy a Sunday roast at one of the many pubs in town.'

'That would be great. I'll book something for Saturday evening. It might be busy then?'

They continued discussing their plans, finishing off their food. James told Luke about the success of the LP, the increased attention and the plans for the band.

•

Band practice was in a new venue which had opened up as a community venue for bands to rehearse. They'd needed to move for some storage space, so they could keep some of their heavier kit there.

This was a big evening as their new agent was coming to meet them and watch them play. She'd also promised to take them out for a drink afterwards.

Rick had been handing over the bookings to the agent, Becky, and had made the introductions to the record label. As a result he was looking a lot more relaxed.

Helen and Grace were keen to meet Becky in person as they'd spoken with her on a video call when they discussed what she could offer. She grilled them about their commitments, so she could start looking at the festivals and gig timetables.

'Hi everyone,' exclaimed Becky as she entered the rehearsal room. 'Great to meet you all in real life!'

She got a warm response from the band, who all said hello, ushering her to a table. James offered to go to the vending machine and get some drinks.

James came back wobbling the cups, along with a couple of bottles shoved into his hoodie pockets.

'I'm so excited about representing you. It has been quite a phenomenon so far. The reaction I got when I called around was very positive on the touring side of things,' said Becky. 'I also had a couple of exploratory conversations with some A&R guys at one or two of the bigger labels, who were keen to know more.'

'That's a pretty amazing start,' replied Rick. 'What happens with our current record deal?'

'I suggest looking into this to find a good angle to negotiate if you'd like me to. They normally try to get a lump sum to buy you out, but I could wrap this into a deal with the other labels, so they'd buy you out.'

'Tricky one. I sort of feel a bit loyal to them, as they did us a good deal, and took a bit of a punt with us. On the other hand, a bigger label with a bigger distribution base may be better for us.'

'Yeah, they also have a bigger influence with the streaming services, which is more interesting as they are key in driving record sales and tickets for gigs,' said Becky. 'Are you guys ready to take the next step up? I can get a full schedule sorted for the summer with the festivals. I should also look into booking a big tour in the autumn, when traditionally the students go back and venues sell out.'

Both Helen and Grace said at once, 'Oh yes, that would very exciting.' Helen qualified it by saying she only had four weeks' notice for her job, and Grace said she was in the same position. James relished the prospect of seeing where this would take them as a band, and joined in by saying, 'I have a week's notice as I'm on a part-time contract at the moment.' Rick replied, 'I'm all in, nothing will stop me.'

'I've saved the best bit until last,' said Becky. 'I have a chance to get you onto a prestigious national prize for newcomers. To do that we need to get a new release out, or turbo charge your existing one to get it more noticed. Don't get me wrong, it has done amazingly so far.'

'If that's what I think it is, just getting on the nomination list is a massive boost,' replied James. 'We would get a lot of exposure from that. Amazing!'

'Let's not get ahead of ourselves yet. What I'd really like is to hear you play, especially if you have some new stuff.'

With that they cleared the table, going to the studio to set up. James knew enough to help Helen, who had the most complicated set-up. Rick helped Grace with her drum kit. The studio was a lot smarter than they were used to. Unlike the old one, it was not a tangle of wires and adapters, and the mixing deck was a state of the art set-up.

They played a set of their newer songs, throwing one work in progress in at the end, which they had some fun extending with a dub section in the middle, before winding it back up to the correct tempo.

'How was that?' asked Helen.

'That was brilliant. I thought I knew what to expect, but this was even better than I could've hoped for. It really builds on what you have done before,' replied Becky. 'Have you got some more you can play?'

'Do you want us to do a couple of the album tracks? We can follow them with a couple of the newer ones,' said Grace.

'Yes, please!'

The band had a quick chat, before deciding what order they would play things, and what they wanted to play. They proceeded to play for about forty minutes.

Becky sat at the mixing desk with the monitors set up perfectly, watching and listening, letting them play uninterrupted.

Once they'd finished, Becky stood up, giving them a big round of applause.

'This just keeps getting better. I promised you a drink. Where do you suggest we go?'

'There's a nice bar not too far from here. It won't take us too long to tidy things away,' said James, unplugging his guitar and moving on to helping the others.

Grace, Helen and Rick had been swapping messages and thought it best to meet in person to discuss the band, with all the recent events. They met in a quiet café that was not one of their usual haunts, greeted each other, placed their orders and got down to the business of the day.

'I want to clear the air as it might be a bit awkward, given my relationship with James,' said Grace. 'I've spoken with him, and asked why he's doing what he's doing. There wasn't a clear answer about why, but a sense of not feeling he's bringing much to the band, even though he's enjoying playing. He pointed out that he's only late for band things, which is confusing him and is possibly subconscious.'

'Thanks for being open. Really appreciate it,' said Rick. 'I also feel a bit awkward as I brought him in. I think we can agree he's a nice guy and a competent bassist, but I think there's something that I can't put my finger on. Grace, you mentioned it might be subconscious, and I think that it's something that he's unaware of rather than it being a deliberate thing.'

'I appreciate your candid thoughts and that it isn't easy for either of you,' said Helen. 'I want to be very blunt and as objective as I can. Like you both say, he's a lovely guy and competent, but, and there is a big but, we are in the process of signing contracts with Becky that will really boost the band's visibility, and we all need to be one hundred per cent in. James did say in the meeting that he only had a week's notice, and sounded keen, but when it comes to it, he's not all in. We have had a couple of sessions where I did the bass on my sequencers, and that worked well, so we do have a viable option if we decide to continue without him. Remember this is definitely not personal. It's about putting the band on a solid footing.'

'I think you're right,' replied Grace. 'We need to make a difficult decision now rather than letting it drift, especially as we are going to be a lot busier with Becky helping promote us.'

'In that case, I think we know what we need to do… are we agreed that we ask James to leave?' said Rick in a heavy voice. He looked at Grace and Helen, who both nodded. He said, 'I volunteer to tell him, as I was the one who brought him in, and it'd be way too awkward for Grace. Unless you want to let him know, Helen?'

'It makes sense for you to tell him. He'll probably take it better from you,' replied Helen.

•

- Morning, George. The treasure hunt is in full flow, although nothing concrete so far. What do you think the impact might be on the planning application if it were discovered?

- Good point, Luke. A lot depends on the narrative. It could help as it would bring history and heritage to the front pages, and put it in people's minds. What would be less favourable is any narrative of plunder or wild stories about the past that could put us in a bad light.

- Do you think it would be less risky to make sure it's not discovered, as without anything tangible there is no story?

- We either slow it down, which could be tricky, or we take control of the narrative. It's important that you stay closely involved and report back. Better to be well informed, even if you are helping him a bit.

- Okay. I'll keep going. We're back treasure hunting in Richmond this weekend. Don't worry, the theories on where it might be are lots of extrapolation on slender facts, probably making 2 + 2 = 5.
- Thanks for letting me know.

TWENTY

James picked up Luke late Saturday morning for the trip to Richmond. James filled Luke in on the band's news, giving a detailed account of what Becky had been telling them.

They talked about the treasure hunt, speculating how close they were to finding the treasure, and how James being away for the best part of summer would slow down the hunt. They concluded that if it had been kept a secret for the best part of four hundred years, it would wait a little longer. They were secure that nobody else had any better ideas. They also speculated whether the people they were wary of even knew about the guild's treasure, or whether they had something else they were looking for.

They got to Richmond in no time, and left their car in a long stay car park. They made their way to the cottage that Luke had booked. It was a self check-in, and Luke had been given the code to the box outside the front door, which had the keys in. The cottage looked just like the picture on the online brochure, other than the paint on the outside wall didn't look as fresh. Some flecks of moss or lichen gave it a slightly mottled look.

They dumped their bags on the sofa, deciding to stock up on some beers and nibbles from the nearby supermarket. Once they were done shopping, they planned go for a walk to the woods, which they'd left in a hurry last time as this time there was still some light in the day.

As they crossed Green Bridge, a van pulled up beside them. The side door opened. Two men grabbed James, bundling him into the van. The men pulled a hessian bag over his head, and tied his wrists together with plastic zip ties. It was all done so suddenly that James didn't know what to do, let alone think of how he could escape. James realised that only he had been bundled into the van, and that they hadn't taken Luke. The van pulled up, and reversed before returning the way it had come. Shortly after that, he sensed that the van was going up a steep road. They stopped at a junction. It was hard to track where they were going. He was sure the van turned off somewhere along the road after the first hill.

The van came to a stop. An authoritative voice said, 'On your feet.' He could hear the door slide open, accompanied by a blast of cold air. James was guided out by his elbows. His captors grunted commands at him when there were steps or other obstacles. The ground became softer under his feet. It became quieter. He could smell that they were in a pine wood.

He was told to stop. The hood was removed, but his wrists remained tied. There were four men in total. The two that had bundled them into the van were young and fit-looking with tattooed arms. They had a military bearing. There was another younger man, who stood slightly apart with a close-cropped beard and hair, again with an air of military about him. He seemed to be the lead muscle. An older man, who appeared to be in charge, didn't have the same physical presence, and looked vaguely familiar to James. He had a resemblance to the visitor James had had in York. At a guess, he was related.

James thought it wise to keep quiet. It was not the time to demand to be let go.

'Right. We aren't going to bugger about here,' said the older man who had a reedy, but commanding voice.

'We know it was you who was digging in the woods recently. We have a fair idea what you're looking for.'

James waited for him to continue.

'Whatever you think you're looking for is probably wrong, so let's start with that. What is it you think is in those woods?' The older man glared at James.

'We are looking for the standard of the Ninth Legion which left York. The legion never made it to Hadrian's Wall. The story tells of a massacre by the Brigantes in what is now the Scottish borders,' said James, as convincingly as he could.

'Utter rubbish. What makes you think it's in Richmond and not in the North?'

'I found some scripts in a digital archive that had a description of a bend in the river and a cliff. By using a GIS analytical script, I found Richmond as a match,' replied James.

'I have no idea what scripts you're talking about, but the Romans were in Catterick, not in Richmond. That whole area has been mined for copper for centuries since the Romans. Evidence of a battle would've been found,' said the older man with authority.

The younger men were beginning to look bored, seeing that James was not going to be a significant nuisance. One of them even got his phone out and began scrolling.

'Why are you so concerned about what we did in the woods? Why kidnap me?' asked James. 'There must be something you're hiding there.'

'That's none of your business. Even if there was something there, why on earth should I tell you?' said the older man.

'As I see it, you're either bluffing and worried we are

about to find the standard of the Ninth, or you have something far more interesting that's buried there?' James said.

'I think you're finding facts to suit your theory. We don't want you near Billy Bank Wood again. Have I made myself clear?'

James replied, 'It's National Trust land. On what authority do you tell us not go there?'

'It can't stretch your imagination too much to think about what we might do if we find you there again. Understood?'

One of the younger men said he was going back to the van. The other two followed, leaving the older man with James.

'That sounds like a serious threat. I have no idea what I've done to deserve being picked up, tied up and threatened,' said James.

'Now, look here,' said the older man. 'This discussion isn't going anywhere. I'm not going to tell you my reasons. I'll say this for the final time. You're not going to go anywhere near Billy Bank. If we find you there again, we won't be so polite. I'm going to call the men back, who are going to cut those ties, and you can walk back into Richmond. It will only take you twenty minutes. If you're brisk, you'll make it before nightfall.'

The muscle returned and produced a sharp knife to quickly cut through the zip ties. Once he was done, he gave James a gentle shove and growled, 'Follow that path, turn right at the bottom and you'll find your way back to Richmond.'

•

The path wound down alongside a small trickle of a stream lined with gorse bushes that were decked in yellow flowers, a few rowan trees interspersed. Before long the path bent around, reaching a style onto a farm track. There was a stream to cross, which could be done by jumping on the stones sticking out above the water.

There was a lot whirring around in James's thoughts, beginning with why it was only him who had been kidnapped. He considered going to the police. It was after all kidnapping, and holding him against his will. Why was he taken and not Luke? Kidnapping is a criminal act, and whoever they were, it seemed thoroughly disproportionate, and seemed an escalation to the burglary. The more practical thoughts were that, even if he did report it, he didn't have a vehicle registration number, and any description of the van would not narrow the search down other than identifying a standard tradesman's van. Even if they found the perpetrators, it would be a case of he-said-she-said, especially as there were no witnesses. They can claim they were nowhere near him, that he made the whole story up. Given who he thought they were, they probably had some community standing that would give them credibility over him as an outsider. The only comfort that James could find was that he believed they were convinced that he was mad, and on a wild goose chase, looking for a Roman myth. He mulled on the idea that they were on their own hunt for something that was nothing to do with the treasure that he and Luke were hunting.

He continued along the valley with his thoughts, through a number of fields each with a sturdy gate. Eventually he went up a hill, emerging onto the old racecourse. He realised that he was on the infamous racecourse that was on the site of the St Martin's Goose Fair, and how it seemed a lifetime away when he was studying the stash of papers he'd bought at auction.

•

James knocked on the cottage door. Luke swiftly opened the door, ushering James in, asking lots of questions. James gave Luke a concise summary of the events, as Luke got beers out of the fridge, pouring them into the glasses he'd found in a cupboard. James then shared his thoughts about what it meant, and his feelings of helplessness in not being able to do anything about it. Luke, like James, was unable to fully describe the van, and certainly could not remember the number plate. Neither of them could come up with a plausible explanation as to why only James had been taken.

Refreshed from a couple of drinks, they had some time before they needed to be at the restaurant for their booking. Luke was keen to drill into the wall, to make a small hole, and to feed in the inspection camera to see what was behind. He got to work by laying out a dust sheet he'd brought with him.

The drill made light work of getting through the plaster, and the inspection camera had plenty of length that allowed Luke to begin exploring. The camera came with an app that relayed the video footage, with a handy feature to take stills. Watching the footage, there was a brick wall about a metre from the plaster. Working his way along, a small gap allowed Luke to push the camera further, revealing a damp tunnel cut into the bedrock with rough chisel marks. The excitement was short-lived, as the tunnel ended about two and a half metres from the brick wall with a wet looking wall with the same chisel marks as he'd already seen. Luke called James over to look at what he'd found, and they concluded that this was not as promising as they'd hoped.

Luke pulled the camera back though the small hole he'd made, and carefully filled it with some readymade plaster. He would need to let it dry, and give it a sanding to smooth it out, and a lick of paint, so the owners couldn't tell they'd made a hole. Luke left up his dustsheet in place, ready for the morning when the plaster was fully dry, allowing him to finish off.

They went to the restaurant they'd booked, and enjoyed a hearty meal. James was hungry from his walk. They didn't discuss anything related to the treasure, or the events they'd experienced as they were not keen to be overheard. They began the discussion on the way back to the cottage where they could talk freely about the treasure hunt, and how, despite not finding anything so far, they'd eliminated some good candidates.

There were a few avenues left to explore, but they needed to do some further research through the online archives. It would not necessarily lead to an 'x marks the spot' revelation. More that they had to find places with connections to the guilds, which would help find places that were likely to be candidates.

James's encounter with the person who had taken an interest in what they were doing, made him less anxious. Clearly the man was not above threatening, even kidnapping, which suggested he would go to lengths to get hold of any knowledge they acquired or even steal anything they found, but not as dangerous as his fertile mind had imagined. He was a determined older man with a motive, but from what James could see, he wasn't part of some sinister organisation.

They discussed what to do next, concluding that while they could involve others, they didn't want to share too much information about what they were looking for, even if they fully trusted the people they confided in.

TWENTY-ONE

Rick met with James as he wanted to speak with him in person rather than being like a teenager and dumping him on social media. They managed a healthy discussion about why James was not fully committed to the band, and how they had a big opportunity to take the band to the next level. They concluded, amicably, that James would leave the band on good terms. They would continue to share the royalties of the first album, and not make any big announcements.

The summer, for the band, was a blur of festivals, concerts and travelling around UK, with spells of doing the continental festivals. The band was getting a very good reception at gigs. Becky was working tirelessly to get them bookings, and negotiating better slots, both in terms of the stages they played and the timeslots they had. They were no longer in the side tents playing mid-afternoon, but were beginning to play the main stages early evening. In a couple of the smaller festivals, they appeared before the headline act.

Becky had renegotiated the terms of their debut album, releasing them from their original contract to much more favourable terms with a bigger label, as she'd promised them. The deal had been possible with some new material, which had swayed the conversations with the prospect of the bigger label releasing their follow-up album. They also had a social media team that kept the content fresh, and engaged with the growing fanbase.

They were beginning to be recognised on the streets. At first it was a novelty being asked for a selfie by some kids in Stuttgart or wherever they were, but it was becoming a more frequent occurrence as their tour continued. They were all getting good at engaging with their fans as part of the job.

They had time travelling between events to work on new material, but equally they wanted to make sure that they all had some personal time to make it less intense being together all of the time.

James made good use of this time that Grace was away with the band to look further into the final period of the guilds in Richmond. Specifically he was looking for connections to buildings or land where they may have been comfortable safely storing their treasure. He knew it had once been in the passage from St Mary's. The big question was where it went next, and what had spooked the people in charge of safeguarding the treasure.

There was a possible connection with the St Martin's site that he'd come across while looking into the Goose Fair, but the timing was all wrong. As a Benedictine priory, they may have had links with the continent, as the glassmakers guild did with their links to Bohemia and Murano, but there was probably little overlap. The records suggested the priory was well in decline in the years leading up to the dissolution of the monasteries, and the size of the buildings was very modest. It would be hard to imagine the priory having the ability to hide the treasure. Not only that, the buildings were heavily quarried after the dissolution. In the process of demolition, secret rooms, cellars or passageways were bound to have been discovered.

Luke was also enthusiastic about researching the digital archives, devoting his time to looking at legal documents from the relevant period. He had the idea of building a picture of the activities of the guild: what they were buying, selling and what land or buildings they were purchasing. A time-consuming process, made more difficult by the language of the day. Some of the digital copies were of poor quality. They'd clearly been scanned a long time ago, when the technology was first emerging, and the images were not the sharpest.

The enthusiastic demolition of medieval Richmond in the Georgian period meant a large part of the town centre could be dismissed as a potential hiding place. Clearly the demolition of the guildhall, and its subsequent rebuilding as a Georgian house, could have totally buried the treasure in a yet to be discovered underground chamber, but more likely, the construction of the new townhouse would've revealed any secrets, and the treasure would've been discovered long ago.

The removal of the town walls and the gates suggested a significant building effort had been undertaken. The remodelling of the town centre was a meticulous, sustained effort to replace the old with the new rather than a more superficial replacement of the façades which left the old structures intact, as seen in many other towns and cities.

It was time to look at the surrounding area to extend the search for the hiding place. Looking at the old maps, comparing them with the modern maps, James could get a better understanding of what was easy to reach from the old roads, some of which had been replaced with new ones. He began with the old Lancaster road which left Richmond towards Applegarth on the right hand side of the river, which at the time was the main route west.

Over time the modern road was constructed on the other side of the valley, rendering the old road redundant. The old road was now a well-loved bridleway and footpath used by the coast-to-coast walkers. James highlighted the area towards Applegarth as a candidate, given the ease of access, along with the terrain that had potential to hide the treasure. The next area of interest was Maison Dieu which passed St Nicholas, which had origins as a Benedictine hospital before being remodelled in the late medieval period as a house. The road continued towards Easby and the abbey. This was an area James highlighted. Although they'd found the tunnel from St Mary's towards Easby that passed close by St Nicholas, so it was more of a possible candidate, he made a note that it was less of a priority.

The road north was onto a moor. James concluded there was no obvious place where a treasure could safely be hidden. The road also passed the barracks and the gibbet, which was probably not a good idea for stealthy behaviour in hiding trunks of treasure, unless the militia were in league with the guild. There was something not right with the possible route north, especially given how the militia were used to gain access to the site of the Goose Fair. It was increasingly unlikely that the guild would've gone along the road leading past the barracks.

The road to the north east that led to Gilling West was a possible candidate for further research.

The final road to consider was the one that left town from the Green Bridge, and continued uphill past Billy Bank Wood. The question was whether there was a bridge before the current one was built in eighteenth century. Indeed whether the Slee Gill Road was built at the time that the guild were looking to hide their treasure.

James was beginning to feel confident that they were getting closer to the treasure. He was going to share the map and his ideas with Luke, but thought he'd wait until he got some more information together.

•

- Hi, James. How are you getting on? Are you managing to juggle the band with the Richmond project?

- Angela, good to hear from you! I've stepped back from the band. Long story. It has freed up time for the project.

- Sorry to hear that you left the band. You seemed to be enjoying it? What have you been finding out?

- We discovered a tunnel complex, eliminated a bunch of possibles and I'm working on the next set of possible locations.

- You should write all this down as it's an important part of history in a turbulent period. There is the decline of the guilds, the disappearance of their wealth and the subsequent vacuum that was filled by the new elite, who then went on to rebuild the town to reflect their new found wealth and success. It goes without saying that it will help make a case for academic research. Especially if you do find the location of the treasure.

- I'll make sure you're involved if I do find it and I'll write it all up. Would you be able to help me search for any references to the guilds, especially in the seventeenth century? I don't know exactly what I'm looking for, but need to find connections in the surrounding area of Richmond.

- I have some ideas around searching for deeds connected with the guilds that I can look into. I'll let you know either way.

Angela had a dilemma around what James was doing. His enthusiasm more than made up for his lack of rigour, and he seemed to be finding things out for himself. She did worry how he was approaching the field work, noting that he didn't elaborate on the tunnel complex, and she assumed he must have been in them, which could've been damaging to the structure and any fragments that could've been useful for the archaeological context. The issue was reconciled with the knowledge that, while she was giving him some help with the research, she was not at all involved on the ground, and that if he did discover something of significance, she was well placed to put proposals forward to do the investigation.

•

Luke had held off contacting George after the trip to Richmond, fearing that he may be too direct and it could jeopardise their business relationship. Equally he would need to say something as it could become very uncomfortable at meetings if they didn't discuss things. George had made no effort to contact Luke nor explain himself.

- You didn't have to kidnap him! I don't know what you were thinking of?

- Luke, I felt we needed to do something after our last discussion to slow him down, at least until the planning committee meets.

- I thought we were going to make sure we owned the narrative if anything did surface rather than trying to head him off?

- I had a chat with Edward and we agreed to have another go to put him off, and thought it would be good cover for you if you were caught unaware.

- Fair point. I was shaken by the experience, which will have come across as genuine. I've had an idea. How about we start a social

media campaign to leak the treasure story? That way we can make sure we take control?

- It's risky, but seems that the other strategy isn't working. I imagine you know a lot more about social media than I do?

- Yes, leave it me, George. I'll get the whole town out looking for the treasure, and create the narrative around heritage and history.

- Good man, Luke.

•

It was Grace who first became aware of the storm on social media, while she was eating breakfast in a hotel in Croatia. She took a screenshot, and sent it James with the message

- You have to see this! Your mate Luke has kicked off something with this. X

James began reading. His face showed his total horror as he continued to read what Luke had written about the Great Richmond Treasure, as he'd sensationally called it. He was offering a generous reward for information that would lead to its discovery, such as stories or legends of tunnels, hidden chambers, false walls. Luke had been careful not to mention James or the tunnel they'd discovered or even the guilds, but he'd cleverly written enough to describe the treasure from four hundred years ago that was hidden in Richmond, North Yorkshire, and that he'd come across old manuscripts that revealed its existence. Luke went as far as describing silver, ornate glassware, silver and gold that made up the treasure, stating that it was likely to be in sturdy wooden chests bound with iron strips. Luke had posted it across a number of channels to great effect. The clamour on social media was real. There was a flurry of commentary and conspiracies, and treasure hunters piled in.

'What has he done?' said James out loud with his hands on his head. Picking up the phone, he replied to Grace.

- We were close to finding it. Now everyone will be out looking for it.

- Does it matter who discovers it? I'm guessing whoever's land it's on will have some claim, and the museums would be best off with the collection.

- Well, assuming more than half of the treasure is gold or silver, that it was owned by guilds that no longer exist and it was deliberately hidden over two hundred years ago, it would be treasure trove and very likely to go to a museum.

- I guess the finder gets some kind of reward?

- That does happen, but there's a whole legal process to assess the find. I was hoping to find it, and involve the archaeologists before anyone else got to it. Although I was a lot less worried about the other people as I think they were looking for something totally different.

- The people that broke into your house and kidnapped you?'

- I think I did a good job of putting them off the scent, but it became obvious that they were at cross purposes, having a different theory all together. I suspect it has something to do with King Arthur, and certainly to do with their family secrets, which I never got to the bottom of.

- Did Luke tell you he was going to go public with this?

- He didn't. I can't think why he has done it without talking to me first. Well, thinking about it. Our last trip to Richmond was a bit stressful with the kidnap. He was very disappointed when he drew a blank at the cottage. He seemed convinced he'd located the site of the treasure. He did seem to really get into the research of a

load of old legal documents, suggesting he was still enthusiastic. I'll see if I can get hold of him. How is the tour going? Croatia today?
  - Going really well, sold out most nights. I'm missing you. X
  - Miss you too. X

James despondently tried to call Luke, no answer, and he left a long voicemail asking Luke to call him back.

•

In the days that followed, the story, which began on social media, was rapidly being picked up firstly by the local press closely followed by the national media, who ran with the story. James received a long message from Luke explaining why he revealed the story. It stemmed from the kidnapping that had shaken him up much more than he thought at the time. Though they'd laughed it off as part of the adventure, it had unsettled him. In the weeks following the event, he began trying to rationalise what happened. He concluded that it was definitely not okay or normal. They should've gone to the police and made a big deal about him being snatched off the street, even if it meant telling them why there were in Richmond. Luke had concluded that sharing the story, so that lots of people would get involved in hunting the treasure, would prevent something like that happening again. By publishing the story, they revealed the secrets they had and would no longer be of interest to the kidnappers. Luke apologised that he hadn't shared this with James, as he was sure that James would talk him out of it. He hoped that James understood why he'd done what he'd done.

Luke also suggested that they leave things for a while,

to reflect on what they'd been doing. They should have a get-together to reflect on how they'd begun with a bit of fun trying to crack a historical puzzle, which turned into a full-blown treasure hunt with baddies breaking into James's house, threats and finally the kidnapping.

James wrote a long response to Luke, saying how sad he was that they didn't talk it through, although he understood why he'd done it. He also added that he was grateful that Luke had not named him, and congratulated him on doing a good job in focusing on the treasure, not on the journey of how they discovered it.

•

The tour ended on a high with a sold out venue in Milan. The band took a day to be tourists, which was getting more difficult as they were recognised in the streets. They could not, and indeed didn't want to, say no to the fans who wanted selfies. Becky had joined them, bringing them the news that they'd been nominated for a national music prize, which was a massive boost to their already rocketing fame.

'Wow, that's amazing,' said Helen. 'This has been such a whirlwind. It only seems like a few weeks ago that we began rehearsing in that room in York, and here we are in Milan at the end of a successful tour, being told by Becky that we have been nominated for an award.' Topping up everyone's glass with prosecco, she said, 'Here's to us!'

They all joined in, chinking glasses, smiling, enjoying the moment, sitting in a beautiful square in a small restaurant in Milan and listening to the chatter of the locals, who were out socialising and shopping.

'A huge thank you to Rick who brought us together,' said Grace. 'It wasn't guaranteed to work, given the different backgrounds we had. I also want to raise a glass to our former bandmate who played a part in the start.' She raised her glass.

'I could only bring you together. The magic happened when we started playing,' replied Rick. 'Becky has done an amazing job. Thank you.' He raised his glass towards Becky.

'I'm pinching myself that this is now my full-time job,' said Grace. 'I really didn't see that coming. Not that I have any complaints at all.'

Becky had organised dinner at a place that a friend of hers had recommended. She gave a small speech, giving them the news that they would be flying home rather than having to go back on the tour bus. She told them that they could travel as light as they wanted as the bus would bring everything else. It would be back in a couple of days. They had worked well as a band, and quickly learned when to give each other space, enjoying each other's company. Although they'd been away from home for weeks, they were having so much fun at the gigs and festivals they played, as well as seeing a lot of continental Europe, that they didn't have time to miss it.

•

Cosmic Fragments met a couple of days after they got back. It was tricky now. They couldn't meet in a bar or pub, and have a private conversation as they were recognised.

People wanted to talk with them and take selfies. Meeting in the studio was the last thing they wanted to do following weeks of touring. Grace had the brainwave of booking a private room at a bar in town.

They discussed renting a secure place for keeping their kit rather than using the studio, and a few other minor administrative things.

'A friend of mine told me about a really nice studio in the Peak District, which is at a farm with accommodation. The best bit is that it's within walking distance of a village, which has a couple of pubs. Apparently there's a footpath through the fields to get there,' said Helen. 'It would be good to book some time in, so we could record some of the ideas while we were on tour, especially as they are fresh in our minds.'

'I'm planning to visit my folks then stay with my sister for a few days. I'll be back in about ten days' time,' said Grace. 'Would that fit in with people's plans, assuming the studio is available?'

'Yeah, I was planning to catch up on one or two things next week. There are a couple of synths I wanted to check out,' replied Helen. 'As you say, we would need to check with the studio. Do you think Becky could look into that? I bet she could make it available. She can be very persuasive!'

'That sounds a very good idea. I'll send her a message to let her know what we are thinking about,' said Rick. 'Is that time frame okay with everyone?' He began messaging Becky.

'From the notes I made, I think we have a lot of interesting ideas to play around with. It will be good to see where it goes,' said Helen.

'Definitely,' replied Grace. 'I really want to bring in a bit more on the percussion side of things. I plan to visit some shops in London.'

TWENTY-TWO

Caitlin had an arrangement with Verity where she would be at the new studio area that Verity had made every Thursday evening. She paid a monthly rent for the space, and Verity had given her a key to her flat as there was no separate entrance. In practice, Verity was there for much of the time. They often painted together, either in companionly silence or sometimes they had one of their phones paired to a Bluetooth speaker that Verity had brought into the room. Caitlin had really taken to oil painting and was a quick learner. Verity enjoyed teaching Caitlin as having to explain or show techniques helped her improve too.

Dutch Masters were not the obvious choice for amateur painters. There were many courses on still life, life drawings or life paintings at the local art college in the evenings, which might have been a more usual path. They both loved the compositions and found the techniques challenging, but fun. Verity had found a good source of paints with the right pigments and varnishes, and they decided to club together to buy a good stock of paints and some quality brushes.

They were both working on a small painting each on wooden boards that Verity had prepared. The subject matter was a domestic scene in the style of the Dutch Masters of a woman sat on a chair by a window with light streaming in, and the sitter concentrating on making lace. In the background was a large dresser and a painting. On the floor lay a rug and a dog curled up asleep. To help, Verity had set up a projector with a high-definition image of an old painting projected on the far wall of the room, which they were using for inspiration.

'It's nice to see the painting taking shape,' said Verity. 'It feels strange that, having put layer upon layer with all the backgrounds, we can now start with the top layers of colour, before we get to the details. After that, we have the layers of varnish to apply.'

'It's a very relaxing way to paint. The image is becoming an old friend already that I feel I know very well.'

'Too true, and I guess it will be the same with the next ones we do.'

'Given the process, we should be able to work on a few paintings at a time to allow drying between coats?'

'Yes, I was thinking about that. On the other hand, what do we do if we start really turning out pictures? Do you think we could sell them to country house hotels or interior designers?'

'I hadn't really thought about that. It seems enough to be able to make the paintings, and I sort of assumed I'd hang one or two at home. Eventually we will need to find a home for them, and I suppose those are good suggestions.'

'The naughty side of me would like to slip one into a car boot to see which unscrupulous antique dealer would buy it up and create some fake provenance.'

Caitlin laughed, and said, 'That's so bad, but I guess on the other hand it isn't you that passes it on as something that it isn't. Let's not go there!'

'Talking of dodgy history, how is Mad James's quest going?'

'He has gone a bit quiet on that front, although I suspect he's doing more than he's telling me, despite the fact that he has got mixed up with some ruthless people. I tried to discourage him, but for some reason he has taken himself on a quest. Who knows, he might get to a complete dead end and it will naturally fizzle out.'

'You have done all you can. He's a grown man.'

•

Grace had asked James if he wanted to come with her to visit her parents and sister. They'd discussed it for a while, and concluded that, although it would be a nice thing to do, it would be much nicer for Grace to spend time with her family. They had a couple of days after Grace flew back from Milan being a normal couple. Although, as Grace was being recognised more on the streets, they had to adapt when in public.

With Grace gone for a week, James had some more time for solitude to put some more effort into the research he wanted to do.

Before he began the research into possible links to the guilds, he called Angela to see if she'd come across anything helpful, as well as to share some thoughts he'd had. The research that Angela had done was to find out more about the prominent guild members of Richmond. She'd cross-referenced title deeds, commercial documents and town registries to find connections. This followed the logic that the guild members, thinking they were securing their treasure for the short term, needed somewhere which was owned by a trusted party.

There were patchy records of the guilds, which meant that some of the documents were either hidden or destroyed deliberately at some point. James speculated that it was more likely that it was deliberate. That would fit with what he'd discovered about the demise of the Goose Fair, along with the subterfuge around the closure and acquisition of the glass makers.

The most promising lead was the connection between one of the prominent members of the glass makers guild with a property at West Applegarth. The property included an area of woodland to the east of the building documented as land for hunting. From what Angela could make out from the incomplete records, the property had been mentioned in the thirteenth century in connection with an estate belonging to one of the local nobility. There had been a sale in the late sixteenth century to the guild member, and a subsequent sale in the 1680s, which mentioned that the house was in poor repair. Angela speculated that the house may not have been lived in for a while to be in such a condition. The new owner demolished the house, building a new one on the plot as it lay near the road, with a clean source of water coming from a spring behind the house.

James and Angela discussed whether there could've been cellars or hidden tunnels, but dismissed the idea as the house was completely demolished, and a new one built in its place. The builders would've come across tunnels while demolishing the buildings. The likely place was somewhere in the woods, given the cliffs along the back of the woods at Applegarth Scar had caves in them. The rock had been quarried over the centuries. It was a good candidate.

They ended the call, with James promising to keep Angela posted on progress.

James had been putting it off for a couple of days, and it got to the point where he had to stop procrastinating, and call Luke.

The phone rang. After a while, it went to voicemail. James was pleased that Luke had not blocked his number or rejected the call.

'Luke, James here. It would be great to get together to have a proper chat about what went on in Richmond and the treasure hunt. Give me a call or send me a message. We could meet at the Royal Oak in town if you like, for a pint and a chat like the old times? Speak soon.' James hung up.

James was not expecting an immediate response, but he wanted to make sure that Luke knew that he was ready to talk.

A message came back a few minutes later from Luke, saying he was tied up at work and he would call James around five o'clock.

It was a relief for James that he'd at least opened up the channel of communication. It'd be good for both of them to talk things over. James had decided not to tell Luke of the latest things with regards to the treasure hunt. No matter what they'd discuss, this was something James wanted to see through. He didn't need to involve Luke with it. It was how he'd handled it with Grace, who'd asked not to be involved as it was his thing. They'd talked about whether having secrets from each other was a good thing and had concluded that this was not a burden Grace wanted to carry.

•

The treasure hunt that had gripped Richmond seemed to have calmed down. The attention on the social media platforms had been directed to the next sensational or outrageous event, or scandal, that had happened locally. Even the online edition of the local paper had moved onto the success of the local pub's cricket team, a quad bike theft and a school sports day report. The landowners around Richmond became be more vigilant about people wandering around, and there was a proliferation of handwritten signs proclaiming 'Private Property. Keep Out' and 'No Trespassing' fixed onto gates and fences around town.

•

It was a warm evening with birds singing loudly, the odd waft of barbeque, snatches of music being played, the hum of a passing plane. James walked to the pub by the river where he'd arranged to meet Luke, and getting there a bit early, he grabbed an outside table just as a couple were leaving.

People watching was always a good sport for James, although these days it was more awkward as people tended to recognise him, so he could not anonymously blend in to fully enjoy the atmosphere as he once could. People knew he was one of the original band members, and despite him no longer being part of the band, in people's minds he was still associated with it and thus famous.

The pub was busy, so he felt that he could blend in a bit more, but that feeling was rudely shattered with the first selfie request. The fans were a couple of lads in their early twenties, with a fine set of tattoos, razor sharp haircuts, approaching him with a certain swagger to mask their shyness. The lads were so excited to meet James, and to tell him how much they liked the music, how they'd been to a couple of the local gigs before the band had become famous and when James was still in the band. James was charming with them, sharing some anecdotes, making sure the lads were happy with their pictures. It got others murmuring, looking over with curiosity, some more furtively than other, as to who the celebrity was, but no others ventured over... to James's relief.

Luke arrived a bit late. They soon settled in, once they'd their drinks.

'Thanks for coming,' said James. 'It really matters to me that we can talk about what happened.'

'Yeah, it's good to see you. Before we get into the events of Richmond and their aftermath, I want to say that I'm sorry you left the band. I'm proud of you as a friend, and that you were a part of it, no matter what happened,' said Luke. 'I've been given a big promotion at work. They have asked me to move to head office in London. They have helped me with a service flat near the office for a couple of months while I get sorted. I start on Monday.'

'Congratulations. That sounds like it could be a big step up,' replied James.

'I'm very excited about the new role. It will be the change I need. I'll miss my friends, and I'll still be the same distance to my family, although they would have to come south not north. I'm sure I'll meet new people, and family will come to visit. I'll be back at weekends.

'I enjoyed the exploring, delving into history with

you, even though the burglary spooked me a bit.' Luke paused before he said, 'We were getting drawn deeper and deeper into what felt like some quest. When I looked back, we had broken into a church at the dead of night to go down those tunnels, and dug in those woods. All of that was getting to the edge of the law, which in my case could've had a big impact on my job.

'That kidnapping was not at all okay, even if it was an old fart with his hired hands and some mad ideas about what we were looking for. I know we laughed it off at the time as part of our quest, but it began to trouble me. I couldn't talk to you about it. I realised that my family would have no idea what I was doing, and why I was potentially getting into trouble, especially given my profession in the property world. It was at that point that it dawned on me that the best way to prevent a repeat of the kidnapping or worse was to put the information in the public realm so that everyone would go out looking. They would no longer have any incentive to threaten us or worse, since we were not the only threat to them. With the secret out, they could no longer protect it. Unless they had a different secret, in which case, we would no longer represent a problem to them.'

'I can see where you were going with that. I can't fault your logic,' replied James.

'The other question was what would we have done if we had found the treasure?' said Luke. 'It'd have been a process of treasure trove, and probably a pissed off land owner who was not happy not to have been consulted before we went hunting. What of the artefacts? Give them to a museum? Sell them at one of the fancy auction houses?'

'I've been thinking about that too,' said James. 'It was never about the money. I guess it was always more of a quest to find some answers, and embrace the passion I have for history. I didn't mean to drag you into something dangerous. It began as an excuse to do some local tourism, and develop your knowledge of tea rooms. The trigger was that book that set me off looking for the mystery barbican. That led to the guilds. Eventually to the treasure. So you can say the treasure hunt was more of a random outcome of the adventure.'

'Are you still looking for the treasure, or has the kidnapping put an end to that?'

'I'm having one last go. Grace has gone to see family for ten days, and I'm looking for some closure on what I began.'

'Promise me you won't go breaking into places or get into serious trouble looking for it?'

'I promise! It's a lot harder to lurk around after what happened with the band, combined with the fact that most of Richmond knows about the treasure,' said James. 'I've written a lot of what we discovered. It feels important that people should know about that period of history, the rich medieval town that Richmond was with the international connections to the glass making centres of Bohemia and Murano. There's also the sub-plot of the individuals, such as the Tubhursts and Heckroys, with their endeavours in modernising the town, demolishing the old buildings, the walls and the gates. You could say they purged the town of its history, leaving the only trace as a mighty castle. That itself became a romantic idea.'

Luke's promotion was prompted by a long discussion with his boss, who concluded that, while he'd done a great job in finding the prospective tenants for the castle project and formed a good working relationship with Rufus, the involvement in an ethical grey area was not healthy. At this stage of the process, they could easily hand over to one of the associates and reassure Rufus that Luke would continue to be involved from a position of oversight. There was no reason why Luke couldn't meet the Rufus team in London from time to time as part of account management and keep the working relationship. Luke didn't disclose what he knew about James, especially the part about writing what the Tubhurst and Heckroy ancestors had done to Richmond.

•

James stayed in a small pub nestled into an equally small hamlet a couple of miles away from where he wanted to explore, a short drive out of Richmond. Arriving in the evening, he managed to eat supper in the restaurant, where he was thankfully ignored by the older clientele who had no idea who he or the band were. There were one or two curious looks from the waitresses who looked school age.

Turning in early, he got a good night's sleep followed by an early, hearty breakfast. James studied the map of the area as he ate, slurping his tea, and had another look at the satellite view to try and memorise it, before setting off.

Parking in a verge leaving plenty of room for cars and tractors, he hoisted his rucksack on, making his way to the start of the bridleway. It was a clear day with a stiff breeze from the west that made the leaves form patterns as they waved in the wind. The grass looked like a green sea with a swell. Stoic sheep were dotted around, lying by strategic drystone walls to shelter.

He caught the sound of a curlew, an oyster catcher and a lapwing, reminding him of the coast where they spend their winters. Walks on empty beaches, with steel-grey skies, foaming seas, flocks of wading birds.

The bridleway, a gravel road with a good spread of potholes formed by the farm traffic, was winding its way through the landscape, bordered by the cliffs on one side and the open vista on the other. A potted collection of gnarled, ancient yew trees lined the banks below the cliffs. Animal tracks snaked their way through the trees and fallen rocks, and the meadows were dotted with flowers and rough grass.

Heading downhill, James approached West Applegarth Farm. A collection of newer buildings housed animals, stored feed and provided shelter for the farm machinery. A chicken shed, long abandoned, with thick spiders' webs acting as curtains on the windows, gave a gothic horror look. A parked tractor, an assortment of trailers, ploughs and harrows were evidence of a working farm. As he passed the first shed, an eerie silence enveloped the building. The animals were out grazing the flower studded meadows surrounding the farm.

James decided against snooping around the farm as it could land him into trouble, coupled with the fact that it was not a likely hiding place for the treasure as the oldest buildings looked as if they dated from the eighteenth century at the earliest. The house, as James had read about, dated from the eighteenth century, replacing an earlier mansion house from the medieval era.

Given the extensive quarrying over the centuries, it was less likely that the treasure would be hidden in the cliffs themselves, even though there were caves. What James was looking for was a barn within the curtilage of the forest of West Applegarth that ran to the east of the farmhouse. The boundary ran above the fields of East Applegarth, the settlement, roughly following the bridleway. A quad bike made its way through the fields, checking on the sheep. A buzzard whistled in the sky as a lone crow bombarded it.

Through a few sets of gates or stiles as the field boundaries seem to shorten, James followed a path leading to the remains of a Romano British fort that he'd spotted on the map and had come across in his research. A distinct set of foundations of the outer walls was covered in herbs, nettles, moss and fine grass, which could take purchase amongst the fragile soil in between the rocks. What appeared to be an entrance was to the east. Stopping to admire the view, he could see that the site was at a perfect vantage point, with views up and down the valley as it wound around. He reached into his bag, taking out a bottle of water and an apple. He sat down on a flat rock to take it all in. Below him small, perfectly formed oak trees, abundant mounds of yellow meadow ant nests, flowers and grasses of all shapes, hues and sizes dotted the pastures.

James continued following the path on the earthworks, which had an ancient feel to them. It wasn't clear to James whether they were connected to the Romano British fort or were part of something much older. It wasn't the time to ponder or get distracted.

•

The ruined barn could be seen through the first set of trees of the woodland that bordered the meadows. This was what James was looking for, picking his way through the brambles, clumps of thistles, nettles in the undergrowth to reach the barn.

There was a missing roof. The east gable was collapsed in what looked like a standard barn in a state of neglect. The wall facing the cliff was of a much earlier date, with much larger, cut stones and a smaller mortar gap. James began by taking pictures of the wall. He scraped away the leaf litter that had formed around the base of the wall like a brown snowdrift. As he dug, a deep aroma of fungi given off by the leaf litter filled the air. A straight line of well-dressed stones was all that rewarded James for his digging.

The adjoining walls were from a later period with rougher cut stones, crumbling lime mortar, and missing sections where the timbers would have been.

James pushed the leaf litter he'd moved back against the wall to make it less obvious that he'd been investigating, before making his way to the back of the building to see if there was any evidence of an older building. Taking a fallen stick from a hazel tree that had once been coppiced, he began to scrape at the woodland floor behind the barn to see if there were any foundations. It wasn't long before a line of broken stones formed, perpendicular to the back wall of the barn. This was the trace of the old building he was looking for.

The act of doing fieldwork without any landowner permission, and a lack of any knowledge of archaeological processes or techniques, would be enough to deter most people. This was not a film or TV drama. This was very real and involved a well-intentioned amateur illegally investigating a potential archaeologically significant site, with very possible damaging consequences.

James had brought a trowel with him in his rucksack. Taking the corner of the back wall of the barn with the newly exposed foundations, he began to scrape away the leaf litter and the top layer of crumbly soil. Sixty centimetres down, he reached stone. Widening the area by scraping more leaf litter and soil, a stone slab was revealed that suggested a floor. Continuing the excavation for another hour, James cleared an area which exposed a neatly constructed floor of large flagstones tightly joined together, connected to the demolished wall.

James took a break. He began considering the next approach. There were options of continuing to clear the leaf litter and soil to establish the layout of the floor, or to continue a narrow strip to find the end of the floor. The depth of the leaves and soil was increasing as James dug away from the barn, making the exploratory strip the sensible option.

At this point James could've stopped, and gone through the right channels to report this to facilitate a professional investigation, but he was way too deep into his quest, and had stopped thinking rationally a long time ago.

The narrow strip showed the floor continuing as expected. James made good progress, reaching the end the floor, revealing the foundations of the opposite wall. The extent of the building was now much clearer, yet it was still a puzzle why the end wall stood and the barn had been built on the back of it. It would take a considerable amount of time to clear the whole floor to reveal the foundations that would bring a clear view of the demolished building. Time was not an option as the longer he stayed there, the greater the chance he would be discovered.

James took photographs of the wall along with his excavations as a starting point. He was beginning to form a plan of what he would do if he discovered the treasure.

Having a clear line of flooring leading away from the barn was a good start. A cross section would be valuable to confirm that the whole area was a stone floor. It was something that James could reasonably achieve in an hour. The excavated cross section confirmed his hypothesis that the floor extended across the area of the demolished building.

That left one more task. James needed to lift one of the floor slabs to see what lay underneath. Rather than wrestling with one of the slabs adjacent to the wall, the slab where the two strips intersected seemed a good place to try.

Cleaning the dirt between the slabs, sweeping the top of the slab to clean it, James noticed a small carved symbol that resembled a cockerel on the right-hand edge of the slab. Cleaning the adjacent slab, there was a matching symbol opposite. For some reason, James chose the adjacent slab to lift, again clearing the debris from the gap. He was now ready to lift it out.

James walked around the wood next to the barn to look for makeshift tools that would help him lift the slab. A thick log from a fallen branch of oak was ideal as a pivot block. James began by carrying it back to the slabs. Continuing, he found a clearing with an old drum held in a frame, which was now a pheasant feeder. At the edge of the clearing an old iron-framed bed had been dumped. Decorated with goose grass, with nettles growing around it, it looked as if the wood was slowly claiming it.

After a bit of wrestling, James detached the longer support linking the two bedheads.

Now was the moment of truth, as James placed the log in the pivot position, inserting one end of the iron bedstead section into the gap between the slabs. Using all his weight at the end of the metal pole to apply the maximum pressure, nothing happened. James then tried jerking the pole down. Suddenly he felt some movement. The slab began to rise as James successfully pulled the pole. He needed to find a way to hold the pole down so that he could move the slab. He needed more wood.

He finally raised the slab, quickly kicking the old fencing post he'd found underneath it. He gently took pressure off the pole, the slab seating on the post.

Manoeuvring the slab to one side, a shaft of sunlight appeared, lighting up a set of steps leading down below the floor.

Using the torch on his phone, James made his way down the narrow steps. There was a small area at the bottom of the steps. Flagged floors and two rounded archways in a similar style to the ones he'd seen in the tunnel leading from St Mary's Church leading to further rooms on either side.

•

James stepped into the room on the left-hand side. He shone his torch around the room. Stone shelves lined the room. A faint musty smell lingered in the room.

It was dry underfoot with no signs of any damp. That was encouraging. Whatever had been stored had a good chance of surviving several centuries. Chests, like the one he'd found with Luke in the tunnel from St Mary's, were neatly placed on the shelves. All were encircled with robust ironwork with a locking mechanism. James counted seven. Examining each one, they were intact, showing no signs of being opened or damaged in any way. Resisting the urge to pull the chests out and open them, James returned to the anteroom to continue into the other room.

The layout was identical. In this room there were ten chests of an equal size, just as in the other room. Walking slowly round, checking each chest, James was in awe of how well preserved they were. Almost at the end, there was one chest that had a small gap where the timber must have rotted. Shining his torch into the gap, he could see one or two pieces of highly decorated glass pieces ablaze with colour. It wasn't possible to make out what they were. James took a series of photographs through the gap. Stepping back, James proceeded to film and take photos of both rooms.

The discovery was significant. James had decided that an amateur raid of the treasury had a significant risk of destroying important information that an archaeology team would be able to collect, helping them with the context of the find.

James took one last look. Climbing the steps, he reached fresh air, and felt the stir of wind in the leaves, and heard the squawk of a crow. Carefully replacing the slab into the position he'd lifted it from was almost more difficult than raising it.

He swept the leaf litter with the soil back into the channels that exposed the slabs, so that it looked exactly like he'd found it. The final act was to return the section of bed to its resting place, and the logs to their original site.

Retracing the path back to the car felt surreal for James. He'd made a big discovery. He knew where the treasures of the guilds had been hidden for such a long time. It was mission accomplished with a slightly sour taste. After all, his quest had been to find the barbican gates, and frustratingly there had only been circumstantial evidence of gates. Nothing to corroborate the illustrations. The treasures were far bigger, opening up the whole chapter of that turbulent era rich in history that had been largely forgotten. It showed the extent of trade across the continent, and how Richmond was largely remodelled in the eighteenth century by design, leaving only traces of the past.

TWENTY-THREE

A welcome shower with a change of clean clothes back at his room at the pub lifted the fatigue that James was feeling from being in the fresh air all day, the walk and the exploration work he'd done.

James was ready to speak with Angela.

'Hi, Angela. Sorry for disturbing you on a Saturday evening.'

'James, great to hear from you,' said Angela, trying to sound enthusiastic.

'Listen. I've made a big breakthrough. I've found the treasure that the guilds hid.'

'Where? How?' asked Angela. Now this had got her attention, and any irritation was quickly forgotten.

'I followed the research you shared with me. It took me to an old, derelict barn in the forest belonging to West Applegarth Farm. The barn had an old wall at the back. Newer walls were built around it to form a new barn with the old one collapsed behind it. To cut a long story short, I did a bit of digging at the back of the derelict barn, and I came across a floor made up of stone slabs. I lifted one of the slabs up which was marked with a cockerel, which I'm not sure of the relevance of. It revealed a set of stairs leading down to two rooms or chambers. The rooms were lined with shelves that had chests stacked on them. I was careful not to touch them. One of the chests had a small gap, and I was able to see some elaborate glassware. I took lots of pictures and a couple of videos, and sealed it back up again. I also covered my tracks as well as I could.'

'That sounds amazing. Well done on finding the treasure. What now?'

'I think it would be much better if a team of archaeologists could excavate the site properly with land owner consent. I naturally thought of you. It seemed wrong to do some cloak-and-dagger operation to remove the artefacts in some kind of Tomb Raider escapade.'

'That's so kind of you to think of me. Can you share the location, the images and videos you took? If you could also share the background documents? I'll get the project rolling as soon as I can.'

'You have been a great help,' said James. 'Of course I can send you everything. If you could leave my name out it, that would be grand. I don't need any more attention at the moment!'

'One small favour to ask...' said Angela, 'would you mind writing up your research? It'd be great to find a way to get it published. There's so much you've dug up about the late medieval Richmond that should be in the public domain.'

'I'd be happy to write it up. I've got lots of notes that should be easy to collect into a document. There are two intertwined stories. The first is medieval Richmond. The traditions, the buildings, the guilds. The second one is the story about the antics of the Tubhursts and Heckroys, with their mission to modernise the town.'

'Now that'd be fantastic if you could write up both. We're naturally interested in the medieval history, but the story of demolition and rebuilding is also very important to tell.'

'Let me know how you get on with the dig. I'm dying

to know what you find in the chests. I hope to see the treasures in a museum one day.'

'Absolutely. I guess it depends on what's found. I suspect that the major museums will be fighting over the collection.'

'I'll send everything after this call.'

They swapped some more pleasantries and ended the call.

•

Grace had come back from a successful trip to the recording studio in the Peak District. It had been a very productive time with the band. They'd transferred their energy and ideas they'd had from the tour. The sound engineers were true professionals who got the best out of them.

James and Grace had a couple of long walks together to talk about the future. They'd decided to buy a place together, especially now that the band was so successful. Grace was earning some good money, with the prospect of more from the tours lined up and the sales of albums and merchandise. James would sell his place, which he'd outgrown. They would buy something bigger where they could have a proper music room for Grace.

James spoke at length about his quest and reflected on how it had consumed him almost to the point of destruction. He vowed not to ever do such a thing again, and had no regrets about leaving the band, with no desire to join another band. He discussed with Grace a return to Davidson and Sons as Caitlin told him they were recruiting again, and she fully supported him. The company was a nice place to work, even if Mr Pickles was a little eccentric, and looking back he'd enjoyed his time working on the publications.

•

The notes, pictures and videos that had been collected in the process of the research were well organised. There was little work that needed doing before sending it all to Angela to help her with the project. James decided that, once he'd sent it all over, and Angela had confirmed she could access all the material, it would be time to delete it all. The books he'd acquired were boxed up and sent to Angela as part of his collection of material.

Before he fully deleted all the materials, James had commissioned a writer to take all the material about the Tubhursts and Heckroys, and write the story about how they'd modernised Richmond, through their determination to demolish the medieval town, the guilds, and the glassmaking industry along with the customs around the St Martin's Goose Fair. One of Becky's contacts was in the publishing industry, specialising in historical books, and was very interested in taking the book on.

•

James had messaged Caitlin. They'd arranged to meet in the café with the Scandinavian lights, tribal rugs on the rough brick walls, and the vintage furniture.

James arrived early and sat at the table at the back. A glass of citron pressé with rosewater and a small bowl of olives were brought to him.

'James! So nice to see you,' said Caitlin, giving him a hug. 'It doesn't seem that long ago that we escaped here on Friday lunchtimes. This place hasn't changed much, thankfully.'

'That seems like a lifetime ago since we huddled here dissecting the office politics. How are things at Davidson and Sons? Mr Pickles behaving himself?'

'Well, where do I start? Davidson's is doing well, and Mr Pickles has bought a couple more small publishers from some old codgers who were retiring. We now have *Traction* and *Steam Engine* monthly, and *Microelectronics* has moved online only as nobody wanted the printed version. And we have a whole range of software engineering online publications.'

'That sounds really positive. Is there enough space in the office?'

'The office refit happened about six months ago. I must say that it works really well. So tell me what have you been up to?'

'I've left the band. Long story, but they have done well without me, and had a very successful tour. Here. Before I forget, I have a little present for you.' James reached down to pick up the LP he'd brought with him, handing it to Caitlin with a flourish.

They were interrupted as the waitress took their order.

'What happened with that historical research you were doing? Did you carry on?'

'That was an interesting story. You know how I bought that book with the illustrations that triggered the hunt for the barbican gates?'

Caitlin nodded, smiling as she recalled the visits to the second-hand bookshops and antiques places after their lunches. James gave a detailed account of the events that led to the discovery of the treasures of the guilds.

'That must have been a difficult decision. I don't know what I'd do if I found a hoard of treasure!'

'I'm really happy that it will be properly looked after. I enjoyed the journey, discovering a lot of interesting things as I explored.'

'I hope you'll write all this up. It sounds really interesting. What next?'

'It was an amazing experience, unearthing all this history. I've shared all the material I gathered with Angela, the university professor, to help her with the project. I've also commissioned a writer to write up the story of the transition from medieval to Georgian Richmond. How it happened, who was involved, and what was lost. I have a publisher lined up for that too.

'As to what's next. I can close this chapter on historical sleuthing. Grace and I are buying a house together, so she has some space for a small studio. I spoke with Mr Pickles yesterday, and I'm coming back to Davidson's in my old role. I realised that, despite all my grand ideas, the thing I actually enjoyed was under my nose. I enjoyed the job. I like everyone at work, and even Mr Pickles isn't the monster I built him up to be. In my spare time, I want to be with my friends, go and watch the band when they are on tour, and get back into walking.'

'I'm so happy for you,' beamed Caitlin.

They ate their lunch while Caitlin filled in James with all the gossip from the office, like the old days. James walked Caitlin back to the office along the usual route, and they couldn't resist popping into one of the antique shops on the way purely for nostalgia. James resolutely didn't buy a single thing.

•

- Verity! I had lunch with Mad James yesterday. You know how he started his big quest when he found that book in the second-hand store? Well, he has only gone and found a load of treasure!

- No way! How did that come about? Was it in the book?

- It was a fairly lengthy story, which included some baddies trying to stop him. It turns out that there were some wealthy guilds who had hidden their valuables, and our man worked out where.

- Has he pocketed a big reward for finding it?

- That was the strange thing. He did it all covertly, and once he'd found it passed on all the notes he'd made and the location to the University of Birmingham.

- What fun. A real treasure hunt. What's Mad James's next project?

- He's coming back to Davidson's, stopped with the band and isn't doing any more exploring. He'll lose the 'Mad' label in no time

- Give it some time, and a bit more delving in the second-hand bookshops, and he'll be off on another mission.

- He seems to be settling down. He's moving in with Grace, who's buying a big pile with the recent success from the band.

•

Angela worked hard over the ensuing months, putting a case together for the dig at the site James had discovered, juggling the documentation making a case while not revealing the extent of James's involvement. There was a good deal of coordination between the university and the landowner, and she put a team together of field specialists, experts from her department.

With the agreements in place, the budget cleared from the department funds, the main dig was scheduled for the following spring. In the meantime, the site was secured with a robust fence, and a site survey was conducted – including geophysics – to understand what they were about to excavate.

What was clear from the preliminary investigation was that there was certainly a buried structure as James had uncovered. The images showed the entrance with the first few steps.

Angela, with her team, worked with the information that James had shared as a starting point, developing the background to the artefacts they were going to excavate. They took care not to widely share the images and video that James had made of the chambers, the chests they held, and the glimpse of the glassware. It would've raised too many questions. The focus was on collating more data on the guilds to give the treasure context. One of the discoveries they made was in the parish records. They found a small outbreak of the plague, which had been one of many. It contained the names of several of the fellows of guild of glaziers, haberdashers and fellmongers dated 1667. It was likely that this would've been the people holding the secret of the treasure who took it to their graves. It would also have been the opportunity to begin the process of dismantling the guilds that led to the modernisation of Richmond in the Georgian era, the process of remodelling, replacing and rebuilding the town.

Rufus Regeneration had a smooth passage through the planning process. There were a small number of objections to the scheme as a whole, or citing traffic issues, but they were satisfactorily addressed in the application pack. The PR team had done a very good job of drawing on people's connection with history, so that the application was all about maintaining the fabric of the historical centre. There was a sense that people identified with the mainly Georgian architecture, and that the castle fit in with the romantic Georgian idea of a ruin. This warm, comfortable feeling of the historic town centre fed into a certain type of nostalgia and with it a sense of place, and the PR company played with these feelings to create goodwill towards the project.

While the Rufus Regeneration project was successful, George and Edward on the board of Rufus Investments became a liability on the publication of the book that James had commissioned. When it emerged that they were related to the Georgian buccaneers who demolished the medieval town, it made their position as part of a major development in a heritage asset untenable. Clearly Rufus Regeneration didn't need the notoriety of the past to haunt the present. Even if it occurred centuries ago, their names would forever be associated with the demolition of the old and their recreation of the new. Ironically it was the new that their ancestors built that laid the path to their demise as that new was steeped in nostalgia.

Verity enjoyed the sanctuary of her study, better described as her project room, which was hidden behind the painting studio.

One of the large benches had a number of prints laid out, which had gone through an ageing process that Verity had developed to ensure that the paper and the ink had sufficient patina to match the pages of the book that was opened. There were bottles of various sizes containing the liquids, powders and glues that she needed. These were the building blocks of the ageing process that she'd refined over a short period of time.

Carefully cutting the binding, and opening the pages, Verity began inserting the prints carefully into the book. The binding glue, a foul-smelling concoction made from animal hide with sinews, was at the ready while she sewed the pages using a thread made from flax. Once the pages were sewn, she applied the glue sparingly.

There was a book titled *The medieval villages of the East Riding of Yorkshire* that was ready to be dropped off at a charity shop. She knew the second-hand book dealers competed with each other to get their hands on the new books first. Verity had also learned to go at busy times, and include a couple of novels of a certain age, with the story that her elderly auntie wanted to declutter, having watched a popular daytime television programme.

None of her friends, even Caitlin, knew about her little secret. Verity had begun the path as a rebellion against her upbringing by her academic parents, who were absorbed in history to the exclusion of everything else, and didn't encourage her to socialise with her friends. Even if she did have friends, the ramshackle house had been no place to bring them to. She had, as a child, moved frequently as her parents tended to have almighty rows with their superiors and would storm out. Fortunately for them, they were very good at what they did, which made finding another post possible.

Verity's mission to fabricate history began at art college when she did her foundation year, learning about the historical materials used in printing and painting. This coincided with the very public unmasking of a serial forger who had gone unnoticed for decades. He'd had his paintings in public art galleries, in famous collections, and in the end it was a sense of legacy and recognition that had undone the forger, who had confessed to a journalist.

Unlike the forger, Verity had no intention of confessing to what she'd been doing in the last couple of years. She'd added many illustrations and photographic plates to a whole range of second-hand history books. She'd been very industrious in her activities.

She was slowing her output now to concentrate on the rare books she could pick up on auction sites, book fairs and car boot sales, being very careful not to go to the same places too often. She'd perfected the art of looking totally unremarkable. She had a wardrobe of very ordinary clothes, sets of clear glasses, and had mastered the way she wore her hair. The same applied to distributing the end product. Verity had a network of charity shops. Sometimes she would send books to regional auction houses.

When she was feeling a bit more daring, she would go to second-hand book shops and just slip one of the books onto the shelves in the appropriate section. She figured if a customer took the book to the counter, the bookshop would be more than happy to sell it and not worry too much about whether it was on their point of sale system.

ACKNOWLEDGEMENTS

Many thanks to Zoe, Gill, Lindsay, Nobby and Tom for listening to me on long walks, rambling about the history I'd made up, and the mischief-making with the real historical events of Richmond.

A special thanks to Nobby Dimon for the thorough and very constructive feedback on reading the first draft.

Printed in Great Britain
by Amazon